BIRDS IN A GALE

A NOVEL

BIRDS IN A GALE

A NOVEL

Ata Nahai

Translated by Chiya Parvizpur and Hourieh Maleki Qouzloo

Philadelphia, PA
Brooklyn, NY
commonnotions.org

First published in Sorani Kurdish, as باڵندەکانی دەم با (*Balindekanî Dem Ba*) by Jiyar publishers, Sanandaj, 2002

ISBN: 978-1-945335-45-7 | eBook ISBN: 978-1-945335-61-7
Library of Congress Number: 2025943030

10 9 8 7 6 5 4 3 2 1

Common Notions
c/o Interference Archive
314 7th St.
Brooklyn, NY 11215

Common Notions
c/o Making Worlds Bookstore
210 S. 45th St.
Philadelphia, PA 19104

www.commonnotions.org
info@commonnotions.org

Discounted bulk quantities of our books are available for organizing, educational, or fundraising purposes. Please contact Common Notions at the address above for more information.

Cover design by Josh MacPhee
Layout design and typesetting by Sydney Rainer
Printed by union labor in Canada on acid-free paper

ABOUT THE NONALIGNED SERIES

The Nonaligned Series is dedicated to fiction, literary nonfiction, and poetry that explores the historical and ongoing legacies of anticolonial politics, the evolving nature of imperialism, and the world-making freedom movements of our times. The series highlights vital and creative sources of internationalist imagination within the fractures and faultlines of the current world order. The name takes inspiration from the worldwide anticolonial and anti-imperialist self-determination movements that sparked a wave of decolonization in the 1960s and '70s across Africa, Latin America, Asia, and the Arab world.

For more information about the Nonaligned Series, visit www.commonnotions.org/nonaligned.

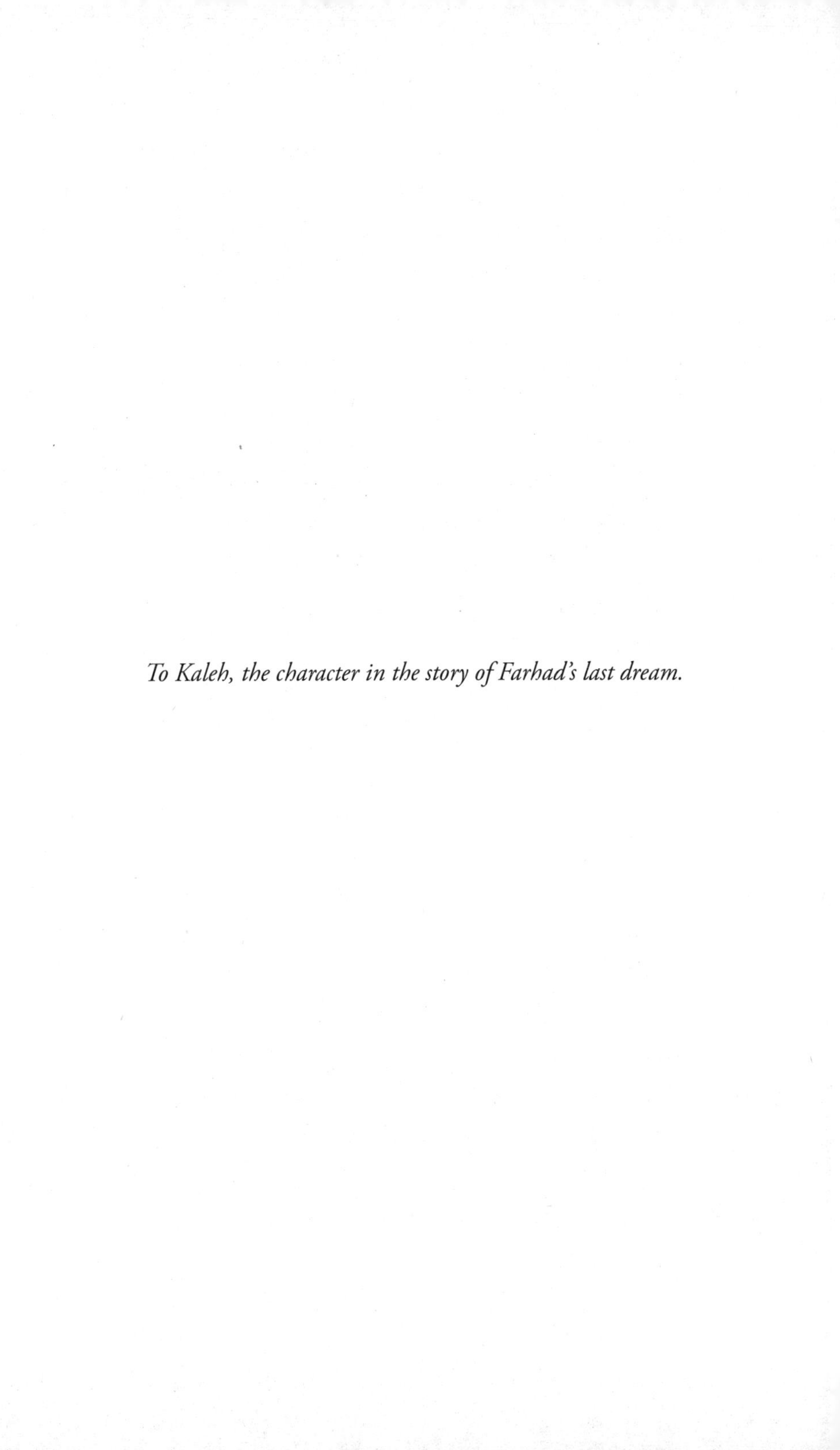

To Kaleh, the character in the story of Farhad's last dream.

CONTENTS

INTRODUCTION
POLITICAL POETICS

Kawan Mohammadpur

It is a given that "small literatures" carry within themselves both obvious and hidden political messages. Such politicization is clearly traceable in both the form and content of these works. Since its emergence in 1913, Kurdish fiction has similarly engaged with political aspects—continuing to do so up to the present day. Politics has been so densely and intricately intertwined with the Kurdish story that it seems almost impossible to draw a line between the history of Kurdish fiction and the region's political developments. Although Kurdish literature is neither uniform nor unmixed—and its development has followed distinct paths across six respective regions, namely Iran, Iraq, Turkey, Syria, the former Soviet Union, and the Kurdish diaspora—it can nonetheless be argued that it falls under the category of political literature.

Political literature does not imply that the writer is deliberately politicizing through their work; rather, the term refers to literature whose form and content are shaped by political developments. This politicization has led to such significant transformations that, in the Kurds' approach to storytelling, narrative forms imported from modern Europe were never received in their original form. In their literary expressions, Kurdish writers displayed an unconscious tendency toward political developments and the realities of their own social lives, rather than merely imitating a specific style of European literature. Even in the early years of the rise of fiction, Kurds had not drawn clear-cut boundaries between the novelette, the short story, and the novel. They used the term *çîrok*—which simply means "story" in Kurdish—for various forms of fiction, regardless of length or structure. The boundaries mentioned above gradually became more clearly defined in the following years, shaped by writers and critics who were more familiar with European literary forms. The history of Kurdish fiction sheds light on the fact that it is the content and its language—i.e. Kurdish—that attract more attention, not the literary structure, particularly for the first- and second-generation writers.

The Kurdish writer engages in a political struggle in an allegorical way through writing stories in *Kurdish*. Although new styles and techniques for novel writing were available to Kurdish writers—albeit second-hand and indirect through translation—they significantly transformed these forms to fit their own social and political models, all in alignment with novelistic goals. These transformations emerged from the writer's political subjectivity within history. In fact, the rise of Kurdish novels in postmodern forms has little to do with literary or philosophical debates within Kurdistan; it stems partly from translation, but much more significantly from political experience. Therefore, it is somewhat difficult—at least for me—to identify these novels as postmodern in the same sense as their Western counterparts. Modernism and postmodernism in Kurdish fiction originate in the political subjectivity of the Kurds, and unlike in the West, they bear no traces of literary controversies or an epistemological history of storytelling. Although such a claim may be made for many colonial literatures around the world, the distinctiveness of Kurdish fiction lies in the multi-layered nature of its colonization. Since the Kurds do not have an independent nation-state of their own, they are also marginalized in theoretical debates on post-colonialism. This double rejection—partly epistemological and theoretical, and partly political by the states that govern them—has further shaped and distinguished the style of their fiction writing.

The best case in point to support this claim is *Birds in a Gale* by Ata Nahai. Nahai is widely regarded as one of the finest novelists across Greater Kurdistan—the four parts divided among Iran, Turkey, Iraq, and Syria—and the most prominent Kurdish novelist living in Iran. Written in a postmodern form and employing metafictional techniques, *Birds in a Gale* exhibits key features of postmodernism—such as uncertainty, short-circuiting, language play, and self-reference, among others. It is, nevertheless, significantly different from its Western counterparts. The origin of this difference lies in the motivation behind the use of these features. While postmodern writers in the West employ such techniques to engage with epistemological and philosophical debates at the literary level, for a writer like Nahai, they are intimately tied to political obstruction and transformation. Postmodernists in the West draw on metafictional techniques to engage with the ontological dimension of the story, subtly reminding readers that the narrative is a work of fiction. In other words, postmodernists aim to deprive the text of any opportunity for the reader to identify with the character or their world. This approach draws the reader into the narration itself, rather than into the story. In *Birds in a Gale*, however, there is no attempt to highlight the story's fictitiousness or to create a sense of distance that prevents the reader from identifying with the characters. On the contrary, the reader is drawn toward the levels of narration and encouraged to believe in the world of the characters. If this is the case in Nahai's novel, then what is the purpose of using the metafictional techniques of postmodernism? I would argue that the necessity lies in a political conflict with history—not a philosophical one with the world, as is often the case in Western postmodernism.

Adopting a subjective "I," *Birds in a Gale* tells the story of a political writer named Mehraban, who sets out to write a narrative about a political figure named Farhad. Mehraban leaves

Iran shortly after the fall of the Pahlavi regime in the wake of the Islamic Revolution of 1979 and lives abroad for many years. Now, he has returned to Iran to write Farhad's story. There is much overlapping among the narrator, Mehraban and Farhad, particularly between Farhad and Mehraban who experience a similar political and emotional story. The similarity in the experience of these two characters is not an unusual phenomenon because Mehraban is writing the story of Farhad with the help of the narrator. The resemblance between writers and their characters is not unusual. Although a large portion of the novel centers on Mehraban, the central narrative is ultimately that of Farhad. The narrator, standing in for the writer's subjectivity, lacks sufficient knowledge about Farhad. As a result, he creates another writer—Mehraban—who, through his perspective and assistance, attempts to commit Farhad's story to paper. It is the story of a political figure who took part in the anti-Pahlavi resistance and came to be forgotten in the aftermath of the Islamic Revolution. The inability to access sufficient knowledge about characters like Farhad stems from political obstruction and the exclusion of such individuals by the government outside the narrative itself.

What is the purpose of presenting a character about whom we lack sufficient knowledge? The need to tell the story of such characters is, above all, a political necessity—a necessity imposed on the writer by the political struggles of the Kurds. The character of Farhad represents those Kurdish individuals who played a role in overthrowing the former regime—the Pahlavi dynasty—but whose political efforts and struggles were later downplayed or entirely forgotten by the rulers of the Islamic Republic after the victory of the 1979 Revolution and the consolidation of power in the years that followed. These anti-Pahlavi fighters have been excluded from the official history recorded by the Islamic Republic of Iran, and it becomes the duty of the Kurdish novelist to preserve their memory and restore their rightful place. The story of Farhad, therefore, serves as the second-level narrative of *Birds in a Gale*—a story meant to be believed. Believability is the key distinction between Nahai's postmodernism and its Western counterpart. In the latter, there are frequent references to the fictitious nature of the story. The Western writer seeks to draw the reader's attention to the techniques used in constructing characters and plot, rather than inviting the reader to believe in the story itself. Nahai employs this approach only at the first level of the narrative—the story of Mehraban—and constructs the second level in such a way that even the character created by the subjective narrator, Mehraban, becomes completely absorbed in Farhad's story. Incorporating Mehraban into Farhad's story is a technique used by the writer to make the second level of the narrative more believable. This technique seeks to show that, although Farhad is a character in Mehraban's story, people like him have truly existed in the social and political history of the Kurds. These forgotten characters possess political consciousness, yet the resulting political obstruction has led to a state in which even they themselves have forgotten who they are. As a result, they must be rescued from the fire of political rejection and granted a lasting place through the act of storytelling.

Politics, in its formal sense, completely rejects individuals like Farhad—and in most cases, this rejection results in their physical exclusion. Therefore, writing about them can be seen as a form of transgression. From this perspective, the plot of *Birds in a Gale* becomes fully justifiable. A story within a story allows the writer to conceal the narrator—who is, in essence, the writer's subjective representative—behind the first level of the narrative, and to tell the entire second-level story through the lens of the first. The second-level story is more political and, by extension, more dangerous than that of the first. In plain terms, it is a guarded secret—one that must be shared, revealed, and believed. Yet each of these acts constitutes a form of transgression in the realm of formal politics. As a result, at the narrative level, most references to specific individuals are concealed, particularly the full names of the characters. A full name signifies that the identity of the individual is known. The subjective narrator never reveals the character's first name—Mehraban is, in fact, his last name. He, too, belongs to Farhad's generation—a political activist who took part in overthrowing the Pahlavi regime. After the Islamists' victory and the rise of a new government and military structure, he was forced to leave the country. The novel reveals nothing about how Mehraban participated in the struggle during the Pahlavi era, after the Islamic Revolution, or during his time abroad. The narrator highlights only his identity as a writer, since speaking openly about such a history within the climate of formal politics would be considered a crime. Interestingly, throughout most of the novel, the narrator refers to Mehraban simply with the pronoun "he," and it is only in the final parts of the novel that the name Mehraban is spoken—this time from the narrator's own perspective, rather than through the voices of other characters. Farhad, too, remains a partially hidden figure. A fugitive student, painter, political activist, and lover—these are the only details the narrator, Mehraban, and the readers have about Farhad. In totalitarian regimes, full identities must be concealed; revealing them is considered an unforgivable political crime. This is why even the subjective narrator of *Birds in a Gale* is unable to provide sufficient information about Farhad's character. Yet these general hints offer enough clues for readers to recognize others like him within the wartime atmosphere of Kurdistan.

In Nahai's novel, even the name of the city where the story takes place is never mentioned. Instead, the focus is on the urban developments that followed the Islamic Revolution—developments that pushed society toward a rentier and disorganized form of capitalism. Banks and clerks serve as clear markers of this transformation.

Therefore, the postmodernism in Nahai's novel is not postmodernism in the Western sense, because—unlike its Western counterpart—it is shaped by lived, experienced truths that take precedence over the text and storytelling itself. For this reason, it may be more fitting to seek another term that more accurately reflects its nature. In *Birds in a Gale,* all of the writer's narrative maneuvers stem from his political subjectivity. The poetics of the novel is, at its core, a political poetics.

What sets Nahai apart from his fellow writers is his deep familiarity with the structure of storytelling. He approaches the novel with complete honesty. This honesty is structural in nature—meaning that every element of the story, from the narrator and narrative levels to characterization and plot, serves the subject of the story with full integrity. The writer does nothing excessive in the novel. Although the subjective writer lives alongside Farhad, he never engages in direct dialogue with him, nor does he ever begin writing Farhad's story himself. Even when Mehraban refuses to write Farhad's story, the narrator, in quiet desperation, still wishes for him to continue. The narrator's refusal to write Farhad's story directly, without intermediaries, reflects the lack of adequate information—stemming from Farhad's forgotten, rejected, and politically suppressed identity.

Nahai himself belongs to the generation of writers who not only experienced the 1979 Revolution but also played a role in it. At the time, he was one of the ambitious young people who closely witnessed the political developments in both Kurdistan and Iran. He is regarded as one of the political activists of that era. In the years following the Revolution, many from this generation either left Iran, were imprisoned, or were silenced in the shadows of political repression. The 1979 Revolution was not merely a political event; it reshaped the entire social structure and transformed Iran's cultural institutions. More drastically, it brought about a transformation in the subjectivity of both Iranian and Kurdish people. Nahai becomes the narrator of a fragment of this change—one that unfolds in Kurdistan across multiple generations. Thus, beyond its cohesive literary structure, his novel stands as a witness to social developments in Kurdistan, and as a testament that history will not be forgotten.

BIRDS IN A GALE

PROLOGUE

And where was he when she was a yarn of fire at a small house and courtyard? Smaller than the small world of her forbidden, haram dreams and fantasies; smaller than the whole collection of her wants; smaller than the share she wanted from life; even smaller than that which wraps her fire-woven body. Her wandering body, restlessly and rebelliously, moved heaven and earth and from the depths of her being, the depths of her tortures, let out all smothered screams of her life. Her rending, dry screams pierced the numb bodies of the mud-brick houses in the alley, whose time-worn rooftops and edges, like the head and shoulders of an awe-stricken stray dog, recoiled and trembled.

And where was he when the tin door of the small courtyard cracked once, twice, three times, shattering the silence and stillness of the alley? The fiery body of the woman leapt out once, twice, three times, disturbing the icy loneliness of the alley. The flaunting fire threatened the sky above, and the gale—the cold, dry, homeless gale—rushed to greet it. Fire was an old friend of the gale, holding it in its arms, missing it, pressing it close, lifting it up to whirl it around. The woman, then, was a yarn of fire in the gale's embrace, dancing the dance of death.

And where was he? The alley was completely bare. Nobody was out there. The windows were the blind eyes of the houses. Nobody could see the dance of fire and gale. Nobody could hear the screams of the woman and death. He was nothing but a pair of eyes and two ears—two eyes like two pigeonholes in a house wall; two ears like two droplets on the edge of a rooftop; like two chips on the body of a wooden lamp post.

He was a pair of eyes. A pair of eyes with no use but to see, and they saw that the woman, repulsed by meekness and modesty, was reveling in death. Her long dress, the pattern of which seemed to have been blue, sky blue, with flowerets that seemed to have been red, happened to be torn into pieces by the gale. The pieces flew—where did they land? Her skin, which seemed both white in hue and rosy from the leaking drops of blood, was scorching and crackling. The walls of the alley were woven with soot and smoke. The sky was dark and dim. His pair of eyes too . . . no—those seeing, beholding eyes were burning as well. Until the gale, weary of its rhapsodic dance, took its leave, and the fire melted into itself.

He was two ears. Two ears with no use but to hear, and they heard that the woman's rending screams had little by little turned into a roar, then a wail . . . and then . . . silence.

And where was he when the black body of the woman, nude and naked, fell in the alley? Was she tall, or did she only seem tall? Her hands were like a pair of burned boughs. The only whiteness in that blackened landscape was the whites of her eyes—eyes whose eyelid membranes have melted away. The pupils were still moving . . . moving? Who were they looking for?

Where was he?

Where did he see that yarn of fire?

Where did he hear that rending scream?

ONE

A rending scream jolted him awake. He frantically scanned his surroundings. The room was dark. Through the eyes of the windows and behind the wavy curtains he saw scattered yellow and red lights. They were too faint to illuminate the room or cast a dim glow on the opposite wall. He rushed to one of the windows. And from there to the balcony . . .

Outside it was just as dark. Nothing caught his attention but the weary movements of the tree branches in the courtyard. He cocked his ear in case the scream came again—or another wailing noise. But he heard nothing beyond the rustling of leaves and branches. He stepped back and closed the window. The ticking of the clock was the beating heart of the room. It ticked loud and fast. Was he frightened too? He groped around, trying to turn on the light. The room smiled bright. Did he see it or not? The beating heart had slowed down. His eyes hooked on the clock at the heart of the wall. Its hands were missing. He searched for his wristwatch but could not find it. Sleep had been driven from his eyes. He did not return to bed. A half-full glass of water from last night was still on his desk, and he drank it to the dregs. His pack of cigarettes was there as well. He pulled one out and lit it.

The echo of the scream still churned in his ears. His body was shaking, and he could feel it. Was it out of fear or cold? He was in two minds. He sat on the chair behind his desk. "Farhad," he asked, "did you hear that chilling scream?"

No one answered him. Farhad was not in the room, nor in any other room of the house. Only his name lingered in his mind—his name and the fragments of his life and past, all tangled in his thoughts with no order.

He drew on his cigarette. The smoke stung the tip of his tongue, and he exhaled a cloud of smoke over the papers on his desk. He had scribbled on a pile of papers. He had been writing for a week . . . yesterday, the day before yesterday, and every other day. Day and night. Since Farhad's birth. The first day of autumn. "The first day of autumn in which year was Farhad born?" he asked me. Then he went on, "If I ever get around to writing his story, I need to know his age. I need to see him. One day, with you . . . why don't you take me . . . ?"

"Farhad doesn't leave home. It's been years since he last left the house," I said.

"It's been years since he stepped out of the house?" he asked, surprised, wondering if he was old enough to be homebound. It did not cross his mind that, in this land, one did not need to be old to be confined to their home.

He snubbed out his cigarette and stood up behind his desk. He walked across the room and stopped beside the bookshelves. A collection of new books . . . ones bought upon his return. He wondered if his old books still remained . . .

"When you left," his brother Baram said, laughing, "one night, our father gathered all the books, piled them in the courtyard, and set them on fire. It made for a big blaze. It brightened not only the courtyard but the whole neighborhood."

But his sister, Monira, spoke with grief: "Roonak and I sat by the fire, weeping till dawn. The next day, when the neighbors asked about the fire, we told them we burned the dry leaves from the trees."

Dry leaves from the trees? Was it autumn when he left? He looked at his books. He had not read any yet, just thumbed through a few pages. "When I go back, I'll take them all with me. The lonely nights of homesickness . . ." he thought.

He chose a book, *A Chink in the Dark.* It was the sixth or seventh memoir he had bought that week. The memory of those men who once tried to revolutionize the world—through their efforts, by leaving their families behind, by enduring prison and torture . . . but they failed. The world has not changed. Has it not? They have simply aged, grown exhausted, and, afraid of being forgotten, they have recorded their memories. *A Chink in the Dark,* a prison memoir. He knew its author, though they never met in person. He spent more than twenty years in jail. He opened the book in the middle. It was the day of prisoners' visiting time. Which day, which year? He could not remember. And it did not matter. What mattered was that the prisoners were allowed to take a shower, to shave, to wear the clean clothes folded under their blankets, to put on the perfumes gifted by their loved ones, to polish their shoes . . . they had done it all. As if they were invited somewhere. They were guests. Guests of their families. Perhaps they talked about that young man whose fiancée had sent him perfume? The meeting of an engaged couple on either side of the iron bars, under the watchful eyes of a young cop with a thick mustache, black eyes, and eyebrows . . .

He closed the book and put it back in place. As he walked around the room toward his desk, the thoughts of the prisoners and their families slipped away. "Farhad," he said, "I'm sure you heard that chilling scream too."

Farhad was still not in the room. He was not in any of the rooms in the house. He gathered the papers on the desk and looked at the first page. A tangle of cold, lifeless words, worn out and repeated. He crumpled the paper and tossed it aside. The second page . . . the sentences seemed alien to him. As if he had not written them. He tore out the second page, then the third . . . and the fourth.

"What do you know about Farhad?"

It was me who asked the question. My voice did not surprise him. He lifted his head but did not seem bothered by my sudden entrance into his room or by me standing beside him. "Many things," he answered. "But scattered and disorganized."

I laughed. He saw a line of yellow, dirty, and ugly teeth, and it filled him with nausea. Was it the first time he saw me like this? Had I never laughed before? Surely I had. I would laugh many more times.

"You laugh too much," he said, angry and resentful. But he regretted it in the blink of an eye. "Of course, laughing's not bad."

He said that because he did not mean to displease me. Perhaps he feared I would sever my ties with him. But I would not. I looked at the crumpled papers. He must have exhausted himself writing them. Yesterday, the day before yesterday, and . . . he crumpled everything he has written that week and tossed it aside. Hopefully, to start over. He began Farhad's story again but remained stuck on the first sentence. The first sentence was a window into Farhad's life. "Choosing the first sentence is the first and last choice of a writer," he said before. "A hard choice. The first sentence determines the life and fate of the character."

"Where does Farhad live?"

He already knew what my answer would be.

"I must see him. He should . . ."

He wanted to say: He should tell me whether he has heard that chilling and piercing scream. But he did not say that. Instead, he continued, "He should help me choose the first sentence of his story. You gave me your word to get us to know each other."

I turned my back on him and walked to one of the windows in his room. I stood there, pulling the curtain slightly. It was still dark outside.

"I've given you my word, and I'll do it," I said.

I did not mention when.

TWO

It was not the succeeding morning of that night; it was the morning of another. He woke, dressed, and left the house. Amidst the noise, the coming and going of the drowsy people in the streets, those in a hurry to run their errands . . . what did he have to do? To enliven the memory of the past, he broke his fast at an old kebab shop in the bazaar. Two skewers of barbecued kebab and two of tomatoes with fresh, hot bread. Many years ago, the restaurant was run by a witty man, *Kak* Yada. He and his comrades used to call him "General." He was illiterate, but he said he had been an officer in Qazi's uprising. He recognized the General inside a black wooden frame. As in those distant days, a smile was frozen on his lips. He nodded in respect. "General, you too? Oh, but it was soon, you weren't supposed to . . . ?" he murmured to himself with a cold sigh. He ate the kebab and left the tomatoes untouched. Then he headed straight to the Cultural Heritage Office. To see Jalali. Jalali was his close friend and an old comrade. He met him a couple of times since the day he returned. As lovely and kind as ever. Not even a scintilla of change. He had not changed? He got married and had three children. He had aged a lot. Much more than he expected. His sight went dim, and his beard and hair turned silver . . . he did not have the heart to tell him how deeply affected he was. He stayed with Jalali for an hour or so.

As he stepped out of the office, he caught sight of me across the street. I was leaning against a tree on the pavement on the other side. He looked surprised—what was I doing there? Jalali was with him too. After a brief farewell, he crossed the street. He was coming toward me, and I stayed there, still leaning against the tree. For the last time, he turned to Jalali and waved. Jalali waved back and walked inside.

He crossed the street. He did not ask, "What are you doing here?" Instead, he said, "If I returned to Kurdistan only to pay a visit to Jalali, it would still be worth it. Jalali is a loyal friend, just as always. I wish you knew him . . ."

It slipped out from his tongue.

"I know him. Been around him for a while. He's the manager of the Cultural Heritage Office—the keeper of the ancient and the forgotten . . . the heritage of our ancestors . . . God rest their souls," I said, laughing.

Did I say it sarcastically? He pouted his lips and walked off without saying a word. Down the pavement, into the crowd of people he did not know. He stared at them—the men and women brushing past him—and sometimes at the shops and buildings he never noticed before. Had they not been there? Or had he wiped them from memory? Big stores and tall buildings . . . banks and offices everywhere . . . He did not look back at me. Did not care if I lost sight of him. Right before the square, he stopped by a newsstand. A few others were already there, staring at the lines of newspapers and magazines behind the glass window. All those newspapers and magazines . . . Most of their names, he had not even heard before coming back. All those writers filling the pages. All those people reading them . . .

The newsvendor was a young boy. He saw him standing off to the side. The boy recognized who he was and came over to greet him.

"Morning, *Mamosta*!"

He waved him in.

"I was just checkin' out your interview. It dropped today. Look! It's right here."

He did not even know about those Kurdish newspapers and magazines until the boy pointed them out. He reached out and took a copy. A small image of him lingered in the corner of the front page, with the caption beneath: MEHRABAN EMBODIED IN THE CHARACTERS OF HIS STORIES.

He smiled. The interview was only three days ago; he did not expect it to be printed so soon. "Ey, good job, Mamosta! You said some real words!" the young newsvendor said loudly and the customers turned their eyes toward him.

"Come, come—sit down, lemme grab us a couple teas or somethin' . . ."

He did not let him. He did not sit. He took the newspaper, paid for it, and left.

Momentarily, he ruminated over the fact that people might have seen his image and they would recognize him. A pestilential feeling came over him. He intended to cross the street. The cars were jam-packed. Vroom vrooms . . . he made his way through the vrooms.

On the other side of the street, among the crowd of people, someone suddenly blocked his way. A man seemingly of his age, but a little thinner. His hair was disheveled and dirty. He asked for a cigarette. He gave the impression of being familiar. So familiar. Unhurriedly, he reached into his pocket while contemplating him.

"Naseri . . . Aren't you Naseri? The one who played *tembûr* and . . . ?

The man recoiled. Something shifted in his eyes. Without taking the cigarette or answering, he stepped back, turned, and left swiftly.

He was stunned. "Naseri . . ." His awestruck and curious eyes stayed fixed on Naseri. "It was Naseri. I'm sure it was . . ." He decided to follow him, quickening his pace. He headed toward the crowded square, scanning the area, but Naseri was nowhere to be found. He lost him. Naseri vanished. Exhausted, he leaned against a postbox on the pavement.

"Seems like he recognized you too," I said. "He didn't even take your cigarette."

The packet of cigarettes was still in his hand. He pulled one out and lit it. Took a single drag, then pressed it out on the postbox. He glanced around and tossed the stub into the gutter.

"I've heard . . ."

He paused. What had he heard? What might they have said?

"Poor Afsana . . ." he muttered.

He tried to summon the image of Afsana's anguished face, her tear-filled eyes—but saw nothing.

"Is Afsana his wife?" I asked.

A bitter, mournful smile curled on his lips. I caught it.

"Was Afsana his wife?" I asked again.

He did not answer. He just kept walking. And I followed—shoulder to shoulder—through the crowd.

"Naseri was a handsome, well-dressed guy. Came from money. Drove a fancy green Peugeot and sometimes played tembûr. That was a long time ago . . ." he said with a cold, deep sigh.

"The kinda guy every girl wants . . . money, a slick car, and all that. She must've been real into him," I said.

"Who? Afsana?" He glanced back again. That same bitter, mournful smile still on his lips. Maybe he was trying to bury the sting of an old scar.

"Things were different back then. If you wanted to win over a girl like Afsana, it wasn't about all that. You needed . . ."

I smiled too.

"A Chinese double-pocket shirt, an American soldier coat, a big Stalin-style mustache, and a pair of plain black-framed glasses . . ." I laughed.

"Was Afsana selling *Labour* newspapers or the *Proletariat Movement*?"

"Afsana wasn't into that kinda thing," he said. "She was into nothing. Just a lonely girl in her own small world. A small world, yeah—but bright and kind."

Now his smile was soft, sweet—spreading gently across his face.

I could not stop myself from asking, "And where exactly were you in that small, kind world?"

He said nothing. It was a hard question. He dodged it, plain and open, but I did not push.

He left the square behind. He had to cross the street again—had to go see his brother, Baram, at his office. It was the second time since yesterday. He needed to ask him to send a repairman for the rooftop. The roof was in bad shape—like the rest of the house. If they did not fix it before the rain and snow came, it would fall apart. A house with no owner . . .

He had not been around all those years. If he had been . . . "If you were here after Dad died, we could sell the house and started that paint factory together," Baram had told him.

He reached the office and stepped inside. Baram was not there, again.

"He's gone to check on the factory. He'll be back soon," the secretary said, a little awkward, a little embarrassed.

He sat on a chair facing outside. The office was across from a cinema. The cinema had been there since he was a child. A teenager. How crazy he was about the cinema. Sometimes, he would stand at its door and stare at the big billboard for hours. At the photos of the actors and actresses—and now at the photo of a young couple on the banner. Standing across from each other on opposite ends of the canvas. The boy was looking up, while the girl gazed down at him. Staring at him. Both were laughing. Though the painter had captured something anxious and frightened in her pretty face, she was still laughing. Nervous and scared, but laughing. Maybe that is just how he saw her. Like Afsana's laughter, when she was still around. Maybe he confused her with Afsana. And the boy with . . . If I were there, I would have mentioned Naseri. But I was not.

Where was I?

I could not follow him around everywhere he went. And I did not find it necessary, either. He did not like it. No character in a story likes being trailed by its author. Maybe not even Farhad—the one who lived inside his story. But he had not met Farhad yet.

I had not introduced him to Farhad.

He pulled the newspaper from his pocket and opened it. Flipping through the pages, he found the interview. The office's tea man placed a cup of tea on the table in front of him. He sipped it slowly, now and then lifting his head from the paper to glance out the window—at the street, the flow of people, the passing cars, at the cinema on the other side of the street and its big banner. The boy was still looking upwards. What was he looking at? The girl's eyes did not lose their grip on him. She was laughing, trying to attract his attention.

It seemed like Baram was late. His secretary checked her watch and muttered to herself, loud enough for him to hear, "I don't think he'll be back soon. He won't be back this soon."

He raised his head and looked at her. She was still a young woman, maybe in her late twenties. She wore a lot of makeup: blood-red lips, ice-white polished cheeks, and she had big black eyes that were shadowed. Maybe it was the heavy makeup that made her look stern and angry. Or maybe she really was. Maybe she was just impatient and restless. Because he was not talking to her? Without being told, she picked up the phone and called the factory. It was obvious someone on the other end was saying Baram was not there. She tried calling his business partner. He was not there either. She hung up the phone. "I don't think he'll be back," she said. "He won't be back."

"Why don't you call his cellphone?" he suggested.

"His cellphone's not with him." She did not mention that it was with his wife. Instead, she added, "If you're in a hurry or need to go somewhere, I'll tell him you were here. He'll call you."

He knew Baram would not call. He knew it. No doubt about that. He would mention the rooftop and its repair. But Baram would dodge the issue. "It's like milking a ram and wasting money," he said before. "A wise man would not put a dead man under the knife. That's just wreckage. We should find someone to sell it to." Baram had mentioned it many times since the day he returned.

He said, "We should sell it as soon as we can. We all need money. Especially our two poor, twisted sisters. For years, their bastard husbands have been licking their lips for the money from this house and courtyard. And . . ."

"We won't sell it. Until the fulfillment of our parents' will, Roonak and I won't sell our shares," Monira responded. She said it that day or maybe a few days later. "Their intention in the will was to throw a wedding party for all their children here, for the sons to kiss their brides in this house, and for the daughters to leave for their husbands' homes," she said, laughing.

The secretary was restless, checking her watch again. She took her eyes off it and glanced at him, waiting in vain for his brother to show up. The look in those big black eyes was . . . He stood up. The young secretary, suddenly delighted, straightened up.

"Are you leaving?" she asked with a smile and a touch of respect.

"I'll leave him a note. Give it to him when he comes back." Then he asked for a piece of paper. The secretary passed it to him, her big black eyes twinkling with delight. He wrote:

> I came to tell you that there's no need to bother finding a craftsman. My friend, Jalali, promised to get one of his acquaintances to repair the rooftop. He'll also renovate the rooms, possibly the swimming pool and the courtyard.

He wrote that just to frighten Baram. Leaving the note, he walked out. He was still at the door when the secretary let out a sigh of relief and picked up the phone. He was an intruder. A non-mahram intruder returning after so many years, unsettling everyone, even that poor secretary.

He glanced at the cinema's banner and the faces of the girl and the boy one last time. In that fleeting moment, the laughter drained from their faces. It spilled. The boy looked melancholic, the girl anguished and frightened. He was reminded of Farhad.

Was he supposed to meet him today?

THREE

He returned home around noon and sat on an old, rusty chair on the balcony, staring into the courtyard . . .

He was reviewing his lessons. NaCl—sodium chloride. Two names for the same thing, and yet it was hard for him to remember them. Both meant salt. The salt his mother used in cooking, or the salt they sprinkled on cucumbers . . . or rhubarb . . . Under the far corner of the balcony, beneath the shade of the courtyard's trees where his father used to sit on the wide wooden furniture, they ate rhubarb. His brother Baram, his sisters Monira and Roonak, and . . . Who else? He rushed down the stairs. He should have gone around the pool in the courtyard. His father was performing *wudu* at the edge of the pool. Was it that day, or another? That year, or years before?

The pool was filled with water. It was surrounded by potted plants with colorful flowers—geraniums, *zhala*, *atrchai* . . . The reflection of the flowers in the water, mingling with the blue background of the tiles, interplayed with the images of the tree branches. The yellow and red evening rays of the sun splashed across the soft, slippery surface of the water, painting the images of tree branches and flowerpots. The image of his father was also carved upon the water. His father was praying, loud enough for his youngest son to hear, loud enough for him to learn. "*Sobhanallah . . . Sobhanallah . . .*"

His father dipped his big hands in the water and splashed a handful of water on his face, smashing the images. The reflections shattered. It also scared the fish away, including his goldfish. "Dad! The fish . . ." he wanted to say.

"Now it's your turn, my son. Come over and do wudu."

He headed toward his father, torn with hesitation. Kneeling at the wet poolside, his image on the soft, slippery surface of the water rippled away. He, terrified, plunged his little hands into the water. It was cold. He hastily pulled them back. Then his eyes tracked the fish, including his goldfish. He did not see it. Amidst the rippling images and the waves of yellow and orange light, he lost sight of it. Or maybe the fish went to the bottom of the pool, hiding in the blue tiles.

"Excellent, my son! Now say, '*Alhamdulillah . . . Alhamdulillah . . . Alhamdulillah . . .*'"

He dipped his hands in the water again. His knees slipped, and a splash startled him. One of the flowers fell into the pool and splattered the water. He took fright, raised his head, and gaped at his father—trying to see his eyes, which were barely visible behind his big nose and bushy mustache. His father's head and chest were half-buried in the tree's branches.

On the other side of the pool, behind the rows of roses, tuberoses, hollyhocks, and jasmines, his mother was lighting the coals for his father's hookah. Baram, Monira, and even Roonak . . . They must have been there for sure . . . They must have been sitting on the wide wooden furniture in the middle of the courtyard and . . . What were they doing?

It was a distant day. It was getting farther away with each passing second. The faces . . . the states of the faces could no longer reach his present moment. But the smells and the voices still lingered in the silent loneliness of the house.

Perhaps he prayed behind his father when he said, "Thank God for keeping my house well-lit. I have a son who prays behind me." But he was thinking about his goldfish. He was sure of it. He was thinking about his goldfish, hiding at the bottom of the pool.

The pool was dried up now. Instead of water, it was full of broken pieces from clay flowerpots. The blue paint on the pool walls was swelling and flaking off. The ceramic floor tiles were cracked and shattered. A pile of pottery shards lay in one corner of the pool, and two gaunt cats were curled up in the debris. They were the abandoned cats of the neighbors, no doubt driven out.

There were no clusters of flowers in the courtyard anymore—only weeds and withered plants. The trees began to shed their red and yellow leaves. The thick branches of the vines, with leaves like bullhide, weighed heavy on the trees and the crumbling old cottages. The courtyard looked like a small park in the middle of a war-torn city.

Who could believe this was his father's courtyard? The courtyard of Mirza Sa'id Mehraban's house?

He asked that on the first day of his return. Did he? Maybe he just talked to himself.

"You haven't been here for years. You've got no idea what's happened to us in the meantime," Baram said. "Why don't you look at us? We're more ruined than this house and courtyard."

But he only watched him.

The only one who seemed untouched by ruin was Baram. But no . . . it seemed he was ruined too. He was. Beyond his bright eyes, behind his chubby, sagging cheeks, beneath the constant trembling of his hands—something was pressing down on him.

Baram added, "We lost our will to live . . . the day you left. Your vanished fate, Father's death, eight years of bombings and exile . . . all that time . . ." Where was he during all that time? Did Baram ask? It did not matter who did. What mattered was the courtyard of the house—the once lush garden of trees and flowers that belonged to Mirza Sa'id—now ruined. And the house too . . .

"Let's go inside, have a look at the house. If it doesn't crumble on top of us," Baram offered. "I left here years ago so it wouldn't collapse on my wife and kids."

He walked up the stairs in fear and doubt. Before opening the two-part door to the corridor, he went out to the balcony. The row of windows—kitchen, hall, and Mirza Sa'id's room—were all shut. The three pillars were still standing firm.

He walked along the balcony. Then he opened the corridor's door and entered. First, into the far end of the house. The back of the house. Toward his old room. Baram's room and the girls' rooms. They were all empty. Ten years of dust have settled on the bare walls, inside the niches, and across the windows. The rooms felt cold and grief-stricken. The small backyard too—cold and grief-stricken.

Baram followed him like a skilled realtor. Like someone eager to snatch the house from its owner, he moved his hands around involuntarily, pointing out the cracks and flaws. Maybe that was all he saw—just the damage. "Come and look at this side. The hall and . . ." he said. "I think it was before you left that we tore down the guest room and built a hall, a kitchen, and a bathroom instead." Baram was wrong. They tore down the guest room after he left. They did not tear it down completely. They just divided it—made part of it into a kitchen and a bathroom. That was before Mirza Sa'id died.

"By dividing the guest room," Monira said, "Baram shattered my dad's grandeur, and justified his wife's excuse that she couldn't go down all those stairs to cook a meal, that she couldn't even go to the basement every once in a while to . . ."

He came back to the corridor and opened the old door of the guest room. Mirza Sa'id's guest room was emptier and smaller than before, but it still had its glory and grandeur. He turned around and inspected every corner. He looked at the niches, the windows opening to the balcony, and the plaster-embellished walls. They have not been dusted in ten years. The kitchen, the bathroom, and . . . his parents' room. Every corner of the house was covered in a decade's worth of dust. Everywhere smelled of his father. The smell of his father's absence. The smell of time passing. The smells of wet bricks, forgetfulness, and death.

He asked nothing. He asked about nothing.

"When we left here, we packed all the furniture and piled it in a room in the basement and locked the door," Baram said. "All of the memories, except for a few photos I couldn't part with. Your photo, our father's photo, and . . . We set the rest of the things aside for you. We knew you'd be back someday. We kept all the family keepsakes for you. We knew how much you loved them . . ."

The roof's shadow moved away from the balcony. The midday sunlight of autumn hit his neck and shoulders. As he sat, he pushed the old, rusty chair back.

The next day, he realized all the so-called family keepsakes were nothing but a pile of broken junk stuffed in the basement. When Baram was not around, his sister Monira and her husband brought in some workers. They cleaned up the rooms—especially the hall—took some furniture out of the basement, washed it, and dragged it back upstairs. The fridge, the stove, the dishes, table, chairs, sofa, and all that. They even washed the old torn, wavy curtains and hung them up again.

"Thank God, at least these remained," he said with a bitter smile.

Monira sighed and said, "These would've been sold too if anybody had made a decent offer. Just like the hand-woven carpets. Just like all them beautiful antique pieces. Like the TV and both telephone lines. I wish I was blind so I didn't have to see our house like this . . ."

They laid out the old rugs, *jajims*, and *kilims*, fixed up the creaky couches, shoved the writing desk and a chair in the corner. Hung up the old pictures, the cracked mirrors, and the clock right in the middle of the wall. The clock still ticked, but the hands had fallen off. Tick, tock. Mirza Sa'id's big radio did not even turn on.

"These were the family keepsakes . . . ?" he said, his heart sinking. He felt small, shattered.

"I hope your sister goes blind too," Monira sobbed.

"We should get a phone line hooked up," said her husband.

He heard the phone ringing inside the room. He stood up. Is that Baram? He was surprised. But it was Monira. She called just to greet him. He felt hungry when he hung up the phone. He went to the kitchen and opened the fridge to find something to eat. He was looking for something to eat for all those years. Wherever he was—on the mountains, in Iraq, in Turkey . . . even in Europe . . .

"May your sister die," Monira said once. "It seems you had no one to pour you a glass of tea or cook for you during all those years."

He completely forgot it. Every man here had someone to make him tea and food. Every man but him. Perhaps Naseri too. What happened to Naseri? A stylish young man, smart, with a high-end Peugeot, who used to play tembûr now and then. And now—he was begging for cigarettes. Miserable Naseri!

Again, he was reminded of Afsana. The poor, twisted Afsana.

He prepared lunch. Ate it. Then he had to wait for me. He hopefully expected me to take him to Farhad. To Farhad's house. Which house? He was indecisive. How long should he loiter in the mire of fear before he could begin writing his story?

Nothing had ever hurt him this much.

One week, two weeks . . . a week or two?

It has been a few months since he was preoccupied with the idea of writing a new story. Even before his return. Before that, he even considered writing a different story. The story of Farhad?

He was not strong-minded about it yet. Not even about me, Farhad, or the other characters in his story.

Writing the story of those among whom you exist and among whom you live is an arduous job. It has always been arduous. Especially when it is about those who are petrified, who sneak into their houses in distress, and who do not open the door to anybody . . .

"Even to themselves," I said. When did I say that to drive him up the wall? Was he outraged?

"Yeah, I'm scared too. I'm a coward. We all are cowards . . ." he replied.

Did I laugh at him?

In the afternoon, he took a shower. He was accustomed to taking a shower whenever he was about to write a new piece or meet the character of a new story. He would wash his body and mind.

He was under the shower. Inside the large mirror of the bathroom. The warm and mild water was raining over his naked body. His body had aged. Since when had he aged that much? His cheeks and eyes were sunken. His body . . .

"I wish your sister would die. You're still a child. Why are you so . . . ?" Monira had said before.

He turned his back to the mirror. He should contemplate something else. Someone else. Since he got out of the shower, he had been sitting at his desk with his head dropped over white paper, thinking about Farhad.

"Farhad is sleeping. He sometimes sleeps at this time of day," I said.

He raised his head. He was not in his house or his own room. He was in another house, another room.

Farhad's room?

The room was dark. Dark and inundated with smoke. It smelled of moisture and burnt rubbish. Farhad was lying in a corner of the room under the dim daylight seeping in through its small window. A torn piece of sheet covered him. I was sitting right next to him, near the brazier. A black kettle sat on the brazier, on the hot coals.

He eyed the walls and ceiling. They were black and dark. The photo frames and the broken mirrors in the niches of the wall were also black and dark. The clock was covered in a thin layer of smoke and soot too. It has stopped. It did not work. As if it had stopped for years.

"Are you living in here? In this house and room?" he asked, stunned.

He meant Farhad and me. I laughed, showing a line of yellow, dirty teeth . . . He did not see it. He walked toward Farhad. Toward the small window of his room. The smoke had tarnished the eyes of the windows. A dim light passed through them and spread over the gloomy blackness and darkness of the room. He rubbed the window clean with his hand. It blackened his palm. He did not care, and continued to stare through the window. Beyond it, there was a big courtyard full of trees. A desolate autumn courtyard. On the other side of the courtyard, there was a big empty house. A basement and a floor. A grand balcony, three pillars, and a row of windows . . .

He was not surprised.

"This house and the courtyard don't seem strange to me. It's as if I've seen them before," he said.

He had seen it. He was pretty sure that he had seen it before. No matter how hard he tried to remember, nothing rang a bell. He added, "I've lost my memory since I came back . . ."

He did not finish his sentence. A big black bird in the window-frame swallowed his attention. The bird was flying over the forsaken house on the other side of the courtyard, then took itself outside the frame of his sight. It vanished.

"Come and sit. I've poured some tea for you," I said.

He turned his face toward me. I poured two cups of tea from the kettle on the brazier. I also set a sugar cube container on the floor. To him, I looked much older and more broken. He pitied me.

"Are you both living here?" he asked again.

I said nothing.

"Are you relatives?"

I did not reply, only laughed.

"Who are you? How is Farhad related to you?"

"My life story is a long one. You haven't heard it because I haven't written it yet," I said. "Your tea is getting cold."

He quaffed his tea. It was bitter. So bitter that no sugar cube in his mouth could sweeten it. "There are so many people in this land whose stories have never been written. Better to say, in this land, no one's story has been written," he declared.

Then he looked at Farhad. He was a motionless dead body under an old torn sheet. "I wish Farhad could wake up and stand."

He lit a cigarette after drinking his tea. I lit one too. "Farhad can't wake up," I said.

He was startled. "He can't wake up? How can't he wake up? I've come to see him. I've come along to talk to him."

The dead body moved. A tiny pale old man crawled out from under the sheet. After rustling and shifting in the dim light of the window, he leaned against the wall without saying a word, without looking or heeding.

"Here comes Farhad," I said.

Farhad wrapped his thin, bony arms around his knee while his head dropped onto his shoulder. His hair and beard were grizzled, his eyes and cheeks sunken. He resembled a thousand-year-old mummified man, freshly extracted from the earth. He leaned against the wall under the dim light of a small window, in a room that was murky and saturated in smoke, a room that smelled of moisture and burnt rubbish.

"Here is the character of your story," I said.

He recognized him immediately. He recognized him behind the cloud of smoke, the blackness, and the weight of age. That lifeless body was Farhad, who was reclining and then leaning against the wall only moments ago. He was not looking at anyone—not even him. The man lingering in his mind. Inside the fragments of his past life. The man who was to be the character of his story.

"What made him like this?" he asked, astonished.

He stood up and approached Farhad, then took two steps backward. "I can't believe . . . No, I can't . . ."

Then he turned his face back to him and moved around the room, pacing. He was scared. It occurred to him to run. It occurred to him to leave that hellish room and return to his house, to stand before the mirror and gaze at himself once more. But he stayed. With the same fear and horror of the lifeless body, he stared at Farhad's sitting corpse.

He wrote:

What happened to this man? How did he end up in here? Why are his broad manly shoulders obliterated? Under the burden of what pain and grief . . . ?

He wrote:

For which deadly sin has this man been sentenced? For committing which deadly sin are we being punished? In which fire of revenge are we being burned? In the inferno of which destiny will we turn to ashes? Inside which landfill of history will we become lost? In the moments of which era will we be forgotten . . . ?

He wrote and wrote . . . Then, in frustration, he flung his pen away and stood up. He stood up only to walk around the room, to vomit these unanswered questions onto Farhad. Farhad, a sitting dead body, a thin and cracked frame; a pale-looking old kid. He wrapped his arms around his knees and dropped his head over his shoulder, looking at nothing—not even at him.

I was still sitting by the brazier. The murky air in the room was thick with smoke.

He was overwhelmed by dizziness. A gnawing feeling in his stomach, followed by nausea, took hold of him. He walked toward the door, his own room or Farhad's? He opened the door and hurriedly left.

FOUR

I did not expect visiting Farhad would unsettle him that much. Perhaps because I have lived with him for many years and have grown accustomed to him. I have grown accustomed to Farhad. But he . . . In those years of exile, he had always been haunted by the fear of losing someone or something. What or whom? He never knew. He just knew he should hold on to all his past life and memories and preserve them in his heart. All his dreams and wishes, and . . . All those people who were part of his past.

He was afraid of forgetting them. Like Farhad, who had forgotten everyone and everything. He had even forgotten himself. He never expected Farhad to be a man like that. "Had I known Farhad was a man like that, I would've never promised to write his story," he said with fury and hatred. "You should've told me that all those broken images piled up in my mind were part of a man's forgotten past. You should've told me on the first day."

The first day? He meant the first day we met. The day our paths first crossed. At first, we met like two strangers. Two people from two different worlds. Two people from two different times. Two people with two different stories, who . . .

"Let me write your story," I said.

He was startled.

"My story?"

"The story of Mehraban, the man who returned home after years of wandering and isolation and . . ." He did not let me finish my sentence. "I've come back to write someone else's story. The story of . . ."

"Farhad?" I asked.

He pondered. Years ago, he longed to write the story of Farhad.

"You know about Farhad?" he asked.

I laughed. It was the first time I laughed and he saw my yellowed, stained teeth. It was on that day we gave each other our word: he would write the story of Farhad, and I . . .

It was early evening when he returned home. Exhausted through and through. He took off his coat and collapsed onto one of the sofas in his room. The sofa creaked and he heard the fabric tear. He sank into the sofa and closed his eyes. He could not shake the image of Farhad from his mind, a broken man who has forgotten his life, his past, and even himself. Why would a man forget his life and his past? His parents, his relatives and friends . . . His childhood, adolescence and youth . . . His memories . . . How could someone forget the memories from his youth, friends, and comrades? That evening right after leaving Farhad's room, he called Jalali: "I want to see our old friends and comrades. I haven't seen them since I got back."

Jalali looked surprised. "OK. One night we'll invite them all over. We'll get together. How about Friday night?"

"I need to see them today."

Jalali was thinking, Why today? "Step outside and wait for me on the street," he said. "I'll pick you up there."

His stomach churned. He stumbled to the curb, fighting back the urge to vomit. Jalali arrived and he got into the car. Jalali saw that he was agitated and pale. He grew anxious.

"What happened?"

"Nothing."

"Then why . . . ?"

"I need to see our old friends and comrades." he repeated.

Then he met them. His old friends and comrades, the few who stayed behind in this land, were now a handful of graying men. They welcomed him. They apologized for not having visited him sooner. Problems . . . The problems of life and work and . . . They were speaking softly and laughing. They were nothing like the lively young guys he remembered. Back then, they would not talk about jobs, salaries, debts, bills, bank statements. They would not talk about work and promotions, or about their houses, businesses, cars, and other people's possessions . . . or their kids' futures . . . They would not say he made the wrong choice to return. You came back to this place, with these people who understand nothing? How is it possible for a man to leave Europe, the center of attraction and glamour? Those guys would not bring it up. He was pretty sure they had forgotten who they used to be. They had forgotten their dreams, their hopes, even how they used to talk. And they had forgotten him too . . .

The ringing phone woke him up. He figured it was probably his sister, Monira. She used to call him often to check on him. But it was Baram. He brought up the rooftop and the note he left earlier that day. Baram was furious. Or at least, he seemed to be pretending. "I'm still not dead. Have I become such a stranger to you that you asked your friend, Jalali, to find you a repairman? Am I really a stranger that you left me notes?"

Then he began to nag about why he had gone to his office instead of coming home, about why he turned his back on them and stopped visiting. He said he was speaking not only for himself, but also for his wife and children. His poor children were delighted that their uncle, their father's pillar of hope, finally returned home after so many years. But now . . . "What a sycophantic, talkative man Baram is," he murmured to himself.

"You should come over to our place tomorrow. We can have lunch together, and in the afternoon . . ." Baram said.

"I'm heading to the countryside tomorrow with Jalali . . ."

He and Jalali had already planned to go to the countryside and stay at Jalali's father-in-law's place for a couple of nights.

They wanted to go hiking the next morning. "You're tired, and so am I. By the way, I haven't seen my father-in-law's family in a long time. We'll go there for two days and blow away the cobwebs in the mountains," he said that evening. Right after bidding their old friends and comrades farewell. He appreciated the invitation.

"You've barely been home two weeks," Baram said. "You shouldn't . . ." He stopped himself from saying that he should not act like he did back when he wandered carefree with his friends. "You shouldn't forget that you have family and relatives, and you've come back to visit them. A wise man . . ."

Baram always talked about what a wise man does not do or what he should not do. A wise man would not come back after so many years just to go to the countryside . . . A wise man would never leave Europe to live here . . . A wise man in an old, ruined house . . . A wise man . . .

Baram was wise. All of them were wise. Since his return, or perhaps since his departure, they had transformed into wise people, always talking about what a wise man does. Baram and his wife. Monira and Roonak, his sisters, and their husbands. His old friends and comrades . . . and even Jalali. All but Naseri. Years ago, Naseri was wise too, when he had a high-end green Peugeot and occasionally played the tembûr. When he used to stalk Afsana, and Afsana also . . .

Tonight, he was determined not to let anyone enter his room, into the quietude of his room. Neither Naseri nor Afsana, nor anyone else. He hung up the phone and stretched out on the sofa. He lay his head on the armrest and his chin sank gently onto his hard chest. He wished someone would cover him with a blanket. But who? He was not supposed to let anyone inside. Not me, not Farhad, not Afsana—Naseri's wife.

FIVE

I woke him up late that morning. He finally shook off the exhaustion from the past two days. But he was starving. He kept getting hungry too often ever since he got back. Maybe it was because the food differed from what he was used to in . . . It was not just the food. Everything here was different. Even the moments themselves. He had to live through these moments. The moments of here. He should write in these moments.

Yesterday on the mountain, Jalali asked him, "So, what have you been up to since you got back?"

He said . . . What did he say? Maybe he said, "I'm going to write a new story. I'll start it tomorrow." Today is yesterday's tomorrow. He headed to the kitchen for breakfast, then to put in order the things that had piled up in his mind.

I followed him and sat in front of him by the small *sifra.* Today's sifra was more colorful: honey, homemade butter, and cheese. They were gifts from Jalali's in-laws. Even the bread was baked in their tandoor.

"You look like you slept well. I doubt that rending scream last night jolted you awake," I said.

I knew. He was so tired that he was out like a light the second his head hit the pillow. The night's frightening scream could not awaken him. Perhaps there was no scream at all, or maybe it was too far away.

"Unlike you, Farhad . . . Till morning . . ."

He cut me off before I could finish. "He until morning, what? He could not sleep? Did he say something? Did he pick a fight?!" he asked furiously.

He was talking with his mouth full. He tried his best to hide his anger.

"He was ill, writhing and wailing in pain," I said.

"Like a wounded snake?!" he said sarcastically, then laughed. As if trying to mimic my laughter. Then he turned grim. "I don't want to hear anything about Farhad anymore," he said. "That's a decision I've made . . ."

He was not even aware of the decision he had made. He had made no decision at all. It was a thought that had crossed his mind in that moment . . . the thought of clearing his mind of everything connected to him, of him whose name is Farhad, who has been afflicted with amnesia for years. "It's rather foolish for someone to devote all his gifts and abilities, all the moments of his life, to the past of a man who doesn't even need a past," he said.

I knew I should not sit in front of someone who was angry with himself, with me, or maybe with both of us. And I ought not to gaze into those eyes where the wrath was so clearly hidden. That is why I got up and stood by the window. To look out through it and, at the same time, say, "What about the story? What will happen to it?"

"The story?!"

He did not say he would quit. And even if he did, I would not believe him. "During those two days in the countryside, I thought about a new project. I intend to write someone else's story," he said.

"Naseri?" I said.

"Why Naseri?! Naseri's story is old and long forgotten. The only son of a wealthy man who falls in love with a poor girl. The girl's heart belongs to someone else. But due to a complicated situation, she's forced to marry him, and after a few years . . ."

He did not say that after a few years the girl would die, and the boy . . .

"So, Afsana . . ." I said.

He had breakfast and cleared the sifra. He held a cigarette between his lips, and its smoke stung his eyes. He turned his face and looked closely at me. His eyes were that of a man plagued and exhausted. "Those who fail in life have already lost at their own game, the game of love and . . ." he said. "I lost that game a long time ago. Years ago."

He wrote the story of that loss years ago. In Turkey, in a small room of a restaurant. An amorous story set against a dark, murky and bitter political background, along with a bunch of slogans . . . Later, in Europe, he published it in a magazine under the title "A Lost Beloved."

He always laid the blame on himself for writing and, specifically, for publishing that story. Even at a literary symposium abroad, he once said, "That story is the worst thing I've ever written." It was the story of a girl who, despite being in love with her fiancé, chose not to join him in the fight for freedom. The girl's fiancé was the one narrating the story, a man who had to step out of her love story and . . . "The narrator of that story isn't reliable. He's not honest with himself, nor with the girl in the story," he said.

"I don't understand what the truthfulness or dishonesty of that story's narrator has to do with you," someone in the crowd said. "Is an author responsible for the good and evil of the characters in his stories?"

He was startled. He pondered himself. "You're right. The author isn't responsible for the good or evil of his characters," he said. He did not say that the author, like anyone else, is responsible for his own good and evil, his virtues and his vices. He had the sense not to say it. They would have realized he himself was the narrator of that story. No one should ever fathom it. It was a secret no one was meant to know. Not even I, who was a story writer like him and stood by the window of his room. I who . . . But I was aware of it. I knew that some authors concealed themselves behind the characters in their stories. I knew he had hidden himself behind the narrator of his story. I had realized it long ago. That was why I laughed. A laughter that . . . He hated me more than ever. He detested me—and all those story writers who stand by the window, laughing as they tell the characters of their stories, "I know. You can't hide anything from me."

I never said anything like that. I was not in his room to say it. I was not in any of the rooms in his house. He was alone now. Alone, standing in front of the broken mirror in the niche. His hair and mustache were mostly white. His cheeks were hollow, and his eyes deeply sunken.

Worried and scared, he turned his face toward the mirror. He heard a munching sound. The munching sound of a small mouse chewing something. Perhaps the moments of his life . . . Where was that mouse which was chewing the moments of his life? He looked for it. Found it. Chased it into every corner, then returned to his desk weary and drained. There were a few white sheets on his desk. He reached for his pen and . . .

SIX

The next day, he flopped down to peruse some pages of his writing. The beginning of the story he was required to write. A beginning after dozens of impotent attempts. Why did these few pages seem successful to him? He did not know yet. He just knew he should not tear them up. He did not crumple them or throw them into the wastebasket under his desk. He had written:

His canvas the painter paints just as his story the writer writes, and, in front of his wooden easel sits the painter. Into the bold whiteness and tenacity of the cloth, the painter stares. Amid the vortex of a harvest of lines and complicated, amorphous patterns, he conceives no shapes. Not even the shape of Kaleh's face. In a far corner of his past, the painter has lost Kaleh. He lost her years ago. At this moment, he cannot find the painting he once painted of Kaleh on a bygone day.

That day, Kaleh wore an all-blue shirt adorned with petite red flowers, sitting on the edge of a pool. She bent over the crystal-clear water. She stared at the tremble and movements of her face on the surface, at the dance of the fish, and at the red flowers. Outside the painting, the sun poured its shining beams onto the water. He who saw her fell for her—fell for the face of a girl in the crystal-clear water. To no one did he reveal that it was Kaleh. He sighed coldly and told the old woman who had accidentally caught a glimpse of the painting, "I fear Kaleh might drown in the water."

He did not even mention it to those tawn *weavers.*

Those ladies who make rugs with their agile fingers in the basements of houses. The ladies who sang the Kurdish folklore song "Kaleh Wey Kaleh." Kind and beautiful were the lady rug-weavers. The painter does not remember their faces. Kind and beautiful was Kaleh . . .

The painter still sits among a pile of colors and small and big brushes, but except for some lines, he has painted nothing on the white canvas.

Some scribbled, tiny black lines—each one taking him somewhere, but none of them to Kaleh. A bullet-like pain passes through his face and neck. The canvas and the easel whirl around and upon his head.

"Where are you, Kaleh?"

He helplessly breaks the silence. "Where are you, Kaleh? Why do you turn your back on me . . . ?"

Then, an unknown hand gives him a glass of water and some pills. He takes the pills while hearing whispers behind him.

"He's not sober. He doesn't know what he says."

His dizziness is gone, but he is still frightened. He fears not being able to finish the painting. He fears no longer seeing Kaleh. Pondering. He'd better follow those twisted lines on the canvas. Unto where? He knows not. This first line takes him to the courtyard of a house. Under the shadow of a tree. The courtyard and the trees are whirling around his head.

"It's better for him to quit painting for a while. He's exhausted. He needs to rest," someone says.

Exhausted is he. The painter is well aware of that. Since he disengaged from that house and that courtyard, through his alley-to-alley journeys, he became exhausted. He sought refuge in the alleys. Then he got lost in one. Just like Kaleh, who got lost and whom the painter can never catch again. The voices keep whispering:

"He is sad. He stands no one."

"He's infected by amnesia."

"Doctor says . . ."

"We shouldn't let him go out of the house alone."

The painter must step out. He must follow another line . . . He must . . . Even if the dizziness keeps lingering and the bullet-like pain passes through his face and neck. Some other pills he should take and into the path he should go. He has set off. He is in an empty alley. Agile and in a hurry, he goes. He does not want to be seen. Knows not why. From that alley into another . . . A white car heads toward him. Startled is the painter. He is petrified. Three well-dressed, well-shaven men get out of the car. Polite and dignified, the men seem. Especially the third one, who is older. They ask him to get inside the car. They want to give him a ride . . . He remembers not to where . . .

He follows another line. That day or another. They've blindfolded him. They take him from one place to another. From one darkness to another. Something like a leg blocks his way. He stumbles. He falls down some stairs. The painter drops to the ground. The same three men pick him up. They nail him to a wall. They're not kind anymore. Never have they been. His eyes are still covered. They kick and punch him.

"Where have you been?"

"Where did you want to go? To see who?"

Dizziness . . . dizziness again and a pain passing through his face and neck. Again, a glass of water and some colorful pills. Whispers again . . .

"Kaleh? Where are you? I wanna see you. I must see you . . ."

He does not see her. Darkness doesn't grant him the opportunity to see her. But he hears her. He hears Kaleh. He knows not how to paint Kaleh's voice on that white canvas. Kaleh's voice amid the mayhem of those voices. In the chaos of those terrifying, sharp screams. All those shrieking shouts and screeching sobs . . . Breathless cries and giggling laughter. Insidious whispers of some people behind him and the ticking of the clock hands on the heart of the walls . . .

"Was it Farhad's last painting that he could never complete?" I asked.

My voice sent a shiver down his spine. He was not supposed to write Farhad's story. So he could not be the character in my story either. He raised his bewildered head. His perplexing look roamed around the room, and I was standing sadly near his desk. He stopped reading. He was thinking. It seemed he could not avoid writing Farhad's story. He should raise the white flag. He did. He surrendered. Surrender? Against which power? My determination, Farhad's forgotten past, or the will to write? That same will which chained the painter to his easel and canvas. Now the painter was one and the same Farhad, and Farhad was also a man resembling all the men of his past. Same as himself. Himself?

"The past of men of the same generation looks so much alike." I murmured to myself.

"But I don't want to write the story of a generation," he said. "I wanna . . ."

He did not say he wanted to write the story of Farhad. He said nothing. He picked up the pencil sharpener. Sharpened his pencil. It jogged his memory—to light a cigarette. In order to dominate doubt and dilemma, he lit it up.

"What happened to the painting?" he asked.

I was sitting on a sofa at that time. "He could never finish it," I said. "He still had a slight consciousness, but headache and dizziness didn't let him. After that, he forgot everything."

Did he forget everything? He did not ask. He knew it. But he could not believe it. He did not believe it since the day he saw Farhad. How is it possible for a man to forget everything? Father, mother, and . . . How can wishes and hopes be forgotten by humans? His dreams . . . The face of his beloved . . . Kaleh's face . . .

"Who was Kaleh?" he asked.

"A lost beloved."

"Which one of us doesn't have a lost beloved?" he asked.

"Sounds like we've lived like losing a person or a thing in order to look for them the rest of our lives. In our paintings. In . . ." he added in mere sadness.

Who was he looking for? He asked himself. He returned from the other side of the world to this side to see who?

SEVEN

It was a tough question. Ever since he returned, he had faced a difficult, challenging question every single day. An unanswered question. He wondered where he should look for the answers to those questions. The questions were only about him, his life, and his past.

"Behind your desk," I said. "Inside the pages you write."

He was neither at his desk nor in his room. He sat on the rusty chair out on the balcony, staring into the courtyard. The pool was still dry and cracked with decay. The leaves were falling, and the big berry tree of their neighbor's . . . He was staring at their neighbor's berry tree, at the empty nest of the storks on its high branches. The storks had migrated the day before he returned. If they were here, he would watch them and listen to the sweet click-clack of their beaks. A big bird with wide, black, veil-like wings occasionally circled the house and the courtyard. He gave his ears to its piercing, scary sound.

A part of the city was visible from the balcony. A portion of the neighborhood. If he turned his head, he could also see the houses beyond the street. A street only recently built, during the years of his absence. A part of their house and courtyard was right up against the street . . .

"The value of the house has grown by leaps and bounds. This street has changed the whole appearance of the neighborhood," Baram said. The city's face had changed. It was renewed. It had grown. The houses spread to the mountains. The houses covered the big hill across from their house. There once existed a beautiful fountain and a pool on that hill. A few fertile trees and . . . When he was a child, he used to go there on Fridays with his school and neighborhood friends, and . . .

It occurred to him to go there once again, to search house by house, courtyard by courtyard, and to find the fountain. I laughed. My laughter did not bother him. It had not bothered him for the past two or three days. "Suppose you will find the fountain, alone . . ." I said.

He did not remember the names of the children—except for one or two who still lived in the neighborhood. Something rang a bell in his mind—to search every house in the city for his childhood friends. Just as he searched for the friends of his youth, the ones from before his departure. With Jalali, alley by alley and door to door. Most of them were not there anymore. Neither in here nor in any place, not in any corner of this country and this world . . . Those who stayed here . . . "They're no longer the same friends you left behind all those years ago," Jalali said a while ago. With grief. Sorrow.

"The pressure of time changed them all. Money made them forget you and hundreds like you," Baram said sarcastically. "You were the only one who was tricked among them. You and some others like you. You were cheated into forgetting your life and your relatives, all to chase a childish dream. Then they turned their backs on you, your dream, and your relatives . . . When you went away, your close and dear friends would walk past us with reluctance. As if we were lepers. And I didn't see most of them at my father's funeral either . . ." Maybe he did not say "most of them," but "none of them."

"They were afraid they'd be arrested if they greeted us." Arrested? Who was he? What had he done?

He heard the telephone ringing again. Surprised but joyful, he moved toward the phone. In that moment, he felt as if he were abroad. In a distant and unfamiliar city, in a room barely forty meters square, he had spent months waiting for a phone call. Waiting just to hear a familiar voice. It was the familiar voice of his sister, Monira. "You haven't forgotten you have a guest this afternoon, have you?"

Guest? He thought. He was not expecting anyone, and Monira knew that. "Nashmil, Laila and me. And don't you dare ask which Laila!"

He did not say which Laila. He knew her. She was a poet, the teacher of his niece Nashmil. Monira's daughter, Nashmil. Monira hung up, laughing.

Laila . . . He saw her a while ago at a literary gathering. At one of those weekly or monthly literary meetings. He was invited and he accepted the invitation. A small gathering in a small hall. About a hundred young people, most of them poets and writers. Before he gave his speech, several of them had stood up and recited poems. The last was a girl. She wore a veil. She covered her rosy face with a black frame. During the time she was reciting poetry, she had a smile on her lips as she looked at him. It seemed as if she recited her poem just for him. He could not remember the entire poem, only the final lines . . .

When the poem's reciting was finished, he stood up and went behind the microphone and . . . The girl, seated beside his niece Nashmil in the ladies' section, kept her eyes on him. He spoke about language and literature, and about the poems that were recited at the gathering. At the end, he answered questions too. Questions from the attendees about himself and his stories . . . When the gathering ended, he was the last to leave the hall. His niece and the girl who recited poetry were waiting for him outside. They walked up to greet him. The girl still had that smile on her lips. She covered her rosy face with a black frame.

"Nice job," she said so friendly and so frankly. "All we know is how to put our artists and writers on trial." Then she laughed. Nashmil also laughed. He looked at Nashmil, his gaze full of questions. "Who is this lady?" He was certain she was not that close to Nashmil. She looked older. The girl did not give Nashmil a chance to introduce her. "My name's Laila. Laila Tolu'i. It's been a year since I became familiar with your stories, and I do thank your niece, Nashmil, for this familiarity." Her eyes were sparkling. So were Nashmil's. "Nashmil is my student, and her mother, Monira . . ." She wanted to say they were friends, but she did not.

"Laila is a kind lady with delicate feelings. We've known her for a year, and during this time . . ." Monira said.

He saw Laila for the second time at Monira's house. By accident? Perhaps not. He was glad to see her again. So was Laila. Again the smile, again that rosy face framed in black . . . They talked to each other. About poetry and literature and about the issues that had been brought up at that moment. He sensed a tinge of sorrow in Laila's face and voice. Even while she was reciting the poem, a delicate sadness lingered on her face. She could not hide it beneath her smile. And her laughter also . . .

"Her father is gone. He was killed when Laila was a child," Monira said after Laila left. Perhaps that sorrow had settled into her face and voice since then. Monira did not mention this. "The first time she talked about your stories, she had no idea she was talking about my uncle," Nashmil said.

"She loves you deeply. She loved you even before she knew you were related to us. Does that mean . . . ?" Monira said.

"She said, 'I wished to see him. To see him in person and . . .'" Nashmil said.

"Then bring her here one day," he suggested. He said it to Monira. They chose today for the meeting.

Monira and the girls quietly entered the courtyard and went up the stairs. Monira had the key to the gate, the iron door facing the street. "We don't knock. We open it ourselves," she said. "Oh, my poor twisted brother. You always have to walk down all those stairs to open the door when you have guests."

Laila thought it would be nice to walk into a writer's room unexpectedly and find him writing at his desk. She did not consider the possibility that he might not be there. He was not at his desk. Nor in the room. He had gone out to buy a few necessary things. When he returned, Monira was washing the balcony. Nashmil and Laila were leaning on the pillars, watching the iron gate of the courtyard. He entered the house through the back door that opened to the alley. No one saw him until he reached the middle of the courtyard. Laila had previously walked through the courtyard under the pretext of visiting Nashmil, then through the house and its rooms. She had placed a bunch of daffodils in a glass vase and set it on his desk, flowers she had brought herself.

"Hosting guests really suits him," Monira said with irony. "We don't mind, but this is the first time Laila has come here. He shouldn't have . . ."

Laila was no longer wearing her black veil. She had on a violet shirt and skirt trimmed with picot. She looked taller. Soft blond tresses tumbled over her shoulders. Though it was her first time in this house, she moved around the room with ease and sat down comfortably. It was a beautiful sight. The sight of a girl in a violet shirt and skirt, a soft blond tress tumbling over her shoulder, walking with ease and sitting comfortably in his room.

The sight of a desk, with a bunch of daffodils in a glass vase on top . . .

"As I was walking through the rooms, I thought this big house and courtyard are the perfect scriptorium for a writer like you," Laila said. She didn't say that this marooned, ruined house and courtyard were the best place for writing.

He nodded with a bitter smile. "Something that I do," he said. It was a strange fate. A marooned, ruined house and courtyard, and how sure she was when she said it was the best place for writing.

"Also, the best place for a wedding ceremony," Nashmil said.

Monira came out of the kitchen with a tray of teas. She had heard their words.

"Something you should do soon," she said.

The mother and daughter laughed, but he still felt that talking about marriage and weddings in front of a young lady guest was inappropriate. Maybe she would get embarrassed and blood would rush to her cheeks. But Laila's cheeks would not. She just changed the topic. "I read your interview. I'm happy you republish your books here."

It was his second interview with Kurdish newspapers and journals since his return. A detailed, all-inclusive interview he had not yet seen in print.

"I'm also delighted you have a new work in progress. A new story . . ." Laila said.

He was startled. He glanced at his desk. Before the guests arrived, he had gathered his writings and set them aside. How did Laila know he had a new work in progress? Had he mentioned it in the interview? What else had he said?

I laughed. I went and sat right beside him on the sofa. "I'm delighted you've revealed it."

He said a few days ago that he was not going to talk about Farhad and his story this soon. He feared he would regret writing it. He feared he would not finish it.

"I don't think I said something. I don't think I revealed it," he said out loud.

"What . . . ?" Laila raised her head and said with a wonder in her eyes.

Monira and Nashmil said nothing. He felt humiliated and shattered. "I've heard you're looking forward to publishing your poems," he said.

Laila was sitting in front of him, a cup of tea in her hand. The usual smile on her lips blossomed, and she stayed silent for a while. Then he said, "I'm still not sure. I'm in a dilemma . . . I think . . ." Doubt and dilemma, likewise, resided in her eyes.

He could see it—even in her words. Laila set her cup of tea down. She took the notebook of her poems out of her purse and, shamefaced, placed it on the glass desk beside her. Then she slowly pushed it toward him with her fingertips.

"I'd like you to read. If you think it is . . ."

He reached out and picked up the notebook. It was a pretty notebook. Its cover was embellished with a girlish taste. Laila's lips gently trembled without letting the smile walk away. Her gaze, from the notebook's trace on the glass desk, followed his hand. Was he the first one who opened the notebook? Was he the first man?

"Some of the poems . . ." Laila said. She did not know what to say. "Some of the poems, I assume, are weak."

He opened the notebook. The first page and the first poem . . .

When the guests left, he put the notebook down. Monira, Nashmil, and . . . Laila collected her soft, blond hair in her palm and locked it at the back of her head. Then she hid it under a gray flowery scarf. She hid her violet shirt and skirt under her black cover. "I'd like you to read them with the eyes of a critic," she said, pointing to her notebook. Her lips trembled again, even as she smiled. He kept them company in the courtyard. Laila looked around once more. "Now I remember. I've seen this courtyard and garden before," she said. "A big pool full of clear water. Rows of colorful flowers. And these trees . . . I thought the big berry tree, the one the storks nested in, must be in this courtyard." She had seen it in a story. She had read it.

He didn't ask which story. "But now, as you see, it is empty and ruined," he said. He meant the courtyard. Laila thought he was speaking about the empty stork nests.

"When the storks come back, they'll bring it back to life," she said. But it wasn't Laila who said that. It was Monira.

"How are her poems? Laila's poems?" I asked.

He still held the notebook in his hands, reading the last page. Some lines from the final poem.

Tear the dictionaries and
Give the cold, dead words to the gale.
In one line,
I write the most beautiful poem of your being
Wipe the past away,
Forget its dark days.
In a moment, I realize your most eternal dream.

Laila had written this poem recently.

EIGHT

"Laila is a dream your sister Monira and your niece Nashmil had for you," I said.

He raised his head. I laughed behind the thick cloud of cigarette smoke. Maybe it was a derisive laugh and . . . he did not take offense. "Watch it, or the story will fall apart," he said.

"Which story? Yours or Farhad's?" I asked. He pondered. He did not know if he was in his room or Farhad's. Was he living his own moments or the forgotten moments of Farhad? Maybe neither . . .

"Or both of them."

His own words startled him. He returned to his desk. I was still there. He turned to me. "I want to see Farhad's last painting. The one in which he wanted to find Kaleh," he said.

"He couldn't find her. He couldn't finish the painting. Just a few thin, twisting lines . . ." I have said that so many times.

"I want to see him. Right now."

He saw it. He reflected on it. I was right. Just some thin, twisting lines . . .

"Where did these lines take him?" he asked.

He pointed to the longest line in the painting. The line that led him to a dark, tiny room.

He wrote:

In a dark cramped room, regains his consciousness. Farhad. The room is the size of a toilet. No window. Not even a hole. A room with one wall made of iron. Feels it through his cold, dry breath. Farhad. When the iron door is knocked, a strange and frightening sound resonates. Like the ringing of church bells. He tries to stand, but he cannot. Every part of his body is crying out in pain. His head . . . his hands . . . his feet . . . It takes him a moment to remember where he is and what has happened to him. He remembers the car, and the three well-dressed men too. He remembers their kicks and punches when his eyes were covered. They asked him nothing but a few simple questions. Happy is Farhad. He is glad his arrest does not seem connected to his past. Not connected? He asks himself. Then why did they arrest him?

Bitterness fills his mouth. His nostrils are clogged with blood and snot. A blood clot clings to his throat. He's struggling to breathe. A broken tooth scrapes against his tongue. Might this be enough for them to let him go? Dizzy and dazed is Farhad. He cannot answer that question or any other. He lies down again.

"Take me with you. Take me somewhere no one knows us, and no one can find us . . ."

Someone tells him. He does not know who.

"Don't walk away from me. I can't stand this sadness."

Has he lost consciousness, or has he drifted into sleep? Once again, the echo of a church bell opens his eyes. It resonates through his ears and into the room.

"Stand up. Turn your back to the door."

He crawls but can't manage to stand. Twisting, he turns his back to the door. The iron door swings open with a cold, dry screech. Light pours into the room. On the wall in front of him, the shadow of a helpless man lying down takes shape. A larger shadow—another man—falls over it. Then two hands, big and heavy, blindfold him. They lift him to his feet. His own legs can't move. They grip him by the chest and drag him somewhere. Forcing him into a chair. His eyes are covered, Farhad. Two or three people surround him. He can tell by their voices and the sound of their shoes knocking against the floor.

"Your name?"

"Farhad."

"Your job?"

"Painter."

"Painter or student?"

They strike him in the mouth. The scar inside his cheek reopens, and a stream of warm saliva trickles from the corners of his lips.

"A painter or a rebellious student?"

"I was a student. I quit. I'm working now," he says.

"Did you quit, or did you escape? Do you work, or do you run organizations?"

Those questions fade his hopes to black. So they knew . . .

He becomes disheartened. Disillusioned, Farhad surrenders himself to a blurry fate.

"A man must be stupid to think they'll forget everything after a while. He's been followed since the very first day he left university," I said.

Then I poured him a cup of tea from the teapot on the brazier. I poured one for myself as well.

So, he was at Farhad's house. Farhad's house—or mine? Farhad was sitting by the door, in the mudroom. Like a pale, sickly child, he did not even bother to play with his shoes. "From the university . . . ? Was Farhad . . . ?" he asked in astonishment.

He was a student, studying art at the Faculty of Fine Arts at the University of Tehran and . . . after two years, he took the university entrance exam again and was accepted to study Law. Most of his comrades were also studying Law. In addition to staying at the university dormitory, they had rented a small house downtown. They would gather most nights. They were a like-minded group who read books and underground publications from the armed and political movements of that time. They would copy the texts by hand and secretly distribute them at the university. Then one day, the police discovered their activities and arrested several of them during the night. "The night his friends were arrested, Farhad wasn't with them. The next morning, they came to the university, but he already knew—and escaped before they could catch him," I said.

For a while, Farhad hid in Tehran. He spent some nights in hotels and others with his comrades. When he ran out of money, he had no choice but to return here. To his father's house. But he quickly realized he was not safe there either. He left that place too. He did not want anyone else to get burned in the fire of his fate.

"Where to?"

He said he was going to start a new life, a secret life. He asked his friends here to help him. They found him a job at a small factory on the outskirts of the city. But he did not stay there long either. He grew exhausted and returned to the city. To the old districts where the poor lived. Soon, he began painting houses with passion. It was a charming career, each day in a house and . . .

"He might've fallen for Kaleh in one of those houses."

Farhad came in through the mudroom and sat cross-legged by the small window. The room was, as usual, dark, and layers of smoke drifted lazily above his head.

"Kaleh was a happy, lively, and beautiful girl. She had a God-given gift for love and passion but she wasn't aware of it. She didn't realize it until she met Farhad. She didn't know that a single loving glance could change her life—and her fate. Farhad's loving glance . . ."

"Then what happened?" he asked.

"Then? It didn't take a year before Farhad was arrested. He remained in prison until the people stormed in and freed him along with the other political prisoners."

It was a hot summer day. The day the freed political prisoners, pale and emaciated men with garlands of flowers around their necks, were carried on the wave of people's shoulders from the prison street toward Azadi Square. Delighted, yet astonished and restless, they waved their small, pale hands at the people, and at him. He scanned the dense crowd, searching for Afsana. Afsana? He could not see her. Where was she? The torrent of the crowd had hidden her from his searching eyes.

Since the night before, when people first heard about the release of the political prisoners, they had been pouring into the streets in crowds. He was at the mosque with some of his comrades. The mosque, too, was overflowing with people, all preparing for the welcome ceremony the next day. One group was writing slogans. Another was making garlands. Another group, who were older, were by the pulpit with the mosque's cleric, writing the manifesto. A throng of coming-of-age boys gathered around a prisoner who had been released earlier. They listened with joy and amazement, all ears for the stories of the prisoners' bravery and resistance, those heroes they would be thrilled to meet the next day. The man knew each prisoner well, and he was recounting their heroism under torture. Did he talk about Farhad? He did not remember. The boys gave their teenage dreams to the gale, wishing they could take the prisoners' place. To them, being in chains and enduring torture was a distant but pleasant dream. The news of people gathering in front of the prison gate reached the mosque. Both the young and the old near the pulpit were glad. He was glad too. "Afsana is there, for sure," he said to himself. She had to be. The revolution was kind, at least kind enough to bring Afsana out of her house, if only for the sake of his heart. Surely, it brought her out. Afsana was a part of the revolution. She was its daughter. Its petite daughter. She was present at most of the demonstrations. Just like him, who took part in all of them. He was the revolution's son as well. If only the revolution had been won earlier. "I'll bite the bullet and won't talk to Afsana until the day the revolution wins," he had told his friend Jalali. "On that joyful and sacred day, even if Afsana is among thousands of people, even if she is at home in the arms of her family, I'll go and reveal to her the secret of my love."

As midnight approached, he arrived near the prison. The families of the prisoners were sitting in front of the gate, waiting . . . With each passing moment, the crowd grew larger. The young were singing anthems in unison. Through loudspeakers, the police pleaded with them to disperse and go back to their homes. Hundreds of armed soldiers stood atop the prison walls and rooftops. Huge floodlights lit the area as bright as day. Afsana was in a corner among the girls. As always, she wore a *jamana* as her scarf. Did she see him? She must have. Their glances flew like letter-carrying birds in the glow of the floodlights. The police spoke again through the loudspeakers . . .

In the morning, the prison doors opened, and the prisoners stepped out one by one. The crowd split in two. Ahead of the prisoners were the girls and women, and at the back of them were the boys and men. He was in between the two groups. He lost Afsana in the thickness of the front crowd. He could not see her or maybe he did and . . . How far Afsana was! His passionate, searching gaze could not catch her. How far away those days seemed! He could not recall every moment. But he had to write them down. He had to breathe life back into each moment of those distant days.

He wrote:

Everyone—men, women, children, the young, and the old—has rushed into the streets. The homebound elderly, from their balconies or behind their windows, scatter bunches of flowers. Onto the heads of the revolutionary people and the freed prisoners. A rain of flowers fell upon them. The city has long been honoring the return of its imprisoned children. It is the day of Armageddon. Armageddon of the faithful people. Elated and successful are the people. Even the police and the soldiers on the tanks and military machines are elated.

The flood that released the prisoners, and especially Farhad, from that small murky room is heading to wherever it may. Petrified is Farhad. The howls, the anthems, the slogans, and tapping beats of the young revolutionary people terrify him. Terrified is Farhad of all that joy and euphoria. He opts for running away. Running away from that carnival of happiness, from the ceremony held in honor of his liberation and that of his comrades as well. Running away from those men who do not want to lose the grace of being under the coffin of the dead, and who now, in turn, want to carry it on their shoulders. To run away and seek refuge in his own loneliness and silence. That same loneliness and silence he has grown used to over the years. To run away and surrender himself to the seclusion of one of those alleys. The alley where he lost Kaleh. There she is, in the stillness of one of those narrow alleys.

"Don't walk away from me . . . I can't bear this sadness . . . I won't be able to . . ." says Kaleh.

"Kaleh, you've endured an ocean of sorrow. You've suffered for ages. Be brave, my girl. Have courage . . . You can overcome it . . ." Farhad said that. Did he say that?

"Can't stand this sadness," Kaleh screamed into the wholeness of the alley. "I can't defeat it." Then she burst into tears.

He set the pen down on the paper and stood up from behind his desk. Both his legs had gone numb. He walked around the room and asked, "Since when has Farhad left that house?"

I was tired. I answered him wearily. Then he promised he would come by someday, to take Farhad's hand and walk out of the house together.

NINE

"You promised. You promised you'd stay committed to writing the story and . . ."

He was not writing. For days, not a single word. They would not let him. They would not let him sit at his desk. They would knock on the door whenever he sat down and picked up his pen. He would close the door. All the doors and the windows. He would unplug the telephone. The moment he turned his head, he would see them everywhere in the courtyard, all around the house. His father, his mother, his siblings, his old and new friends . . . It has been some time since they brought Laila here as well. Laila Tolu'i. Monira and her daughter, Nashmil, brought her in and walked her through the house. Then she put a bunch of daffodils on his desk. Each day, she would buy a bunch of daffodils and place them on his desk. Every day, she would peel away her black veil. Her soft blonde hair tumbled over her shoulders. "A big house and courtyard like this, is the perfect place for someone like you to write," she would say. She never called it a marooned house or a ruined courtyard. She would say it with a smile on her lips, every single day.

It would be the perfect place if only they let him work. But they did not. Naseri would not let him. Naseri, with his high-end green Peugeot and the tembûr he sometimes played, was now begging for a cigarette. Oh, poor, twisted Afsana . . .

"Forget about Afsana. Keep writing your story," I said.

"I can't. Some nights. Again. That piercing and chilling scream . . ."

I did not know what connected that rending scream to Afsana.

"It's too late. The days come and go in a blur. I'm scared . . ." I said.

He interrupted me, "You scared? Of what?"

He was thinking, What was I scared of? Was I supposed to believe that he—he, as Farhad—would . . . ?

If only he knew what Farhad thought about in those moments, sitting in his dark, smoke-filled room, thick with the smell of damp and burnt rubbish, beneath the faint light trickling through a small window, his head hanging from his neck. About whom? He had heard him speak once or twice. Just a bunch of broken, incomplete words and sentences . . . What did he say? What was he talking about? Nothing rang a bell. His words were not clear enough to stick in his mind.

"Sometimes he talks. He murmurs things to himself that I can't understand. And neither can he," I said. Because behind those words, there's nothing he remembers. He thinks about nobody and no one."

He could not understand how a man—even one who had lost his memory—could think of nothing and no one. He said, "I'm sure he thinks about someone . . . Kaleh . . ."

If only he knew what Naseri was thinking about . . . He could not have forgotten everything. Maybe he was thinking about Afsana. About her children. Do you think Afsana has a child? A girl or a boy? Maybe a girl and a boy. Hiwa and Hero . . . Hiwa and Hero Naseri. He does not remember if he and Afsana ever talked about having children. In those days, Afsana and he would talk about themselves. About themselves and their life. About the days after the revolution won. Days when the city longed to have a break. A break to recover from a hundred years of weariness. Who stopped the city's dream from coming true? Those were days marked by sound and fury, by fighting and ferocity, by seizing and letting go. "The city is getting used to all this fighting and ferocity. Let's leave here. Let's go to . . ." Afsana said.

"The fate of the revolution, the fate of the people, and . . ." he said. What else did he say? What was Afsana's response? Just a few days ago, he wrote:

Kaleh said: I can't hold this grief. I can't resist it.

The door was being constantly knocked. I said "Go. Go and open the door."

He just heard it. Who might it be? Baram? "Tomorrow, I'll bring a workman to repair the rooftop," Baram had said, but that was some days ago. He brought the workman and he had repaired the rooftop. It means . . .

It was Jalali. "Good guy! I've been knocking on that poor door for an hour. I was about to give up!"

He forgot again. It was the third day since the Cultural Heritage Office opened an exhibition of the Ziwiyeh district's treasures at the city museum. A treasure found after three thousand years. Unearthed. Under the feet of those people . . . The fortune of a nation . . . Every day, he promised to attend—but he never did. This morning, Jalali called. He said he would come pick him up and he did. "You don't seem to care much about your ancestors' cultural heritage," Jalali said playfully.

It reminded him of something Baram, his brother, once said. "I fear the ancestors' heritage . . . Like that of my family . . ."

His fear was not irrational. He saw a large portion of Ziwiyeh's ancient artifacts displayed in foreign museums. Daggers, bows and arrows . . . maces . . . saddles, helmets, shields, and buckles.

"The outsiders took all the weapons and ammunition," Jalali said furiously. "And the seals . . . the historical tablets too. Even the pots, the spoons, the dishes . . . They divided everything among themselves. They stole a part of Kurdish history . . . What's left behind is just . . ."

The remainders were locked in glass display cases. In the museum's hall and . . . He stared at the jewelry—the gold and silver—still bearing the faint traces of the goldsmiths' fingers after three thousand years. They have not even wiped the sweat from their foreheads. The earth had kept the treasures safe, like a mother.

But the memories . . . The wishes and the yearnings . . . Even the names and the addresses . . . Which of those three-thousand-year-old ancestors had crafted that intricate gold necklace? For whose neck? Whose beloved? Around whose wrist had that delicate, snake-shaped bangle once coiled? From whose ears had those lotus earrings once dangled . . . ?

Jalali pointed to a broken piece of ivory no larger than a child's palm. "Look at these palanquins, carts, kings and viziers, the horsemen and the infantry. All of them are carved onto this tiny piece of ivory," Jalali said in astonishment. "It inspired a current artist to draw big graffiti. I bet you've seen it. By the way, it's no longer necessary to swear on the Quran to prove that we've been the native people of this land for three thousand years. We had our own corps and troops, our kings and queens."

The necklace, behind the thick glass of the display case, still carried the scent of unfulfilled wishes. The little snake was still hissing and the lotuses still held on to the thirst for amorous whispers—buried beneath the earth for three thousand years.

"The history of this nation is the history of its lovers' unfulfilled love," he said.

"They still don't believe in our history—even after discovering this treasure," Jalali added.

He could hear the beating of the goldsmith's heart—that lover who had lived three thousand years ago. He heard it . . . he, and perhaps the veiled girl who had just stepped into the museum. Laila?

I said, "Laila's here to see you. Look at the joy on her face when she sees you."

He raised his head and saw Laila. It seemed as if she was coming from a long way away. Her steps were tired. Tired but heavy and firm. She was not happy. He was shocked. He did not ask if she came here to see him. He did not ask how she knew he was in here. He said nothing.

Laila went to welcome him. At a fast pace. Her eyes were twinkling. The smile on her lips was a part of her face. A part of her rosy face that was irresistible to the eyes. When she approached him, she said, "What a serendipitous encounter! I didn't think you would be here."

She said it closely, with warmth and familiarity. Like a longtime acquaintance. He welcomed her. He turned to Jalali and said, "I'd like to introduce you to each other. Miss Laila Tolu'i . . ."

They already knew each other. Perhaps from long ago. Jalali was elated. "This is the third day we've opened the exhibition, and Laila has been here every day."

He said it with a grateful smile and thanked her, thanked her for coming every day, for watching over her ancestors' treasures and heritage. Laila wrapped her veil around herself and turned her eyes to the hall. The hall was empty. A stream of colorful light poured into the hall through the thousand eyes of the great window. Faint music floated through the space—the sound of a piano . . . It sounded like a singing stream flowing through the bottom of a valley, a song for an empty hall. Laila's gaze shifted to the glass display cases. "I'll definitely visit this exhibition every day until it closes. I've never seen so many beautiful things before. Three-thousand-year-old beautiful things . . ." She turned to Jalali. "I couldn't have imagined that the creations of the people of our land, three thousand years ago, could be this stunning."

He smiled. "Since the beginning of the world, humankind has loved creating beautiful things," he said.

"Why?" Laila asked, blushing. "Sorry for the silly question, but I was just wondering—what might be the reason for that?"

He did not reply immediately. He stared at a point for a moment, then said, "Perhaps to decorate their surroundings. Embellishment has always been part of human endeavor. Adorning themselves and the world around them."

The museum attendant approached them. He wanted to speak with Jalali and whispered something in his ear. But they heard it too. "Tea is ready. Should I bring it here or . . . ?"

"No, we'll go upstairs," Jalali replied.

A man and a woman entered the hall. A young couple. They wandered among the glass display cases and stopped near them, in front of the golden necklace, the bangle, and the earrings.

First with enthusiasm, then with a touch of greed, the woman looked at the jewelry. Her eyes sparkled at the sight of the jewels. Also, the man's eyes. But the man glanced at the woman with embarrassment. I wish he knew what the couple was thinking in that moment . . .

I said, "I'm not sure about the woman, but the man is thinking about why he hasn't been able to make his wife happy."

Why could Naseri not make Afsana happy? "My family insists I marry Naseri. The man with the green Peugeot and . . ." Afsana said. "They say that in these dark days, only Naseri can make you happy. He's not a man of politics, patriotism, the colonized motherland, or any of that stuff . . ." she said, laughing. With grief. "They say he's a rich man, and he's supposed to pour gold coins at your feet," she said, laughing. Laughing? Maybe with regret . . .

"Let's go upstairs and drink our teas," Jalali said.

While they were going up the stairs, people were entering sporadically. A lonely, swarthy boy walked in. He caught his attention. But the boy quickly slipped out of sight. Where has he seen that swarthy boy before . . . ? They went upstairs. To the museum manager's office. Jalali sat behind his desk. From the other side of the desk he stared at a small statue of a woman on a stool, placed in the far corner of the room. The woman placed her clay head in the clay bowl of her palms, her clay eyes fixed on the ground. Laila sat in front of Jalali and looked at the statue. How far were they from each other, Laila and that clay woman who had her head buried in the bowl of her palms? He asked himself, and his gaze moved back and forth between the two. From clay to flesh and blood. From flesh and blood to clay. From Afsana to Laila. From Laila to Afsana. How far were they from each other, Laila and Afsana? The day he saw Afsana for the last time . . . Perhaps Afsana placed her head in the bowl of her palms after his departure, her eyes fixed on the ground.

The museum attendant brought them tea. "It seems the statue has caught your attention," Jalali said.

While sipping his tea, he said, "It's a nice statue. It's the work of an artist . . ."

Nice? So that statue was made to decorate a space. To embellish the sculptor's surrounding world. When the world is adorned with the fruits of human sorrow and regret . . .

"I've said it before. This city is full of young, gifted artists," Jalali said.

Then he talked about Laila. About her poetry. That girl had been waiting for this moment for a long time. She pulled herself together. She looked at Jalali; her lips began to tremble. At that very moment, he wondered if she had come to hear his thoughts on her poetry. She has been here for three days in a row, hoping to see him here and . . . She must have been absolutely dejected not to find him here. He felt embarrassed. He should have spoken about her poetry much earlier, at least when she rushed into the museum hall. Why did he not heed her? Why did he not notice her waiting eyes? The burden of waiting that lived in them, in her question-filled gaze? "It's been a week that her . . ."

He didn't say "Laila."

"It's been a week that I've been living with Miss Tolu'i's poetry." Miss Tolu'i? It was a cold name. He added, "I've read her poetry notebook a few times this week." Then his gaze shifted toward Laila. Laila was exultant. Exultant because he had read her poetry. She was waiting to hear the rest of what he wanted to say. Jalali was waiting too. He sensed it, and so he began to speak about poetry. First, he spoke about the form and language of the poems, then about their content and themes. He looked angry and withdrawn. Perhaps it was because he kept the girl waiting for days, or because he knew Laila wanted to hear more about her poetry. Mainly, it was about the content and themes of the poetry and about his thoughts on the concepts. The concepts of love, sin, and . . . "The dominant theme in most of the poems is love . . ." he said.

"The first poems are girlish, and to some extent, filled with a childish passion and emotion toward her deceased father," he said. "A father whose death is not confirmed by the poet. A father who lives in the poet's mind . . . someone she carries with her everywhere, as an inseparable part of her being:

> That heavy, warm hand
> Remains on my shoulder forever and
> Within me, I carry
> The ardor of those sorrowful eyes.
> I take you with me
> To everywhere,
> Even to where you should not be."

While he was reciting the poem, he looked at Laila. Tears welled up in her eyes. But now, the teardrops were gone. He could see his own reflection in her pupils. "There isn't anything new in poems like these. Everyone loves their father and even those who aren't poets might use similar language to express that love. But Laila . . ." She was rejuvenated when he said her name. "But Laila will gradually move beyond this stage and begin to change her mind about the general ideas and central themes of her poetry. From now on, she no longer uses the language everyone else uses, nor does she portray love and affection the way others do. From now on, she turns away from the well-trodden path, seeking to separate her way from theirs, her language from theirs, even her thoughts from theirs. For a girl living in a traditional society like ours where even love and affection carry fixed, unchangeable meanings such traits are seen as a clever effort. From now on, the poet's engagement with everything and with the central theme of her poetry becomes more personal and distinctive. It shifts with time and changes according to her inner moods. For example, in one of her poems, she writes:

> I love you forever.
> You deserve to be granted this sacred gift.

But in another poem:

> I will trap you in love,
> And I will rain down
> All the hatred of the gods upon you."

He did not remember the poems exactly as they were. He hoped Laila might help him, but she kept her head down and said nothing. "We can no longer say with certainty that the poet is only addressing her father in these poems. Suppose it is the father, but this one doesn't resemble the father from her earlier poems. A wise old man or a sage on the stage, living in the poet's mind. But it's a beloved who exists in the mind of the poetess . . ."

Then he continued, "If we read the poems from this perspective, we see that, bit by bit, she brings that wise old man, that beloved, out from her mind and seats him before her. To me, two main features of this process stand out. First, the poetess draws closer to herself as she becomes separated from that imaginary man. To knowing herself. She draws closer to her own independence as a human and as a woman. Secondly, she connects with this beloved man through dialogue. This marks the beginning of the poetess's freedom. To live and to write, to truly experience her own poetry, she needs this freedom and independence. Even if within this freedom and independence, within this encounter with the counterpart there exists a kind of revolt and fury. To me, this is, to some extent, entirely natural. A womanly revolt at the threshold of freedom and independence. For instance:

> The snake deceived you not.
> The red apple,
> And the desire for wheat,
> And the Tree of Knowledge,
> They were all alibis.
>
> The snake deceived you not.
> It was me.
> It was me craving you to descend.
> It was me craving you to sin,
> To sin and to repent.
> Sin, repent.
> Sin, repent.
> The Eve repents her sin not."

Now he was certain: the poem was far more beautiful than the way he had recited it. He kept watching Laila. Still hoping she might help him correct his mistakes. She still had her head down, saying nothing. He felt a strange coyness in her face. He had felt it before. At his house, on the day he took her book of poems. Her lips were trembling. Now, her lips were trembling again. She seemed like a girl undressed before the eyes of strangers, or worse, a girl being forced to undress. He could not quite understand it or perhaps he did. Perhaps he imagined her remembering past moments—the ones when she had written these poems, or the events that had driven her to write them—forcing a flood of blood to rush beneath the white and red of her skin. He went on talking. Mainly to say everything he could about her poems, or to make up for his earlier indifference. Or maybe he enjoyed his speech. Jalali liked his words too.

"Unfortunately, I don't remember her poems and Laila hasn't helped me either," he said.

Laila raised her head. Her moments of coyness vanished, and the smile returned to her lips. Then their eyes met. Just for a moment and in that fleeting instant, he saw something strange. In Laila's gaze. His heart collapsed. He said:

> Tear up the dictionaries,
> And give the cold, dead words to the gale.
> In a single line, I write
> The most beautiful poem of your being.
> Wipe out the past.
> Forget its dark days.
> In a single moment,
> I fulfill the most eternal dream you've ever had.

Was it he who uttered it or was it Laila? Jalali, who was listening intently until that moment, said: "I've never heard any of these poems before. What I heard was a collection of beautiful and deeply emotional poems that . . ."

He did not say that she had written them for her father. "These poems are beautiful," he said. "But this last one, this is a dreadful demand. To tear up the dictionaries, to wipe out the past . . . What will remain of us if we follow our poets?" He said it with laughter. Maybe he was thinking about the Ziwiyeh treasures. About the heritage of his ancestors, down on the lower floor in the museum hall, inside the glass display cases. Maybe he felt a quiet relief that Laila did not have the power to erase them. "What does humanity have without its past and its language?" he said.

"A short poem and an eternal moment," Laila said.

He smiled as well. The door to the room had been left ajar, and the museum attendant stepped in. Someone was calling for Jalali from outside.

"I'm coming, and . . ." And he left.

After a while, the museum attendant came in again with a tray holding two cups of tea. "What happened to Jalali?" he asked.

"It's been nearly half an hour since he left. One of his friends came for him, and he had to leave," the attendant said.

"Didn't he say goodbye?" he asked with surprise.

"Did he say goodbye?"

"Sorry. I think I kept you waiting," Laila said.

He did not understand. Did Laila mean that Jalali had said goodbye or not? She looked at her wristwatch. It was late. She stood up and wrapped her veil around herself. He stood up too. Then they stepped out and went down the stairs. The museum hall was crowded. The man and the woman were still there, watching the golden necklaces, the snakelet bangles, and the lotus earrings. They left the hall indifferently, without even a glance of curiosity.

CHAPER TEN

Today was the day he promised to take Farhad out of the house. To where? Downtown. To alleys and streets and . . . to the world he had forgotten. When was the last time Farhad left that dark, smoke-saturated room smelling of dampness and burnt trash?

"Years ago," I said. "Taking Farhad out is like showing a dead body to people. Don't hope he remembers anything. Nobody remembers him either."

"So why should I write his story?" he said in a low, heavy tone.

Then he turned to Farhad. It was like he knew he was going out. He looked around nervously.

"How are you gonna take him? By car?" I asked.

"I'm scared he'll get overwhelmed by all the street noise, the crowds, the sound of traffic. It terrifies him."

I knew where he planned to take him. He gave me a signal to get him ready. I did not know how to dress him. I searched the room, opened the doors of the old chests, found his coat, and dressed him. His old hat and scarf too . . .

He was still watching. A bitter smile played on his lips.

"When people see him like this, in these clothes . . ." he said.

He did not finish the sentence. He did not say what the people would remember when they saw him like that. Farhad was ready. They left together. I had to follow them.

It was cold outside. A sharp gale was blowing. Thick gray clouds twisted and tangled in the arms of the sky.

We slipped into an alley.

He wrote:

Tight and narrow are the alleys. The houses are small, their roof-edges worn down by time. The walls are adobe, the windows painted blue. The flowerpots on the balconies, behind and along the edges of the windows, are old, lidless metal gallons—some big, some small. Full of geraniums, basil, and . . . The smell of fresh bread from the corner bakeries have flooded the whole alley.

He stood right at the crossroads.

"Which alley should we take?" he said.

He hesitated, turned to me, waiting for an answer. But I was not following him—I was following Farhad into one of those tight alleys.

He quickened his steps, trying to catch up.

"These narrow alleys all look the same. Be careful. We might mix up the paths."

"Which path?"

He asked himself, but had no answer.

Farhad had come back to life. He was young again—just like in the old days—slipping through the twisting alleys, quick as an arrow, hands buried in the pockets of his worn coat. The icy wind bit at his face and ears. He reached me.

"Men get lost in these alleys. Where's he trying to take us?"

"It's not far now. Just down to the end of this dead-end. An old wooden door . . ." I said.

"That is, if it hasn't crumbled after all these years."

Which door? The door to which house?

No time to ask.

A middle-aged woman stepped out from one of the houses. She saw Farhad and froze. A soft, grateful smile—like a light, beautiful butterfly—rested on her lips.

She asked Farhad something. He answered with quiet dignity, measured and reserved.

A few steps away, an old, frail man sat on a bench by another doorway, hunched over a fire burning in an iron gallon. He did not stand to greet him. Maybe he did not notice him at all.

"We're here."

At the end of the alley, in front of the wooden door of a house, Farhad stands. The door is ajar—but not closed.

Farhad knows. Before reaching for it, he glances around, as if trying to bury a sin in the loneliness of the alley.

From the corner of his eye, he looks toward the window of the opposite house. A small, blue window. Behind the glass, he spots a clay flowerpot. A mini pomegranate tree. He leans in. A tiny red pomegranate, just bigger than a sour cherry, presses softly against the windowpane.

"Wish it hadn't fallen?" Farhad's heart sinks. He grips the handle and knocks—softly. So gently, it could only be heard by someone behind the window of that house . . .

"Now, a delicate white hand will pull the curtain back from the other side of that small window and water the mini pomegranate tree. Then Farhad, calm and uplifted, will open the wooden door and step inside," I said.

He liked it. He said, "That's a beautiful, romantic image."

He wrote:

Again, he glances at the window of the opposite house. No delicate white hand draws the curtain. No water is poured into the mini pomegranate tree pot. He is frightened. Farhad. He knocks again—this time, a little louder.

He watches the window closely, then the iron door of the house across the alley. Nothing moves.

"Maybe she's not home."

The color drains from Farhad's face. He knocks louder than before. The gaunt old man lifts his head from the fire in the iron gallon and slowly rises. A pigeon flutters, then lands on the roof of the opposite house.

"Who is that? The door's open!" a voice calls from behind the wooden door.

It's the voice of the old landlady. Farhad freezes. Panicked and disappointed, he pushes the open door and steps inside. A dark corridor swallows him. At the end of the tunnel is the stairway to the upper floor. Just before he climbs the stairs, the old woman shouts from the other end of the corridor, beyond a small courtyard. She sticks her head out of her room's window, talking non-stop:

"Who's there? Who is it?"

"It's me. Farhad."

She hears the sorrow in his voice. As kind as ever, she says: "My son, you know I never shut the door because of the pain in my legs and back . . ."

Farhad doesn't wait to hear the rest. He hurries up the stairs. Upstairs, both doors to his rooms are open. He steps into the one facing the alley, walks to the window, and looks across: A small one-story house. A large pigeon coop rests on the rooftop—a wired cage. All but two or three of the pigeons are scattered across the roof. The rooftop is pigeon land. White, blue, spotted, black-and-white, crowned and uncrowned pigeons—cooing restlessly, circling one another.

Just under the roofline is the small window overlooking the alley. The mini pomegranate tree still hasn't been watered. Farhad shifts his uneasy gaze to the courtyard below. A small courtyard with an iron door. Pigeons loiter there too. One, with many-colored wings, raises its head at the edge of a tiny pool. It opens its beak toward the dripping tap, thirsty for each falling drop.

No. No one's home.

Lonely and unsettled, Farhad walks into the other room. The one facing the courtyard and the old woman's house. Poor, bent old woman—still talking non-stop, unaware he's upstairs. Maybe because of the pain in her legs and back . . . Farhad looks around his room.

His eyes catch on an empty bucket. He grabs it. Under the pretext of fetching water, he heads back down the stairs—into the dark corridor, and then out to the courtyard.

The old woman's courtyard has not changed. Still messy, still untouched. The vine by the wall was still there too. The old woman always used to complain about it. "It's a fruitless vine. Not even a sour grape," she would say. The ladder was still leaning against the wall, its middle rung still broken. "It just needs a piece of wood and two nails, but . . ."

He walked over and stood beside the ladder, placed his hands on a rung, and looked up—as if he were inside a well and the only way to reach the surface was through the ladder's rungs.

He places the bucket under the tap in the courtyard. The old woman has stopped talking. She closes the window. But after hearing the rippling of the water, she hesitates. Her eyes wander.

"You're here, my son?"

Farhad leaves the bucket and walks toward her. A shameful smile rests on his lips. He asks for forgiveness—for knocking on the door, for forgetting that the old woman never closes it.

"I don't know why I thought you might have someone with you to open the door for me," he says.

The old woman understands. A smile sneaks through the wrinkles of her face. She knows. She's aware of the longing in Farhad's heart.

"Do I have someone, my son? Once in a while, that girl in the neighborhood comes over. But today . . ." she trails off.

"Is she sick or something?"

Freezes. Farhad. Horrified by his words.

The old woman pities him.

"She stopped by before noon. She didn't seem sick. In fact, she was very cheerful."

"Maybe she went somewhere."

"She was supposed to come back in the evening to clean the courtyard for me. I wish her all the happiness. She even said she'd tidy your room up if you weren't home."

The old woman knows how to choose her words carefully. She's always known what to say. She knows how to calm Farhad's heart, the young boy who calls her Daya*—and sometimes* Daya Gian, *dear Mom. So kind, the old woman. She always has been.*

Farhad breathes a relieved sigh. Color returns to his face, and light fills his eyes once more.

We went up the stairs through the dark corridor before Farhad. When we got upstairs, I said, "This was Farhad's house. Many years ago."

It was Farhad's house. Two rooms opened onto a small corridor. "This room was his workplace," I said.

We were in the room facing the alley. All its walls were covered with paintings. In the center of the room, an unfinished painting stood on an easel. A bunch of oil paints and brushes were scattered on the floor beside it. He felt cold among the sharp specks of color, the frowning faces, and the chill tones of the paintings. A pain stabbed through his body. He lit a cigarette and sat on the chair in front of the easel. The thick smoke of his cigarette spread through the room. "He painted most of these before he came to this house," I said. "The ones he did here aren't even hung up." He looked at the unfinished painting on the easel. A man stood against a black and blue background of . . .

He stood up and went into the other room. I followed him. "Here's where he used to sleep, eat, and sometimes host," I said. He flicked the butt of his cigarette out the window into the old woman's courtyard and scanned the room. Nothing caught his eye except for one or two old photographs and a clock whose hands were missing.

"Whose photos are these?" he asked.

I was tired. I laid down on Farhad's bed. "That one's his father." Behind the dusty glass, a good-looking man sat beneath the shade of a tree.

"The other one . . ." I said.

The broken words slipped from the corner of my mouth. My eyelids gently closed . . .

Farhad came upstairs. Through the window of the other room, he looked out at the emptiness of the alley and the house across the way. Now or later on . . . The last drop of water falling from the pipe froze mid-air. The drop before it, just before reaching the beak of the many-hued pigeon, stopped and hung suspended. The soft drift of the dirty, tangled clouds vanished. Time went on strike, and everything stopped.

The tip of his pencil had vanished inside the wooden barrel. He set it down and lit another cigarette. He was in a rush. He had to leave the house in less than an hour—a house that had once belonged to a sick, lonely old woman, and in whose rooms Farhad had once lived for a while.

He had to take Farhad out with him, and bring him back to his present house. To his present dark, smoky room . . .

He had to pass through the winding alleys, the thatched walls, and under the blue windows . . .

"Some parts of this neighborhood and the alleys haven't changed over the years," he said during the first days of his return. "Some parts never seem to change."

He was wrong.

When he walked through the alley for the first time after coming back, he realized just how wrong he has been. The houses, the thatch of the walls, the blue-painted windows, the geraniums and basils in tin cans . . . even the people had changed. He did not recognize a single one of them.

Just like Farhad.

Not the Farhad of many years ago—but the body of Farhad, who now recognized no one. Farhad had forgotten everyone and everything.

He thought to himself, Will I . . . like Farhad?

He abandoned the thought. It frightened him. He stood up from behind the desk and wandered around the room—then through all the rooms of the house. Every corner reminded him of something. Of someone. He did not chase those memories. He returned to his desk.

The desk was piled with papers—blank sheets on one side, scribbled ones laid out before him. He glanced at the scribbled pages. The words, like mischievous children, stood on crooked lines. The sentences, like the contours of Farhad's last painting, were twisted and unsure. They led him nowhere.

"Your handwriting's always been illegible," I said, chuckling. "The teacher's punishments and your father tweaking your ears didn't help one bit." He looked up and stared at me. My eyes were open. I was awake, sitting on Farhad's bed.

"It was a sweet, light nap," I said. "I feel refreshed."

"It's late. Real late," he said. "I've been here a long time now, but I still don't know what Farhad's looking for . . . or who he's waiting for."

A few raindrops settled on the window and slid down in crooked lines.

"Rain's started too," he said.

"Farhad's waiting came to an end too."

He rushed to the pencil sharpener with a sudden joy. As he turned the handle, the crooked raindrops on the windowpane multiplied. Then he stood up and walked into the other room.

Still lingers behind the window. Farhad. Into the alley he gazes, where soothing rain falls like crystal threads. The wet pigeons on the roof of the opposite house have fluttered into the coop. They coo in chorus. The hammering rain and the patter on the roof of the pigeon coop have frightened them.

A man appears at the far end of the alley, two teenage boys by his side. Farhad lights up at the sight. He steps back from the window, not wanting to be seen. The man is young. He takes the boys' hands, dragging them along the alley. They approach the iron door of the house across the way. Once they vanish from sight, Farhad leans forward again. He stretches his neck toward the other end of the alley. A girl is walking—graceful under the rainfall. The lady of rain and water, she is. She walks light and gentle, raising her head now and then toward Farhad's house, toward his window. She doesn't seem to see him, but she feels him. The closer she gets, the more graceful her steps. She wears a long blue dress. Tiny red flowers dance with the wind and rain, sliding over one another. Only the flowers on her chest cling tight, like stubborn butterflies. They tremble with the rise and fall of her breath. Her firm breasts have loosened the buttons of her bodice, her sokhma.

All-eyed is Farhad. He grabs the handle and opens the window. The scent of rain and rooftop petrichor rushes into the room. Desirously breathes it in, Farhad.

The girl still doesn't see him—but she feels him. She raises her head again. Rain drips through her hair and down her forehead, along her temples, by her bright eyes, over her cheeks and lips. The rain carries the nectar of a smile, of cheer. It runs down her neck and over her chest.

In fear and wonder, Farhad lowers his head in greeting. He sees the girl and revives. He raises his hand and waves, less afraid now. His fingers disturb the rainfall and scatter the raindrops. The bud of her lips blossoms—whispers a silent hello. Then she disappears into the door of the courtyard, disappearing under the rainfall and the gaze of two thirsty eyes.

Farhad steps away from the window. Agitated and frantic, he leaves the room. Where to? He returns immediately. Restless is he. Bereft of peace . . .

"Why is Farhad acting like this? Why is he turning around himself?"

"He's in love," I said.

"In love?"

He returns to the window again. Stares at the window of the girl's room. Behind the window, a tiny pomegranate, bigger than a sour cherry, inside the delicate branches of the mini pomegranate tree, sticks to the glass. It conjures up kissing a beloved behind a window. Farhad sees her. He sees her beyond the transparency and crystal of the rainfall and takes a breath of relief.

Lovers do not quit their habits. The signs and the symbols must not be forgotten. This was the spell of those white, delicate hands. Surely, she must have watered the mini pomegranate tree with a glass of water. She did. He did not notice it.

"You think that girl is Kaleh?"

Kaleh was their neighbor's daughter back when Farhad was a teenager. Just a little girl then—a photo framed in a blue window. At that time, Farhad was just hitting adolescence. His mustache started to grow. His voice cracked. Two nuts pressed against the skin of his chest. At night . . . every night, once the neighborhood fell asleep, he would sneak to the rooftop without letting his parents know. He would sit there till dawn, staring at the window of Kaleh's house. At the darkness behind its glass.

"The same story of a boy's first love," he said. "So what happened?"

Her father, like every other story like this, sold the house. Moved out of the district—and even out of the city. Took the whole family. When Farhad found out, he came down with a sickness. When he got better, he rushed to his pencil and paper, and started drawing the face of a girl he had never actually seen well.

"And after that?"

After that, Farhad grew up. Finished school. Got into university. One evening, when he was heading to Tehran, he saw Kaleh again—on the bus. Only this time, Kaleh turned into a Persian girl from Tehran, heading back home with her mother after visiting her brother in the army. The mother and daughter were kind. Friendly. They were sitting in the two seats to Farhad's right. The girl could not resist talking to a boy who reminded her of her brother—so respectful, so shy.

That night, under the faint glow of the roof lights, Farhad gave in to her delicate whispers, or snuck hungry glances at her face from the corner of his eye.

After midnight, Kaleh wrapped herself in a silk blanket, leaned her head on her mother's shoulder, and fell asleep.

It was a spellbound night for Farhad. He did not sleep at all. They arrived before sunrise. Kaleh's mother got them a taxi. Amirabad Street. Right then and there, Farhad realized he had not asked for Kaleh's address. He raised his hand. Chased the taxi with his eyes. But it kept going. Fading down the street.

Once again, Farhad lost Kaleh. Without even having her address.

A bitter smile, like hemlock, settled on his lips. "He never saw her again?" he asked, quietly.

He searched hard. He would skip out of class just to wander around Amirabad Street every day. Southern Amirabad. Northern Amirabad. Even though he knew she was done with school, he would hang around a school nearby every day. Staring at every girl who passed.

But he never found her.

It was like she never existed. Like Kaleh was just something he dreamed that night.

"Who knows?"

It no longer rains. Beyond the window of Farhad's room, the girl in blue appears. She comes out to sweep the courtyard. The young man climbs the ladder and scatters seeds for the pigeons on the rooftop. One by one, they flutter out of the pigeon coop and begin pecking at the still-wet roof. The two blind boys, hand in hand and afraid of slipping, stumble out through the iron door of the courtyard. Farhad is no longer at the window. He's left the room too . . .

"And who is that beautiful lady?" he said. I was getting tired, but I endured it—the joy of remembering Farhad's forgotten moments, his craving to know, to listen, to write . . .

"Kaleh? It's been a while since he found Kaleh again," I said.

He did not ask how. I have already told him—someday, somewhere.

"After dropping out of university," I said, "he came back here and started working as a painter. He painted the doors and windows of houses in the old districts. Most of the houses in this neighborhood were painted by Farhad."

"Then he saw this girl and was completely swept off his feet . . ." he said.

ELEVEN

He had sat down to review his life, as he always did. He felt a danger—a familiar feeling that had always kept him company. In a far corner within him, at a moment like this, it would rise to threaten him. What danger threatened his life? His entire life had been stitched together from fragmented memories of the past, a heap of broken images, and now . . . Since he returned, a crowd of people, close or distant, had gathered around him; and some events had taken place too, mostly tied to the people and events of his past—all past but Laila.

Laila came back again yesterday. With Nashmil, to take back her poetry notebook. She seemed to have aimed to get it typeset.

"I wanna dedicate my first collection of poems to you," she said.

She said "you" and it surprised him. Dedicate to me? He did not ask. He did not even say that she had dedicated it to her father on the first page.

"I've learnt many things from you," Laila said. "From your stories and also from what you told me at the two recent meetings."

Then she left.

Monira called him at night. She was cheerful. She heard Laila was going to dedicate her collection to him; she talked about Laila. About Laila's family. About Laila's father who was killed many years ago. About her mother who remarried. Laila was a keen and strong girl who studied in such a quagmire, attained her bachelor's degree and, at this moment, was possibly scheduling to continue her studies.

"You should be much kinder to her," she said, chortling. "You should also be much kinder to us."

Afterwards, she invited him for lunch tomorrow. He could not make it. Within the following two weeks, he could not make it to visit them as frequently.

"If you called me and I couldn't answer, don't get worried. Sometimes, I unplug the telephone," he said. "I should . . ."

He did not say he should write Farhad's story. He said: "I have lots of unfinished things to do."

"The best thing you've ever done is coming back after all those years. Now, you should care more about us and your life as well," said Monira.

"The life of the story writer is the story he writes."

He had said it before somewhere. Or he had written it. Therefore, he started reviewing his story. The story he was supposed to write. He was writing it, and in the first few pages, he met a woman—someone he did not know. He thought to himself, except for my mother and sisters . . . but even then, I don't really know them. What about Afsana? Did he know her?

I said, "To love someone, there is no need to know them. But to write someone's story you must know them. An all-inclusive and a full-fledged knowing."

He giggled. He sneered.

"How is it possible to know a person who didn't exist?"

Did not exist? She did exist, for sure. She did exist even if the painter had been unable to paint her face in his last paintings. There are numerous clues substantiating her existence. The narrow alley, thatched walls, a tiny blue window, a mini pomegranate tree in a cracked clay pot . . . A small pomegranate bigger than a sour cherry that occasionally rests on the window glass. When a young painter comes back home, he knocks on the open door three times and waits for a delicate white hand to water the pomegranate plant beyond the window with a glass of water. If a young painter, in an alley, knocks on an open door, a white delicate hand must . . . Well, there must be Kaleh. She did exist; therefore she could set her foot in this story.

He thought, I might know many things about Kaleh. But he did not ask me anything. He turned to Kaleh and said, "You yourself talk to me, Kaleh. Talk about your past."

"Past? There is no past. Everything starts from now. From the moment in which I see Farhad," Kaleh said. In his mind, she said it infuriatingly. He had his head down on his papers. I laughed, like always.

I said, "Do you feel shattered?"

He was shattered. He felt inferior. Not before Kaleh and her anger, but before himself and the work he should have done. Something was missing. To continue writing the story of Farhad—the story of Farhad and Kaleh—he lacked something.

He said in disgust, "I don't understand. Why is this girl disconnected from her past? Why does she hate her past?"

"You don't understand?" I said.

"It is not good . . . I must take a tiny look at her past at least. But I know nothing about it."

"You know it. You know a bit about her. You know her parents passed away and she's living with her brothers . . ."

"Her big brother is a gambler and pigeon-fancier, and her little brothers are blind . . . With this insufficient information, no story can be written."

As soon as I wanted to say something, he uttered, "Or, better to say that a hundred different stories would be written."

"Write one of those hundred stories," I said.

"Well, how can I bring it to an end?"

"It's out of your control. It had ended before you started writing your story. We all know it. Even Kaleh knows it's finished."

He raised his head from his papers on the desk. Weariness was still traceable on his face. He lit a cigarette and said, "I can't understand. You say everything ended in the past, and Kaleh says there is no such thing as past. So how is this story ever gonna be read?"

"Don't worry about its readership. Just write it," I said.

He wrote:

As she walks through the alley, she notices something. Another window, one among the row of quiet houses, has been painted. Sky blue. She pauses. A thought sneaks in—who's painting a window a day? She steps into a doorway. The house with the freshly painted window. Down in the basement, the women are weaving rugs. Their rhythmic tapping fades as she enters. The chorus of their Bartawnana *song trails off. They greet her with joy. She gazes at the blooming pattern of their rug, eyes sharp like a seasoned craftswoman. One of them, distracted, knots a bit of red where yellow should be.*

"That jerk cheated on you again?" she blurts out.

The weaver bursts out laughing. The others join in. Upstairs, Farhad hears the laughter. So does the mother of the tawn weavers. Her heart swells with the sound.

"That girl—our neighbor—she's a harbinger of happiness. I wish she'd come upstairs," she says.

The girl climbs the stairs. Her steps echo, firm and bright. The door upstairs stands wide open. Farhad sits in the middle of the room, mixing colors, facing the open door.

"Is that you painting the windows blue?"

She hadn't meant to say it loud enough for him to hear. But Farhad's heart skips a beat.

His heart skips a beat at the sight of her.

"Kaleh, is that you?!"

Did he say Kaleh? Whether he said it or not, the name hits her like sunlight through a cloud. She blossoms. Kaleh . . . What spell lies in that name? She forgets her own the moment she hears it.

"Since that day, from that very moment," I said, "that girl turned into Kaleh."

In time, even the neighbors forgot her old name. Everyone in the neighborhood began calling her by the new one. Kaleh had said to Farhad, "I wanna change my name on my birth certificate too."

That day, Farhad was working in the old woman's house across from Kaleh's. The house had two sections, split by a small courtyard. The side where the old woman lived had just two rooms. The other part was a two-story building that faced the alley. The first floor had a dim, narrow hallway and an abandoned storage room, full of dust and memories. Upstairs were two small rooms and a narrow corridor. A young couple used to live there, but they had just moved out. Hoping to rent it again, old woman had called in someone to paint.

"I'm ready to take it," Farhad said.

And so, she rented it to him. For the first time in his life, Farhad had a place of his own.

"The windows of old woman's house were the last in the alley that Farhad painted," I said.

He looked up, lit another cigarette, and said, hesitantly, "The last house? So, you mean he had painted Kaleh's . . ."

He did not finish. He picked up his pen. Maybe he meant to walk over to Kaleh's house. But Kaleh was not home.

So he wrote:

In Farhad's house is Kaleh. "Neighbors should look out for one another. I'm going to tidy up his room and arrange his things," she says. She also tells the old woman. It doesn't surprise the old woman. She knows Kaleh is quick and full of energy. She even helps her every day, cleaning her rooms and the courtyard as well.

"Shall I go?" she asks, with a shy smile. The old woman is uncertain.

"I'm afraid he might be tough on it."

"Tough on it? If he was, he wouldn't leave his doors open."

The old woman gives in. She's kind-hearted. She nods in agreement. Through the dark corridor, Kaleh heads up the stairs. First, she goes to the room facing the alley. That room is his studio. There's still no curtain above the window. She looks out the window, at the alley, at her own house, at the rooftop, and at her brother Rahim's pigeon coop. She doesn't step further. She's afraid someone might pass by the alley and . . . pass a dead-end alley? She scans the room. A pile of small and large paintings hang on the walls. She glances at them quickly. The yellowish, jaundiced colors of the paintings, the broken portraits, and the disproportionate protruding eyes scare her. She finds herself caught in the fierce war of maniacal men and women. She's unable to intervene for them. Helpless, she backs away.

She moves into the other room. A bed is pushed into a corner of the room, covered with things. She rolls up her sleeves and gets to work. First, she sweeps the room, then the corridor. She looks around. There's nothing to lay down except a torn blanket. One by one, she unloads the things from his bed—the clock, then the photos. Whose photos are these? She hangs them up. Then the lamp, the dishes, the kettle, the cups—all new, recently bought. She arranges them neatly by the window. There are some boxes left. One is filled with papers. She unpacks it. Each paper has a sketch on it. The other boxes are filled with books. She's never seen so many books in any other house. She arranges them on the empty boxes by the wall.

What else is there to do? "I'll go set up your furniture and . . ." she says. Kaleh's thinking. Is this really all Farhad has? Some unappealing paintings and a pile of books . . . She looks out the window. The old woman is still in the courtyard. She drags herself into her room. "I wish Farhad would come back now," she tells herself. Chasing the spark of a thought. She hurries into the other room. Back to the window. Rahim's pigeons are out of the pigeon coop. The blind boys are squatting down, shoulder to shoulder. She stretches her neck toward the alley. The alley is empty, and Farhad isn't there. It's not Farhad she's waiting for though. Disappointed, she goes to the other room again. "I wish Farhad were home." She sits on the blanket beside the books. She picks up a large book. "Jean . . . Chris . . . tof." She puts it down, then grabs another one. It's written in a different language and alphabet. Maybe English? "Does she know how to read these books?" she wonders. She opens it, and it's filled with photos—photos of various people. A photo of a naked woman catches her attention. She's surprised. She looks up and around the room. No mirrors. Why is that? "Why Farhad . . . ?" She stares at the woman's figure, from head to toe. "Could he . . . ?" She doesn't say a word but turns the page. A picture of a man and a woman, both nude. The woman is asleep in the man's arms. Kaleh bites her lip, blushing. She closes the book but opens it again. This time, she flips through the pages more quickly, fearfully.

Farhad has returned. He hears a voice on the stairs. An unfamiliar voice in the emptiness of the house, the darkness of the stairs, and the hallway. He is stunned. Farhad. It's a womanly voice. A song, a woman singing to herself. The sweet flow of her voice stops him at the top of the stairs. He holds his breath. Both room doors are open, but the voice isn't coming from the studio. He quietly sticks his head into the other room. She's sitting a few steps from the door, her back to him. A lock of her hair hangs over her shoulder, draped across her chest. Her neck and ears glow brightly, almost white. The radiance of them sparks Farhad's shame. He doesn't blink, his eyes tracing the two lines of her neck, down her shoulder, and her back. Kaleh wears a black men's shirt. The fabric clings to the skin of her body. Her sweet voice and the scent of her body fill the rooms and the hallway.

Her voice is weakening, now barely a whisper. Kaleh's whisper blends with the beating of his heart. A shiver runs through his knees. Something inside him urges him to retreat in silence. He steps backward, his trembling steps impossible to conceal. The sound of his shuffling feet catches Kaleh's attention. A chill runs down her spine. She spins around like a lithe deer . . .

Farhad doesn't know how he will look to her. Disheveled and agitated, or happy and longing?

"I wish I could just look at you and listen to you like this for a thousand years."

Did he say that out loud? Ashamed is Farhad. Of himself, and of her who is standing before him with her fingers intertwined. A sweet smile rests on Kaleh's pale lips. Her fear still lingers. Farhad walks inside, embarrassed. His room is neat and tidy. He silently thanks her delicate, white fingers. Then he sits down on the bed, helpless. Kaleh remains standing. Why doesn't she sit down? Farhad gestures toward the other side of the bed.

"I know you must be tired . . ."

He cannot say anything more. Even if he could, Kaleh wouldn't hear. She's still caught up in the weight of his first words. She sits— not on the bed, but on the blanket spread on the floor, leaning against the wall. Likewise, Farhad slides down and leans against the bed . . .

Silence fills the room. The girl and the boy are speechless, hiding from each other's longing glances. She surrenders her body to the shy gaze of Farhad. Silence is the pumpkin of alienation's soul; she drops it to the ground and shatters it:

"The old woman thought you might be tough on me if I entered your rooms."

She laughs, haunted by a strange feeling. There's been a question hanging over her for a while now. She pushes it aside, not voicing it. Instead, she asks another question. "Did the old woman know you were back?"

She doesn't give him a chance to answer.

"I told her I'd clean up your room before you got home . . ."

She stands as she speaks, looking around once more. She wants to say, "There's nothing left to do." But she doesn't.

"She didn't see me. The old woman doesn't know I'm back," Farhad says.

A smile blooms on her lips. She feels at ease at once. She's no stranger now. She giggles, then sits on the edge of the bed.

He put his pen down and snuffed out his cigarette in the ashtray on the desk. The ashtray was overflowing with butts, and a few empty cigarette packets were scattered next to him. What if his sister, Monira, were here and saw this scene . . . ? He stood up, emptied the ashtray, and tossed the empty packets in the trash. He did not return to his desk. He was exhausted. Instead, he lounged on the sofa and stretched his legs. I sat across from him. He looked at me.

"It's useless," he said, "this meeting, in this way . . ." He didn't finish the thought—didn't say that it would lead him astray. "The girl in this meeting doesn't look anything like Kaleh."

"Doesn't look like Kaleh?!" I said, surprised. "How do you know? You don't know Kaleh, do you?"

"I don't know her," he said. "But I know Farhad. And I still remember some of the ethics and morals of those years. Those years, maybe now, for an artist like Farhad . . . A committed political student . . . Kaleh may not have been that kind of girl. A simple and lively maid . . . There must've been something eccentric in her character that fascinated Farhad."

"Something eccentric?"

I thought about it. What's eccentric in the character of a lady? What could be captivating enough for Farhad? "What was eccentric in Afsana's character that enchanted you? In Afsana's—"

He interrupted me. "I don't want to depict Kaleh based on Afsana. I don't want Kaleh to be Afsana, or resemble her. I don't want the story of Farhad and Kaleh to be the same as the story of Afsana and me . . ."

He spoke more to himself, lost in his thoughts. "Farhad has to be himself. A man with amnesia, living in a dark, smoke-saturated room that smells of dampness and burnt rubbish. Kaleh has to be herself, too. A girl who, many years ago . . ."

"She lived in a narrow alley with her gambling pigeon-fancier brother and her two blind brothers. She was enchanted by a painter; one day she entered his room and sat at the edge of the bed, and . . ." I said. "How sweet it is. Two lovers, sitting shoulder to shoulder at the edge of the bed, and . . ." I laughed. As always, he saw a line of dirty, yellowed teeth.

"I still believe there must've been something unusual in Kaleh's character. I can't continue writing the story unless I understand it," he said.

"You won't understand it until you keep writing." I may have sounded ironic, but he did not notice. He got up and went back to his desk. He reread the last page of his draft.

A smile blooms on her lips. She feels at ease at once. She's no stranger now. She giggles, then sits on the edge of the bed . . .

TWELVE

"I wanna see all Farhad's paintings," he said one midnight. So I brought him all the paintings—except for the ones he had already seen in Farhad's house. The house in which Farhad had lived in recent years. Lots of portraits covered the studio walls; lots of frowning, frenetic faces that had scared Kaleh.

"I don't want these paintings. I can't find Farhad in them," he said.

I brought him the paintings Farhad made after meeting Kaleh. He dusted them off and hung them on the wall of his room, his own room. The paintings were old. The colors were cracked and scattered like dust in some parts. The canvases had tears in places, but they were sewn up with fine thread and tiny stitches.

"Where have these paintings been all this time?" he asked. Then he scrutinized them, one by one. At first, he closely examined the cracks, the scars, and the dried, scattered colors. Then he stepped back a bit, made his way to his desk, and pondered them. He would ponder them every day, and if anyone—Baram, Monira, or anyone else—came to visit him, they would find him gazing at the white wall of his room, lost in thought.

"What are you thinking about?" I asked.

"About Kaleh," he said. "Behind that blue window, Kaleh must've been waiting for Farhad's return for a long time." Then he pointed to one of the paintings. It was the first painting Farhad made of Kaleh's house.

He wrote:

There, behind the window of her room, stands Kaleh. In the dark and solitude, she ruminates over her past shining days. Not her distant past—she has forgotten that. Since the moment she saw Farhad . . . it is Farhad's return that Kaleh waits for. Only a pair of waiting eyes can understand the message of other waiting eyes. She senses the thirst of the flowers in the vases. She waters them. The last glass of water, meant for the mini pomegranate tree on the edge of the window, is in her hand. One, two, three knocks on a door. She hears them. The familiar knocks on the old woman's door—Farhad's home. Kaleh draws the curtain. Her hand rests on the dry pot, and her other hand pours water onto the plant. She sees Farhad in the alley behind the wooden door. As she looks, her hand trembles. The pot swings, and so do the delicate branches of the mini pomegranate tree. A tiny pomegranate, bigger than a sour cherry, sticks to the cold glass of the window. Farhad sees her, and Kaleh bursts with joy. She sets the glass down and opens one side of the window. Farhad enters. But the wooden door is still open, leading into the darkness of the corridor. Kaleh raises her head toward Farhad's room window. On the white background of the still-closed curtain, a pair of pigeons fly and twist around each other on the rooftop. Then the curtain is drawn. Farhad appears behind the window. The pigeons now fly on Farhad's chest. Farhad beckons her. Kaleh sees him and joyfully closes the window. She leaves the room . . .

Rahim, her brother, is not at home. He is not supposed to come back that soon. Also, the blind boys are sitting beside each other in the courtyard and . . .

"Don't go out till I come back," Kaleh says.

She doesn't even trust them that way and locks the door to the alley. The alley is bare. The wooden door of the old woman's house is still ajar. She enters and closes the door on the loneliness of the alley.

The loneliness of the alley is an alibi for the love of those lovers to remain veiled.

"Up to when are you going to keep the love of Farhad and Kaleh out of the eyes of the alley?" I asked. "Till when do the people of this alley have to sneak into their houses and close their windows when the lovers meet?"

I said it playfully. Ironically. He said nothing. He lit a cigarette and thought to himself that it was impossible for the people of the alley to be blind to Kaleh's going to Farhad's house.

He wrote:

Love cannot be obscured. Loving looks and whispers, clandestine dates and trysts are irresistible to the eyes and ears of people in a tiny, deadlocked alley. Kaleh knows it well. Liberated is she. Why liberated? Exultant is she. Let the alley shout her love. Friendly are the whispers and smiles of people. Let the rug-weavers chant louder. The look of Farhad's old landlady is kind.

But Farhad . . .

Sad and silent is Farhad.

Sad and silent?

"Why should Farhad be quiet and sad in these moments?" he asked.

He was talking to himself. He put his pen down and raised his head from his draft. He stared at me for a while, then at the wall of his room. Then he stood up. As usual, he roamed around the room and headed to one of the windows, and then to the balcony . . .

The gale was blowing intensely. This whirlwind was also blowing last night. Slamming the doors and the windows of the houses, the gale had been howling till morning. And now it was pushing itself. That big black bird, usually flying over the house and the courtyard at this time, disappeared. Where was it? He did not ask.

The gale was shaking the half-bare branches of the courtyard trees. It was sweeping the dry leaves and the dust of the courtyard into a corner. It swept his gaze as well. My gaze too. I saw the tiny old house in the corner for the first time. A house? A room—the small window of which was facing this house and courtyard. I wanted to ask who was taking a sojourn in that small and old room. I did not ask. I was reminded of Farhad, who was living in a dark and saturated-in-smoke room, smelling of moisture and burnt rubbish, and sitting under the dim light of the small smoky room. In the mind of a writer. A writer who was in a hurry to write his story before his death—whose death? A story that was forgotten many years ago.

He did not stay long on the balcony. The wind harassed him and he felt cold. He had to go inside. It was obvious that he was thinking about his question during this time. And about an answer to his question.

"Why should Farhad be sad and silent in these moments?"

"There are numerous reasons for being sad and silent for a person like Farhad," I said.

He turned his face toward me. I followed him inside the house. He looked at me. He was searching for those numerous reasons in my eyes and my tired look.

I said, "Farhad is a fugitive student and the police will possibly discover his place at any moment and . . ."

He nodded his head as if something had jogged his memory. He likely forgot that Farhad was a fugitive student who, with his comrades . . . But Farhad did not forget it. Farhad had not forgotten anything yet. His running away from the university, coming back to the city, living a secret life, his promise to his comrades—those young guys with whom he shared his dreams and wishes.

His friends, those young boys, were as old as he was. At first, once a week in the darkness of night, they would spring up one by one from the end of the alley, walk along the mud-brick walls, and sneak into Farhad's house. Kaleh had seen them a few times. Through the window of her room—when they were entering the house through the wooden door. Or when they set foot inside the alley after peeking into it.

Kaleh was scared of them. She was frightened. Farhad's friends resembled no one else. They did not resemble anyone she knew. Once, she told Farhad with a derisive laugh, "Your friends look like thieves. Like thieves, they hide and—"

Farhad interrupted her angrily: "They're the most innocent and honorable boys in this city."

Kaleh said nothing. But the old woman, the landlady, said, "Take care, my dear son. You're a poor worker. You should mind your own business. You should just care about your life and your future."

Why did the old woman say that? Farhad was thinking to himself. He wished he was a poor worker. Like all the other poor workers. Like the kind the old woman and Kaleh thought he was. If only he could just care about his own life. The life of Kaleh and himself.

He should tell Kaleh he was a student. A fugitive student. He should tell her he lived a secret life.

He was at his desk again. He dropped his head over the papers and wrote:

Sad and silent is Farhad. Lone and lugubrious. Behind his easel and canvas, he sits. He has mixed the colors—black, blue, and . . . He plucks the brush and strokes the canvas. Another line, another bar. Then he slides back and gazes at his painting. A man behind the bars . . . Incarcerated is the man. Chained. Through the dark blue background of the painting, he watches a pomegranate beyond the bars. A big red pomegranate. It's neither dropped from a branch nor laid on a plate. Is it beyond the bars or in the man's dream? It lies in the wetness of his lightless eyes.

Flustered is the man. His hands are glued to the bars. His thin, bony fingers press against the cold iron.

Still slid-back is Farhad. Still gazing at his painting. At the chained man. They will look alike a lot, if he becomes chained too. If he looks at Kaleh behind the bars. Hears the shuffle of Kaleh's feet, Farhad. He is startled. He shouldn't let Kaleh see that painting. Not this soon. He stands up. With his back to the painting, and to the man behind the bars . . .

"Until when is Farhad going to conceal that painting from Kaleh? Until when will he postpone introducing himself to her . . . ?" Did he say it or me?

"Till the end of the date."

Farhad is also dejected, even in the other room. Even beside Kaleh. As if the burden of a question is loaded on his body. Or an answer. Kaleh cannot understand. At first, she thinks he might be mad at her. Mad at Rahim's friends who come and go from their house repeatedly.

"Rahim shouldn't let himself gamble in a house where you live," Farhad had angrily told her before. "You shouldn't let that pack of riffraff come to your house . . . It's a pity. It's a pity that you're Rahim the gambler's sister and . . ."

"Rahim is the man of the house. He's the owner. I have no power over him except for not showing myself to his friends and locking the room with me and the blind boys inside," Kaleh cried.

Farhad trusted her. He trusts her. Kaleh is thinking. She picked a fight with her brother Rahim last night. She wanted him to quit gambling, to make a clean break from his riffraff friends. Farhad might have heard their brawl. Maybe he's worried about it.

"I made it all clear to him. I told him he had no right to gamble in that house. I told him, as long as I'm there . . ." she says.

She says it courageously. Merrily, daringly. Hoping to soften Farhad's brows, to shake off the sadness and worries that burden him. But they don't. Well, he's concerned about something else. He grieves over something else. Over what?

Kaleh leans against the wall. Facing Farhad, she stares into his eyes. He averts his gaze. His gaze is as loving as ever. Loving and fatigued. Fatigued from hiding a secret. This time, Kaleh understands.

"Why do you hide it from me?"

Farhad is startled.

"What?"

"That secret which fatigues your kind look." A smile, like the shadow of a sin, passes swiftly over her lips and cheeks.

"There is no secret in my eyes." The tremor in his voice and his eyes prove him wrong.

"But there's a secret in my heart. Not a secret, but an untold."

What is that untold? Kaleh doesn't ask him. She dares not. She cuddles her own body, her chest, as if to make sure of her being.

"I'm not who you think I am. I'm not a poor worker," Farhad says.

Kaleh must laugh, like always. She must blush.

"I'm a student. A student who . . ."

She doesn't hear what he says next. She's perplexed. She sweeps her gaze around the room. Some things have been added. A bunch of books and . . . She abhors the books. It's the first time she has ever abhorred something related to Farhad.

"So you and I . . ."

So you and I what? He raised his head from his papers. He shifted his gaze toward one of the windows. Again, the rain. I should have known this whirlwind would be followed by a nice rain. He set his pen down and stopped writing.

"I don't know what surprised her more. Farhad being a student or his fugitive status," he said.

Kaleh did not understand Farhad's intention until then. She did not know that a fugitive student was like a real criminal. Someone the police were chasing after to imprison. Just like the man in the painting who was imprisoned . . . Kaleh had not seen the painting of the imprisoned man before.

Now, like Farhad's other paintings, the one of the imprisoned man was on the wall of his room. He looked at it. He stared at the bars, at the man behind them. The man was still staring at the pomegranate on the other side of the bars. The pomegranate was no longer red. It was discolored—red and yellow and . . . orange? It was fiery. He stood up and moved closer to the painting. What a remarkable resemblance the imprisoned man bore to him— to his present self, now, after so many archived years, watching Afsana once more.

"I must go out," he said.

THIRTEEN

He had to go out on such a frigid day. These cold days were just the beginning of the cold season. When the cold season begins in this mountainous land, it does not easily come to an end. He dressed, then wrapped the woolen scarf around his neck. The one his sister Roonak wove and sent from Tehran.

"To where again?" I asked.

He turned his face to me. From his eyes, I could tell he was longing to say, "Leave me alone. You know very well that . . ." But he did not say it. He said nothing. I knew he was tired and restless. And when he was like that, he needed to wander the alleys and streets. Or into the parks and quiet recreational grounds that had once been their lonely rendezvous in the afternoons. On fall and winter days, in the distant past, they used to walk there hand in hand—Afsana and he.

The phone started ringing just as he stepped out of the room. "He's coming back to pick it up," I said. But he did not. He headed down the stairs and crossed the courtyard. The fallen, soggy leaves clung to the mud-brick walls of the courtyard's corridor. He went out through the door that opened to the alley and shut it behind him. That old wooden door. He always passed through it. After a short while, he opened it again. The telephone already stopped ringing. Why did he come back? Monira and her husband entered behind him. Her husband had just arrived in the city. He had been to Dubai or Kuwait. He brought him a small radio cassette player as a gift and placed it on the niche, next to his father's big radio. "Unfortunately, there's no cassette in it," he said.

Monira's husband laughed and pulled three cassettes from his pocket.

"These are mine, from back in the day," he said. "They'll bring your old memories to life. I bet you'll enjoy them." He was thrilled. But Monira . . .

"Did that couple call you from abroad?" Monira asked.

Anwar and Nasrin . . . They were his friends and neighbors. A day before he returned, they had said, "As long as you're in Kurdistan, we'll call you once a week. And once a week . . ." But during all that time, he called them back only once.

"From now on, I'm giving this number to anyone who calls you. I don't care if you're writing a story and don't want to be disturbed," Monira said. "I'm tired of telling people over and over that you're not home and I'll ask him to call you back. It's embarrassing."

Monira's husband played one of the cassettes. It was a song by Taher Tofeq:

> Once I passed by my beloved's house,
> I saw her standing alone like a rose.
> Her gaze was soft, her heart unknown,
> A quiet beauty, all on her own . . .

"You like it, don't you?" he asked.

Monira stood up and turned the volume down. "You had another call," she said. She looked worried. Worried and slightly angry since the moment they have arrived.

"Who? From where?" he asked.

"I don't know who he was, but he said he was calling from the provincial government. He said you're supposed to go to the office of . . ." She spoke with fear in her voice. "What do you think? Could it be again . . . ?"

He smiled. Mostly to soothe her. "Don't be afraid. I'm sure it's nothing serious. Maybe they just want to remind me that my three-month stay is about to end, and I should—"

Monira interrupted him. "What about your marriage? What about my dad's will?"

Monira looked at her father's photo hanging on the wall. She had not seen him in a long time . . . in the courtyard, Mirza Sa'id was sitting in his chair, in the shade of the tree, smoking his hookah.

"Today, I came to tell you that Laila . . ."

"Monira, Baram is dead serious about selling this house. He brought customers over this morning," he said.

The customers were bank employees. Melli Bank or Mellat Bank . . . They were experts, agents, and officials. They entered the house through the iron door that opened onto the street and walked around the courtyard. "The biggest bank in the city could be built here," one of them said. Then they went up the stairs. He greeted them.

Baram whispered, "All authority is in these two men's hands. They can easily tilt the scales." He said nothing. Baram laughed.

"I'd like you to take a look at the rooms," Baram said. "This is one of the oldest houses. Though we've had them repaired a few times, much of the plaster embellishments and many of the windows are still the work of craftsmen from a hundred years ago."

"Mr. Mehraban," the other agent said, "we're not buying broken doors and windows. We're buying the land. The day after the deal is made, we'll tear it all down. The embellishments, the windows, and the rest . . ."

Baram thought to himself that this deal needed to be done and dusted. The bank would pay a good sum, and he needed the money. The customers liked the house. When they left, Baram walked them to the courtyard's gate. "I didn't know there weren't any sweets or fruit. I didn't like serving them only bitter tea," he said when he came back. He gathered the empty cups and took them to the kitchen.

"Do you know how much money each of us gets?"

Baram said it loudly, just to make sure he heard. He was washing the cups. Baram started toward the kitchen, but his eyes landed on the photo of their father. He stopped. Then he walked toward it. "Eighty million Tomans each. Maybe more. But with that eighty million, I could buy all the shares in the factory and fire that upstart co-partner," he said. Mirza Sa'id was smoking his hookah. He did not hear it. Was it the bubbling of the water inside the hookah that drowned it out? Or was it the clatter of Roonak and Monira's tawn-making down in the basement? Perhaps it was in the afternoon when Monira and Roonak came back from school and went down to the basement. Maybe they were weaving one of the largest carpets for the guest room. Most likely, they were working on one of those big carpets, just so they could say, years later, "Those carpets Baram sold were woven by our own hands."

Baram was frightened—afraid Monira and Roonak might resist again. And him? He just laughed. Money can melt stone, he thought. Provided that . . . "They say chance knocks on a person's door only once in a lifetime. But this is the first time it's ever knocked on ours. Only the bank can afford to buy this house and courtyard. I've done my part convincing the experts now it's up to you to convince Monira and Roonak," he said.

"This house and courtyard still carry our father's name. It's the only legacy left to two brothers and two sisters. Until our other brother returns from abroad, we . . ." Monira and Roonak said earlier.

"I don't covet my brother's share. I'm sure he needs the money more than I do," Baram replied.

"And what about us?" Monira and Roonak asked.

"I'll give you your shares too according to sharia and law," Baram said.

"Our share of our father's house," they said, "is visiting it once a month, cleaning the rooms and the courtyard, changing the pool water, tending to the flowers. Sitting in each room for a while and weeping our hearts out in memory of our parents."

Baram thought to himself, Now that the house is empty, the pool drained and crumbling, the flowers and flowerpots gone . . . maybe they will agree to sell it. Especially if they knew how much the bank was going to pay them. Out loud, he said, "I've been waiting for years to buy the remaining half of the factory and take down the current sign above the entrance. Then I'll have a new one made with 'Mehraban Paint Factory' written on it."

But he did not hear it. Or maybe he did and simply said nothing. He appeared from the kitchen. Baram was still standing, happily, in front of his father's photo. In front of his own father. "I'll carve the name 'Mehraban' in Kurdish, in bold letters. So, it catches people's eyes. I'm doing it for you. I hope you like it. I'm sure if you were still alive, you'd be proud of me," he said with joy. His hands moved as he spoke. Then he turned his back to them and walked into the other room.

Mirza Sa'id lost his temper. He took a final puff from his hookah and set it aside. "Proud of what? One of you never even steps foot in the house, and the other wants his inheritance while I'm still breathing. Get outta my face, both of you . . ."

Baram recoiled, stepping back. That was when he saw his mother emerging from the basement. Did she have a ladle in her hand? Monira and Roonak were following her, as always, walking just behind their mother. But when they saw their father's anger, they quietly turned back, following their mother down to the basement again. What was Mirza Sa'id angry about? None of them could quite remember. "My dad died of Baram's gaucheries," Monira said.

Cold air seeped in through the window seams. "This house is freezing. Why didn't you turn on the heater?" Monira's husband asked. It had run out of fuel. A couple of days earlier, Monira sent him an oil can, but it ran out the night before.

"I was just about to go and get another one," he said

Monira's husband did not believe him. "As if you could! Bet you just remembered now, huh?" he said, sarcastically. He was right. The fuel and even the cold only crossed his mind when they started talking about it.

"You can't find oil in the evening," Monira said. "We'll go to our place tonight, and I'll have someone bring it to you tomorrow. I'll also ask a carpenter to come and fix these doors and windows. If it gets any colder, no one's gonna be able to live in this house."

He smiled and said, "Baram wants me to empty the house so he can sell it. And now you wanna fix the windows and . . ."

Monira's husband smiled too, but Monira hit the roof and said, "If you don't bring a bride into this house, Baram can keep dreaming about selling it."

She added, "I'm not the only one saying it. Roonak says the same. Poor Roonak. She calls me from Tehran every day asking about your wedding."

He did not ask which wedding. He did not ask whose wedding. He simply turned off the cassette player and left the house with Monira and her husband.

FOURTEEN

After his guests left, I asked, "Is someone coming to see you?"

A woman and two men were his guests. He saw the woman before either at the Cultural Heritage Office or . . . "At the painting exhibition . . ." the woman said. "I told you that my friend is a director, and he's really eager to adapt one of your stories into a film."

The director was a romantic man. He had his glasses hanging around his neck, resting on his chest. After listening to each person speak, he would immediately say, "Brilliant! Fantastic! Unique!" He was from Tehran. He said he studied graphic design in Germany and made a few short films since returning. He liked speaking in German and would occasionally switch into it. I could not understand it, and neither could the woman and the man who were with him. "I'd like my first cinematic experience to be here in Kurdistan. A Kurdish project," he said. He heard the summary of the story from that woman and man. Were they his friends or his colleagues? "As they talked about it," he said, "I realized it was a fantastic story . . . Brilliant . . . It's unique! I asked them to translate it for me."

It was the story of a countryman. Years before the event, Braymok was utterly bewitched by a girl named Parikhan. He borrowed the names of his characters from the lovers in a *bayt*, a Kurdish folktale.

Because of Braymok's misfortune, Parikhan's family was against him. He brings the Mullah and a few graybeards to ask for her hand, but her family refuses. Even Parikhan's weeping does not help. Her parents force her into a rushed marriage, to a man who . . . Braymok leaves his hometown in grief. With dust in his throat, he wanders from village to village, city to city, and disappears for years. When he finally returns, he is wracked and worn out. He does not go back to his village, but settles alone in a vacant cottage nearby . . .

"The movie begins here. Braymok is busy with his chores. When he hears the roar of warplanes, he lifts his head. The sky is clear and sunny. A sudden explosion startles him. His gaze, shared with the camera, drops from the sky to the village below. The village is first veiled in dust, then swallowed by thick smoke. Above the tent of smoke, a few black-winged scavengers appear. That's a powerful opening . . . Brilliant . . . Unique"

He wrote the story years ago, during the Iran-Iraq war, when warplanes bombed cities and villages daily.

Braymok's blood runs cold at the sight. What if Parikhan . . . ? He rushes back into the village, the first to arrive. It has been razed to the ground. Most of the inhabitants are dead, wounded, or lying unconscious on the ground. The survivors climb into the mountains, coughing with rattly, phlegmy breaths. The dust has settled. The thick smoke has thinned. A sharp, penetrating smell hangs in the air. The bombs were chemical. Braymok realized it. He scrambles over the rubble, stepping over the dead and wounded bodies of his relatives and acquaintances. He still remembers the address of Parikhan's house. Also her husband's. Parikhan and several others lie on the ground in the courtyard. Are they dead or wounded? Braymok does not hesitate. He embraces her. Parikhan has grown heavier, her body fuller. But

Braymok feels a surge of youthful strength. He lifts her onto his shoulders and runs . . .

"He's finally doing what he should have done years ago," the woman said. Then she looked at the other man. He nodded. "Fantastic . . . Wow . . . It's unique," the director said.

Braymok does not set her down until he reaches his cottage. He lays her on the prayer stone beside the fountain and the pond. It's the first time he has seen her in years. Her body and her face . . . Blisters cover her hands and face, hiding even the lines of her wrinkles. Her eyelids are closed. She breathes heavily. It suddenly occurs to him that he needs to remove her clothes. The thought gives him goosebumps. But he must. He has to tear off her clothes. His hand touches her collar. His hands tremble. His knees feel weak. He sweats with embarrassment. Shutting his eyes, he blindly undresses her. Then he washes her in the pond. The clear water rinses away the dust and smoke. He has to open his eyes to pull her out of the pond. He lifts his gaze. Gently, he lays Parikhan's soft, white body on the prayer stone. Is this the body he has not even dared to imagine for all these years? He quickly turns his face away from her. He goes to his cottage and brings her his own shirt and trousers. With his turban, he gently dries her hair. A strand of hair clings to the cloth. Parikhan's hair is falling out. Now and then, a cough shakes her chest and head, and a thick stream of pus and blood congeals at the corner of her lips . . .

These scenes are told in flashback. The story begins with Braymok on the peak of a high mountain, hanging a swing between two oak trees. He has laid Parikhan on a millet-husk mattress. It is the final day of the event. Three or four days after the bombardment and . . . Braymok does not stay long in his cottage. Not out of fear of the chemical bombing, but of Parikhan's family and relatives. He packs up after washing Parikhan. He loads his mule with a sack of food supplies and other essentials. He spreads a ragged quilt over the mule, lays Parikhan on it, and heads up toward the highest part of the mountain.

In the story, Parikhan does not regain consciousness, not even for a moment. Day and night, Braymok rocks the swing, singing an old love song filled with sorrow. At times, he wets his turban and gently wipes away the blood and pus seeping from Parikhan's wounds.

"In the film," the director said, "Braymok becomes infected too. Parikhan's breath and wounds pass the illness to him. Little by little, his entire body begins to itch, as if he's been bitten by chiggers. Blisters form on his sunburnt skin. And his breath . . . The film ends with the simultaneous death of the two old lovers. It's a bitter ending but brilliant . . . truly unique." Then he looked at his friends, the man and the woman. They nodded in agreement. He looked at him.

He said nothing. He had already said what needed to be said, about the story, about filming it, and . . . He said that he needed to see the script. The woman and the two men stood up to leave. "I'd like to walk around the city a bit," the director said. He also invited him to join. He apologized, saying someone was coming to see him. The guests then bid him goodbye. He accompanied them to the door. When he returned, the sorrow from that bitter story was still etched on his face and in his eyes. He watched *me*. I was grief-stricken too. "I didn't expect him to go into such detail about the story of Braymok and Parikhan," he said. "I don't see how that extra episode is relevant to the story you're writing."

I wondered if there was any connection between the story of Parikhan and Braymok and the one I was writing. "By the way, is someone coming to see you? Laila?" I repeated. He was startled. "Why? What day is it today?" he asked.

"Wednesday."

Laila called him a couple of days ago. She said, "If it's not an imposition, I'd like to meet you this Friday afternoon."

"But I go out on Friday afternoons. I go to a park named . . . I'd be glad if you joined me."

"I will," Laila said.

He let out a breath of relief, smiled, and said, "I have to meet someone."

I did not like it. Not one bit. "These constant comings and goings are getting in the way of your work," I said. "You should know you don't have much time left to finish . . ."

I expected my words to frighten him, but they did not. He shook his head with sorrow and said, "I'd like to visit Farhad and take him out again, if possible."

Then he took a cigarette from the pack on his desk and sat down. "Don't you want to tell me how Farhad's doing? I haven't seen him in days," he said.

"He's not okay. I've never seen him this devastated. Before, he used to lie down or sit beneath the dim light by his window, his head hanging low. But now . . ."

Farhad, like an animal sensing an approaching volcano or earthquake, paced restlessly around his room through the haze of his cigarette smoke and mine and hurled himself against the dark, black walls. Suddenly, his shoulder struck the old, worn-out clock on the wall. It jingled and fell. He picked it up. Its dark, black glass was not broken. He placed it back on the wall. Farhad did not seem to notice. Did he even realize what was happening? Like a thin, gaunt sleepwalker pacing back and forth, he was trembling, speaking in vague, broken words, saying things he could not understand. I embraced him, carried him, and laid him down beside the small window. Then I sat down. He was in my arms. I could feel him trembling. His pale, chapped lips were quivering, and so were the lids of his petrified eyes. I pulled him closer to my chest and gently patted his head and shoulders, like a child. "I wish I knew what was wrong. I wish I knew where it hurt," I said.

He was still standing beside the clock. His whole body was trembling as well. He said, "Don't you think this storm and whirlwind . . ."

He could not finish his sentence. "What if taking him into those tight, dark alleys . . . what if writing his story . . ."

He did not finish his sentence again. He walked to the window. "I'm scared this isn't his story. I'm scared it's my story . . . your story . . . or anyone else's . . ."

Why did this windstorm not stop? On the other side of Farhad's window, in that dark and bitter atmosphere, the leaves of the courtyard's trees were swirling in the whirlwind. Like a flock of blind, wandering birds, each flying in a different direction and landing in some place. Where?

How could these blind, wandering birds, these old and crumpled photos, these pale and colorless memories, these distant, forgotten days, these moments in gale and storm ever be assembled? How could these events, both lived and unlived, be joined together? How could these torn, fragmented body parts ever form the same body again? How could these scattered and shattered pieces of time come together into a single, linear thread? How could these forgotten stories be remembered and rewritten within the frame of a story?

"How can I trust this writing?" he said.

He once wrote that Farhad was a lifeless body . . . a corpse that only seemed alive. But how could this restlessness go with such an inanimate form? Was it he who asked that or was it me?

"I wish I could glimpse the world beyond Farhad's petrified eyes," he said.

Farhad's eyes were saturated with fear. As always, his gaze lingered on nothing. Neither in this room nor in this world. I struggled to dress him. Then I said, "If you want to take him out, he's ready."

He looked at him from head to toe. His clothes were no longer dirty or stained with paint as they had been before. "Who washes his clothes? Kaleh?" he asked.

I laughed. "Kaleh's an eccentric girl," I said. "Whenever she washes his clothes and cleans his room, she asks the old woman not to tell Farhad. She wants her to say that she did it herself."

"Why does she hide it from Farhad?"

I laughed more loudly. "The funny thing is she doesn't even try to hide it from him," I said. "It's like a childish game. When

Farhad leaves the house, Kaleh does the chores, and when he returns, he thanks the old woman with fake embarrassment. Later, when Farhad and Kaleh meet, they laugh about it together."

He chuckled and said, "Kaleh's a smart girl. Maybe this is her way of trying to —"

I cut him off. "There's no cleverness in it. It's just a game, a three-sided game."

"A three-sided game? So, the old woman . . ."

"Yes, the old woman knows it's a joke and she enjoys it. She says, 'I did nothing, my son. I just washed your clothes and swept your room. Which mother wouldn't do that for her child?' And Farhad says, 'Thank you, Daya Gian, dear Mom.' The old woman is enchanted every time she hears 'Daya Gian.' And Farhad repeats it, without hesitation."

"Doesn't she have any children?"

The old woman had two young daughters, but no son, did she? Maybe not. Maybe she had three or four sons who died of measles in childhood. Or perhaps one of them survived the illness, grew up, and drowned in a river. Or maybe he fell from a rocky mountain alongside his father. Or . . . Whatever the reason, she was living alone at the time. She has been living alone for many years. Her daughters were caught up in life's troubles and could not visit her often. But Kaleh . . . The old woman said that if she had a son, she would have married him to Kaleh. She said it with sorrow, as if she has missed the chance for a perfect bride. "A lady must be well-tempered and kind. Kaleh is not only honest and kind; she's beautiful too. If only she had a proper family . . . a father, a decent brother . . . But alas, she's the sister of Rahim the gambler," she told Farhad. "Damn poverty . . ."

"Damn the oppressor. Damn the tyrant regime," Farhad said.

Did he say that? He certainly did. He said it everywhere, to everyone. At first, Kaleh did not hear him. She did not listen to him. But when she realized that Farhad, the poor laborer, was an educated man, she was startled. Stunned. She stared at him for a moment, then looked away in embarrassment. "You're educated?" she said. "Then you and I . . ."

Farhad did not let her finish her sentence. He stepped closer and gently placed his finger on her lips. "It doesn't matter who I am or what I am," he said. "We love each other. That's all that matters. Forever . . ."

Forever? It is a hard question. Harder than that question upon which man's life is based. It is the first time that he questions himself. It is the first time that he ponders the consequence of that love and his involvement in it. Cannot sleep. Farhad. That night and the subsequent nights. He restlessly comes and goes in his room. He tosses to and fro. This issue has touched him. Twists around himself. Like a snake, not an injured snake, but a man in love. How can he convey it to Kaleh that his promise will not make their dreams come true? The dreams of Kaleh and . . . Who knows what Kaleh dreams? Who knows what happens within a woman? Reveals it not. Kaleh. She has not expressed it. She may have expected to hear those words uttered by Farhad.

Forever. A sweet answer. Sweeter than what a woman craves to hear. Kaleh has heard it, and her sweet sigh of certainty like an ever-chained pigeon has been unshackled from the cage of her chest. She does not smile. Nor does she chuckle. Neither that day nor the other succeeding days. She surrenders herself to the destiny of Farhad's arms.

We left the room. Farhad's room. As always, Farhad was walking ahead of us. He was still uneasy. From one alley to another, and . . .

Through the tight alleys, Farhad heads home. His hands linger at the bottom of his coat pockets. He takes heavy, firm steps. Steps of certainty? His tie with himself is severed clean. It is no game. It must be horrifying. It is horrifying for Kaleh. If a woman relies on her dreams—if she weaves her destiny into a man, into a man's destiny, into the destiny of a word . . . Words make sense to men and women differently. The promises too. Should interpret to Kaleh the meaning of that promise. Farhad. He does. He has prepared himself for it for a while. "Kaleh, darling, it's true that you know I'm a student, but I'm a runaway student who is being chased by the police and SAVAK," he has whispered it to himself so many times. "Don't ask what I'm guilty of. My only sin is that I can't make your dreams, our dreams, come true. That's why we have to . . ." Has he forgotten what they had to do, or was he just unable to say it?

But he has to express it today. He must do it. He must say: "Kaleh, darling, I know you've had hard days and a bitter past. I even know that you are resting in the shadow of this love. I don't want. I never want that past to return and defeat this love. It's possible for you to turn this love affair into a sweet memory for your future life. A future life with no me. A future life . . ." Poetic is what he must say. But he knows this kind of poetic, fluid language cannot be spoken when he is with Kaleh. He reaches the square, but he doesn't notice it. He cannot smell the fresh scent of bread. Nor does he notice the bakery on the corner of the alley. He takes one or two steps more. The baker calls out to him.

"Kak Farhad, don't you want bread today?"

Turns his head. Farhad.

He scratched out the last sentence of his writing. He wanted to write: "He cannot hear him. Therefore, he does not turn his face."

"He's not self-collected. His heart is with the pigeons on Kaleh's rooftop," I said.

When he stood in front of the bakery, he tried to see Kaleh's house. But he could not. He could not even see its rooftop. Still, he saw the other pigeons flying above it, circling over the rooftops of the neighborhood houses. So Rahim was at home, up on the rooftop.

Farhad bought the bread and left. He followed him. He, too, knew the alley now, house by house. The first house belonged to Dervish Fatah, an intertwined house with a long, narrow courtyard. The people of the neighborhood called him Maniac. Whenever he saw Farhad, he would always say, "May the mystic sage protect you. Draw a picture of Kak Ahmad Sheikh for me.

I want to hang it on the wall of my room, between the *daf* and the swords."

Farhad's comrades assumed he was a member of SAVAK. "All the houses at the mouth of dead-end alleys belong to SAVAK," they said. A few houses ahead was the house of Ra'na the Seven Pants. At first, Farhad thought Madam Ra'na might have worn seven pairs of pants. Or perhaps, on some bygone day, she had once worn seven pants. But then he realized Madam Ra'na had seven daughters, and wherever she went, she would tearfully moan, "The expenses are high. I can't afford it. People buy a pair of pants; I have to buy seven pairs."

Farhad wondered why she did not say seven shirts or seven pairs of shoes. Mashalla the Postman's house was just a few steps farther on. He was that old, emaciated man who always sat on a platform by his house. He would set some wood on fire in a lidless metal gallon and curl his arms around it. Farhad's comrades were all certain the old postman was a SAVAK member, and they were afraid of him. Across from Mashalla's house was Lady Parizad's. A gregarious, kind woman. Farhad saw Kaleh in her house for the first time. Next, just behind the second corner of the alley, was the house of Haji the Lame, an aged man who dyed his hair and mustache. He even dyed his eyebrows. At night, he would climb up a ladder to peep into the bedrooms of men and women. They said he even eyed the mullah of the mosque. He had a crooked, dwarf son whom they called Haji Carlos. He was a thief. He could snatch a baby from a mother's arms and was said to be able to shoe a skylark in midair. But he never harmed anyone in the alley. The Turkish barber wizard was also one of Kaleh's neighbors. His wife took pride in having a husband who had circumcised all the boys, men, and most of the girls and women in the alley. There were others who lived there too. Another family . . . one he already knew. "Why haven't you written anything about the people of this alley all these years?" he asked me one day.

"I might write their story after I write yours," I said.

He wrote:

The voices of the lady rug-weavers echo through the basements of the houses. The fervor of their singing snakes through the alley. Hears it. Farhad. He hears the voices of the women and moves through the fragrant waves of their song. Approaches the house. Farhad. Near the wooden door of the old woman's home and the small window of Kaleh's. Kaleh's blind brothers are at the door, in the alley. They recognize the shuffle of his shoes. Sliding their hands along the thatched wall, they move toward Farhad to greet him. Gently smiles. Farhad. The blind boys' affection fills him with euphoria. Follow the shuffle of his steps. The blind boys. They wrap themselves around his feet. He bends down and gives them some sweets and candies. Rahim is watching him from the rooftop. "You've got them used to it, Kak Farhad," Rahim calls out loudly.

Rahim holds a huge Yazdi handkerchief in his hands. He flips it, forcing the pigeons to flutter. The tired pigeons fly aimlessly, above Kaleh's house and above the other houses. They dare not land, held back by the thread of the handkerchief in Rahim's hands. The most beloved is a black-winged king pigeon that somersaults in flight. It makes its master cock-a-hoop.

Farhad says hello to Rahim. His gaze moves from the pigeons to him, then to the small window of their house. The glass of the window has painted the thatched wall and one side of the old woman's wooden door onto itself. The mini pomegranate tree sits behind the window. Farhad greets Rahim more loudly. The fragile white hand draws the curtain behind the pomegranate plant pot.

"They say you're gonna paint the blind boys," Rahim says.

There they are in the alley, the blind boys. Hand in hand, as always. They lick the sweets and candies.

Who says? Farhad does not ask. Who said it? "I wanna paint those poor blind boys," he'd said the day he was painting Kaleh by the side of the pool. He looks at the window again. Kaleh does not appear. Is she upset with him? Grief takes hold of him. He forgets why he came back and what he meant to tell her. Once, twice, three times, he knocks on the wooden door of the old woman's house, his house.

"Kak Farhad, don't you see? The door is not shut!" Rahim says.

I laughed. "He's gotten used to it," I said.

Farhad felt embarrassed and walked in, disappointed. He followed him, and I followed them. The old woman was in the courtyard, at the end of the dark corridor. She did not say, "Well, my son, the door wasn't closed." She has not said that in a long time. "Don't go upstairs. I need to talk to you, my son," she said.

Reluctantly, Farhad walked toward her, toward the small courtyard. The old woman brought him a large box and handed it to him.

"Your spectacled friend brought it for you just before you came in," she said worriedly.

Farhad understood. He knew it was books. He took the box from her. "He shouldn't have . . ." he said.

"Where were you last night? I wish you'd been at home."

What had happened? He shifted his gaze from the old woman to Farhad and asked me what was going on.

I said nothing. The old woman said, "They had a fight again. A heavy fight that brought all the neighbors out."

Farhad understood. He shook his head and sighed coldly.

"What happened?" he asked again.

"Come upstairs. I'll tell you," I said.

While Farhad and the old woman were talking, we went upstairs and entered the room facing the courtyard. It was now a neatly furnished room. He sat in Farhad's chair and stared at my mouth.

I said: "The struggle between Kaleh and her brother Rahim isn't new. But their problem has worsened since Farhad moved into this alley. They argue over something almost every night and end up grappling with each other. First because Kaleh wouldn't let him gamble in the house. Then she said Rahim's riffraff friends shouldn't be coming around here. And last night, she kept nagging him to find a job and let go of . . ."

Their struggle grew more intense. "I'll file a complaint and have you arrested," Kaleh said. "If I get no response or help, I'll pack up and walk out on all of you," she added, tears streaming down her face. Rahim was drunk. He hit her. Kaleh ran out of the room. She climbed the ladder. She said she would decapitate his pigeons. Rahim threw her down. He drew a knife on her. He tried to stab her in the stomach. The neighbors saved her and wrestled the knife away. Kaleh scratched her own face with her fingers. She cried. So did the blind boys. Farhad's old landlady took Kaleh into her home. She held her close and rocked her to sleep until dawn . . .

He was all ears. Tears welled up in his eyes. Farhad was still in the courtyard beside the old woman. Tears might have been welling up in her eyes too. He stood up and looked through the window. At the old woman and Farhad. Then he turned his head to me. "Well, why does Kaleh stay away from Farhad? Why doesn't she show herself to him?" he asked.

"It's not Farhad she's staying away from," I said. "Her eyes are bruised and swollen from Rahim's kick last night. She doesn't want Farhad to see her like that."

Then I stood up. I had to go out of the house to do something; out of Farhad's house and . . . to leave him alone. "I'm going out. You can write about what happened that night in detail, the fight, the brawl until I come back," I said.

He was still behind his desk. Behind the desk of his room with the pen in his hand. He stared at the last sentence he has written:

"Kak Farhad, don't you see? The door is not shut!" Rahim says.

FIFTEEN

Fire again, wind again, and the frozen loneliness of the alley. The dance of fire and wind—and that scary, rending scream again . . . Whose rending scream shattered his midnight dreams?

He jolted awake before sunrise. Dizzy. He had been dealing with dizziness for a while now. But this morning . . . maybe it was from last night's drinking. His friend Jalali was here last night. It was Yalda Night, and he showed up in the afternoon with a bottle in hand.

"I came to let the sadness of your life blow away with the gale on the longest night of the year," he said—like most Friday nights, when he tried to drink his grief away.

Jalali wandered across the courtyard, singing. Then he spotted the radio-cassette in the room and laughed.

"Looks like someone's replaced me in the couple weeks I was gone," he said. "Congrats! You're settling in. Doesn't seem like you're in a hurry to go back."

"Monira's husband gave it to me. Came with three tapes: Taher Tofegh, Ali Mardan, and Banan. Which one you want?"

"Ali Mardan and his *Chan Jarm Wt.*"

The calm voice of Ali Mardan resonated inside the room. The cups were filled, emptied, and refilled. Jalali was singing along with the cassette:

> *I swear I told you time and again—*
> *I'd drink what you pour, even poison or pain.*

He said, "I haven't listened to Ali Mardan's voice in a long time. Since the time that . . ."

He could not remember since when. Jalali could. Those days when Ali Mardan was singing and he would close his eyes, remembering Afsana. Were they in his room or Jalali's? They used to shut the door on themselves:

"Let's stay away from 'Ey Reqib' and all those revolutionary songs."

Did he say that? Or was it Jalali?

Jalali clearly remembered the days of demonstration. Days when people would pour into the streets for any reason and . . . there was always a reason. A massacre in a city, and people would rise up in anger. The leaders would call for a demonstration, and people would embrace it. One person—sometimes more—would be martyred, and the crowds would carry the bodies on their shoulders, heading to the cemetery.

He was with the people. As always, he was searching for Afsana in the crowd. And Jalali . . .

"The third day, the weekly, the fortieth day of the martyrs, and . . ." Jalali said years ago. Jalali had seen it coming—those days when people would flood out of their homes, into the alleys and . . .

"You'll have a date every day. A revolutionary date."

He felt embarrassed. Humiliated. Ashamed of himself when he saw people risking their lives and . . . Even Afsana's look embarrassed him. He could never tell if her gaze was full of contempt or love.

Jalali still remembered Afsana. A girl in blue, wearing a jamana scarf, her fist raised in every demonstration. Like all the young people, she sang the anthems, and when the march ended, she slipped alone into the narrow alleys. She walked in small, light steps. Every now and then, she found a reason to glance back—and she saw him, following her at a distance. Him and Jalali.

"You keep that poor girl waiting," Jalali said. "You've put her in a dilemma. You should be ashamed of that. Ashamed that you don't go to . . ."

"On the day of victory," he cut in firmly. "That day I'll go and wherever she is . . ."

Jalali remembered that day too. The day the whole city spilled into the streets and roundabouts. The day everyone danced. The dancers carried rifles instead of *sarchopi* handkerchiefs, firing into the sky once in a while. Afsana and a group of women and girls were near Azadi Square. He stood far off, in the shadow of an alley.

It was a beautiful day. The red-letter day of his life.

"You swore you'd talk to her today," Jalali reminded him.

"Among that noisy crowd . . . ?" he asked, shrinking.

Jalali uttered no more words. He went into the crowd. He walked up to the group of women and girls. He stood next to Afsana.

"That friend of mine wants to talk to you, madam," he said. He pointed at him with his finger. He was drenched in sweat on that cold day. His knees were trembling. He wanted to run away, but he did not. He just dropped his head.

Surprisingly, Afsana looked at the women and girls in fear and shame, as if she craved their help.

"Talking to me?" she said.

"Yes," Jalali said, gulping down his spit with difficulty.

"But I . . ."

Afsana did not know what to say. Helplessly, she stepped forward. Embarrassed and . . . He saw the blood rush into her cheeks. She glanced around in fear while taking light steps.

"Hello."

He was out of breath, shivering. "Hello," he replied. Afsana should have smiled. Far from them, Jalali must have smiled.

"I've sworn an oath to . . ."

The uproarious crowd and the gunshots drowned his words.

"We should talk in a less crowded place," Afsana said. Did she? Then she left, and he followed her.

Jalali was completely drunk. After listening to Ali Mardan's cassette several times, he did not take it out. He played another of his songs:

> She calls me Uncle
> As if I'm old.

He took two painkillers before noon. Then Baram came. Baram brought him a computer. It was his son's. "He doesn't use it for nothing but gaming," he said. "And now it's exam time. It's better it stays here for a while."

Baram was a good brother. His smile and the gentle movements of his hands showed he was a good brother. "I think it might be of some help to you." Then, he took it inside the room and set it on the desk.

"I get really ashamed of myself when my writer brother doesn't have a computer on his desk."

"If I need a computer, I'll buy one," he said angrily. Baram did not even frown.

"I know. You didn't buy one 'cause you're planning to go back."

Baram plugged in the computer and turned it on. A bunch of red flowers appeared.

"Did you talk to Monira about selling the house?"

He had talked about it. But he said, "No, I completely forgot about it."

Baram laughed. Perhaps he knew he was lying. He knew it hurt him. "I should take you to a good doctor. If you keep going like this, you'll get amnesia."

He was shocked. He did not know what to say.

"I'll go to Tehran. I'll also visit Roonak, even if her spiteful husband's at home," Baram said. "I know the news of selling the house will make them happy. Tell Monira too. We can make a fortune selling this house and courtyard. Then we can . . ."

Baram left in a hurry, just like he had come in a hurry. He was still suffering from a headache. He had a headache? He reached for another pill, but just then the phone rang. He picked it up. It was Monira.

"You should've come here last night. It was Yalda Night, and it would've been perfect to be together," she said, complaining. "I prepared a whole Yalda Night meal. I bought watermelon and all kinds of things. Nashmil was hoping we could invite Laila. We were supposed to invite her family too if you were with us. Her grandma, her uncle and . . ."

"I had guests," he said, apologizing.

He did not mention it was Jalali.

"You don't have guests now. Come over here for lunch."

"Why?"

"It's Friday, and we'd at least like to be together this afternoon."

Friday? He had looked forward to this Friday—but he had forgotten it. That scared him. Baram's bitter sarcasm was still rattling in his head, If you go on like this, you'll come down with amnesia. He remembered my words too. I had told him he did not have much time left to finish his story. He conjured up all those nights and days when he was just like Farhad—frightened.

What a strange fortune, that everyone is polluted by amnesia—or has been. Everyone?

"I forget everything too," Jalali said last night.

Around midnight, Jalali got totally drunk. He stood up, was about to leave, but he wouldn't let him.

"I won't let you leave like this. I'm scared that . . ."

Jalali cut him off while the words were still pouring out of his mouth.

"I'm a married man with children and . . ." He laughed.

"I'll call your wife. I'll tell her you're staying with me," he said.

Jalali's wife was kind and womanly. One of those women who, when others see her, they say, "She looks so much like my mom."

He stormed toward the phone. Jalali blocked him.

"During these three or four years that I've been the man of the house, there hasn't been a single night I didn't spend with my family," Jalali said. Then he stood. He stumbled.

"What about before that?" he asked.

"I don't remember before that. I've forgotten it."

Jalali got married a few years ago. But he would say, "Ever since I haven't been able to dream and have fantasies, I feel like I have a wife and three kids."

He did not understand his words.

I said, "Only those men and women who've lived together without love for years can understand that."

Was I drunk too?

When noon neared, he went to Monira's place. "I'll go to the park this afternoon. Laila's supposed to . . ." He already said that before. As he was about to leave, he asked again, "You sure it's okay for me to be with a young lady at the park?"

"Until a few years ago, the police would arrest boys and girls hanging out without being blood-related," Monira said, then laughed. "Don't worry. They won't suspect you."

He got it. A decrepit man like him . . . Who would suspect a decrepit man? He asked himself that bitter question more than once, all the way to the park.

Who doubts a . . .

The park sat on a hilltop. When he came with Afsana a few years ago, the trees were not this tall and autumn was not this mute and sad. Autumn? Today was the first day of winter. Yesterday autumn, today winter, but not much had changed. He made his way to the park through one of the narrow streets. He was tired. He sat down on a cement bench and lit a cigarette. The city beneath him did not steal his eyes. Instead, it was the narrow street, the trees along its edge as well as the rows of withered flowers, the trampled grass, and the dry fallen leaves gathered in the concrete curb . . . Autumn's leftover relics were all staring at him. Staring at him—and at the men and women who sat alone, far apart, on the hard, cold cement benches. Or those who were walking under the bare trees. He took a long drag of his cigarette and let his eyes loose down the slope of the street. Waiting? He saw Laila below, hurrying up the street like someone was chasing her. Just like Afsana, who used to hurry that same way—and he knew Naseri was following her. Naseri with the fancy green Peugeot. Naseri who sometimes played the tembûr with the youth.

Afsana would say, "He doesn't let me be. He stalks me every day. God, he gets someone to propose to me every night. I'm scared that finally . . ."

He lost control. "Someday, I'll get someone to stop him in the middle of the street, drag him out of his car, and beat him."

Afsana was scared. "Beating doesn't work. People will find out and it'll drag our name through the mud."

"I have some armed comrades. I'll have them petrify him. He's a rich-born man and my comrades . . ."

Afsana said . . . He did not remember what Afsana said.

Maybe she said, "Love has nothing to do with being born rich or poor! You too aren't poor-born. They say your father . . ."

Or maybe she did not say anything at all.

Laila was approaching him now. She was not there yet, but with a smile on her lips, she pulled her hand out from under the black veil and waved at him. Afsana never wore a black veil. She used to wear a blue manteau and a jamana scarf. Laila reached him, and the blood rushed to her cheeks, her bright eyes shining.

She said politely, "I'm sorry. I know I interrupted you. I know you like to be alone. Alone with your memories . . ."

With his memories? He was thinking Afsana has been lying under the ground for years. Not in this city. In another. In Tehran. That was why he smiled bitterly.

Laila turned to look around. She was at the highest point in the city. Had she ever been here before? The houses, the streets, even the cars sliding along them were all visible down there. It felt like she was in a car floating in the sky. She got scared. The smile on her lips faded. She felt like she might tumble down the hill. She felt nothing under her feet. She sat down on the cement chair and pressed her palms against it. The cold, hard chair reassured her. She took a breath.

"Here is a very good place but . . ."

Then she took another deep breath that revealed her fatigue. She gathered all her strength to conquer the fear. "What were you thinking about?" she asked.

He said nothing. Or he said something that had nothing to do with her question. He was sitting beside her. He rested his arm across the back of the cement chair. He was staring at Laila's cold-bitten face. Her smile still lingered on her red-and-white cheeks. But fear and . . . fear? She could not shake the shame and anxiety off her face. His eyes stayed on her. His gaze was heavy. Laila's face was not used to the look of a decrepit man. He realized that. He turned his neck to follow the direction of his own gaze. Toward the narrow street . . . No one walked in it. He lit another cigarette. Laila asked for one, shyly. It was the first time he saw her smoke.

He said—

Laila did not let him speak, "Just every now and then. And without anyone knowing."

Then he stood up. They stood up. Two by two and shoulder to shoulder, they strolled along the street at the edge of the park, beside the withered flowers and the bare trees. What to talk about? They had nothing to talk about. Or . . .

> A yellow bridal veil
> A bunch of fading flowers
> Soaked my cheeks wet, the autumn's tears

Laila sang softly.

"Is it folklore?"

Laila turned to him. Her inherent smile and . . . he realized it. Why would a young woman like Laila speak of yellow bridal veils and fading flowers? "You could recite happier poems," he said. "You're still at the beginning of your life, of your youth. Those are the kind of words spoken by the people in my stories. The ones whose life and youth . . ."

Laila stopped walking. He stopped a few steps ahead and turned to face her.

"Did I say something wrong?"

Laila did not hear him.

He slipped his hands into the bottom pockets of his coat. A blue wool scarf was wrapped around his neck and shoulders. To Laila, he seemed a graceful, quiet man—but one shadowed by sadness and disquiet.

She stared at him deeply. Mehraban has returned to the characters of his stories, she thought. Her eyes, out of her control, drifted to the background behind him—to a field, all yellow at the bottom of the park, a distant gray mountain, and a scowling sky. It was a bitter, cold view. Even more bitter than that poem she had written years ago for a reason. For what reason?

"You wanna say a young girl like me can't be a character in your stories?" she asked.

Why did she ask that? He stepped closer, closing the distance between them. Now he was standing directly in front of her, gazing into her eyes—eyes full of confusion and questions, the pupils trapped in a heavy whiteness. His eyes slid down her cheeks—red and white, as delicate as rose petals. Her lips trembled. Maybe her whole body trembled. A body longing to collapse into his arms, but his hands remained buried in the depths of his coat pockets.

Laila asked again, this time more shyly, more fearfully.

"Can't I be the character in your stories? The new stories you'll write from now on?"

"No . . ." he said.

He spoke with a bitter seriousness, with grief and heartache.

"I've got no time left to write a new story," he said. "All I can do now is revise the old ones. Or maybe write the ones I never had the chance to put down."

His eyes stayed fixed on Laila's face. The pupils were trapped in a thick, wet whiteness . . . Then his gaze drifted toward the city—toward the invisible noise and chaos of the houses, the alleys, and the tangled streets. Laila was still standing in front of him. Close. So close that an old man passing by coughed deliberately, as if to split them apart. A lonely old man shuffling along the narrow street.

They began to walk again. Shoulder to shoulder, they passed the bare trees and the withered flowers. Then they sat on a cement bench again. It was cold. Especially at that height, in that sharp weather. He started telling Laila the story of Kaleh and Farhad. It was the first time he shared that story with anyone.

"It's a strange fate," he said. "A merciless destiny. They have to separate. Each one pulled in their own direction. I know where Farhad ends up. He's a fugitive student, wanted by the police and SAVAK. I'm sure they'll catch him sooner or later and . . ."

"What about Kaleh? What happens to her?" Laila asked.

"I don't know yet. I've written Kaleh's story on a daily basis. Which means I only know her present, not her future. Just like her. She lives only in the moment, blind to what's coming."

It has always been that way. Women live in the now, in the moment—unaware of tomorrow or what lies ahead.

"Unlike men. At least men know they'll be arrested, killed, or wiped clean by amnesia."

Did Laila say that?

The cold pushed them to their feet. Together, they descended into the narrow street.

SIXTEEN

By the time he returned, he kept saying, "Two or three months is a very short window. I'm scared I'll run out of time."

Time for what? I did not ask. I already knew.

Two weeks have passed since the bank employees visited the house, and he still has not taken the matter seriously. The matter of selling the house, the courtyard, and . . . He kept forgetting. Only when Baram—or Monira and her husband—brought it up . . . he remembered it. He got scared. But he forgot again. As if he was forgetting on purpose.

Baram, on the other hand, put his job, the factory, and even his family completely out of his mind during this time. He put all his eggs in one basket to sell the house and the courtyard. He should have seen it coming . . . If he had not been so indifferent to the things happening around him, he would have known.

Baram brought the bank employees again. This time, they acted more familiar, more at home. Baram did not mention the age of the house—the doors, the windows, the moldings—and they did not talk about tearing anything down. They measured the house and the courtyard, ate fruit and sweets, and left. The next day, Baram went to Tehran. After years of exile and estrangement, he visited Roonak's house. When he came back, he paid a visit to Monira. He also went to his parents' grave. Word was, he had his father's headstone redone. Baram managed to do all that during this time.

But he . . .

He was thinking about Farhad and Kaleh all this time. Dreaming of Afsana and . . .

Today, his sister Roonak returned from Tehran. After years, and for what reason . . . he did not know. All he knew was that they all planned to gather at Monira's house tonight, and tomorrow night at his house . . . His house? At Mirza Sa'id's house, their father's house. All four siblings around a sifra . . . They would gather to bring back the memories—memories of the years gone by when Mirza Sa'id was alive, when Lady Ra'na was alive.

This evening, they met at the cemetery, by their parents' grave. They recited prayers together. Then they kissed one another's cheeks. They embraced, cried on each other's shoulders. They cried on his shoulders too.

"We all go to my house," Monira said, once they calmed down.

He and Roonak went. But Baram and his family . . . Baram and his family did not attend for dinner . . . after dinner, they . . . They said, "You were all here, and we just couldn't stay away. All of you together . . . and us, all alone . . ."

"Since my dad died," Baram said, "this is the first night I've felt peace in my heart."

Peace?

"I'm sure Dad and Mom are happier tonight. Their souls are more at ease," he added.

"My dad and mom's soul . . ." Roonak started.

Monira tried to finish her sentence. "Dad and Mom's souls are at peace when—"

Baram cut her off. "Tomorrow night, when we gather at our house, we'll settle all matters, and especially that one."

That one? What matter?

All three looked at him. Smiling. They were kind. All of them were kind. Baram's family. Monira's husband, her daughter, and . . . Roonak has come alone, without her husband or children. Her husband said he could not come because of the kids' school and homework. He sent his apologies to everyone—especially Baram. Said if he got the chance, he would come and finish the chess game he started with him. That night, a while ago, when Baram visited them in Tehran, they started playing. Around midnight, after years of tension has finally thawed and they became friends again, they brought out the board and arranged the pieces. That same night, Baram called him from Tehran.

"I'm at Roonak's place," Baram said. "Her husband and kids say hello."

"Roonak's house? Really? But you and her husband . . ." he said, surprised.

He did not say, "But you and her husband fought like cat and dog . . ."

The day after, Baram came back from Tehran. He came straight to him and said, "Roonak's husband, that son of a bitch, turned into a whole different man when he found out how much the bank paid for the house and the courtyard. A completely different man than the one we thought we knew."

But he did not know Roonak's husband. He had never even seen the man—until the day he went and spent a few nights at their place in Tehran. Roonak's husband came off as calm and dignified. A quiet, responsible employee, busy with his work and his life, like a bee.

"He's not that bad," Roonak said.

But Baram replied, "He's fire under straw. Sly as a fox."

Baram then turned to him, "What about you? Did you talk to Monira? Did you tell her about selling the house and the courtyard?"

"No, I forgot," he said again. This time, it was the truth.

Baram, feeling proud of his triumph in Tehran, did not press him to see a doctor. He did not say, "If you keep going like this, you will lose your memory altogether."

"Don't worry," Baram said, "better I go to her house myself and patch things up again. It's no good for the siblings . . ." Then, as always, he stood in front of Mirza Sa'id's photo, hanging at the center of the wall. Mirza Sa'id said nothing. He has not said a word in a long time. He spoke less after his wife, Ra'na, died. When he came home, he used to open the courtyard door, walk into the garden, and pass slowly through the row of colorful flowers. But after Ra'na's death, he no longer glanced at the flowers by the edge of the pool. He would go straight to the chair under the trees and sit, waiting for his daughter Roonak to bring him the hookah. Roonak used to take care of their father after their mother passed. And after she got married? She got married years after he left.

"Oh, poor twisted Roonak," Monira said. "We forced her into that marriage. She didn't want to, she swore she wouldn't as long as my father was alive."

She could not hold it back. Tears welled up in her eyes and spilled down her cheeks. "The day she left as a bride, it was like she'd buried seven brothers. She cried her heart out. I felt worse. And we were right to be upset. That was the day Dad had his second breakdown."

"How about Baram and his wife?" he asked. "Didn't they serve my dad?"

"Serve him?" Monira's voice tightened. "I wish I'd been blind during those days. They didn't just ignore him—they hurt him. They tried to grab his property while he was still breathing. Pushed him to sell the shops. Tried to force him to sell the house and courtyard too. But my dad didn't budge. So they turned their backs on him. Stopped listening. Stopped talking to him."

She took a breath, steadying herself.

"I was pregnant. Still, I'd go make the hookah. I'd bring him tea. And my heart sinks every time I think about what Baram and his wife did to him. I never go to their house. I won't let them in mine. I'll never forgive them."

But now, she has forgiven them, and they were reconciled. Now, they were all at Monira's house, making plans for the gathering of tomorrow night.

"You gotta be my guest. Early in the morning, I'll get meat, rice, and everything we need, and my wife'll cook a good meal," Baram said.

"No, your wife can't handle it alone. Roonak and I will go and . . ." Monira said.

He refused. "You're my guest. In that case, I'll . . ."

They all burst out laughing.

"You mean you really think you got the guts to cook for all these people!?"

"I'll bring take-out from the restaurant. I just want y'all to break bread with me," he said.

They did not accept it. "That's a shame . . . Really too bad," they said.

"Too bad is you don't just settle him down and tie a knot. Too bad is . . . the way he came back, he's gonna . . ." Monira's husband started. But Monira cut him off before he could say, "He is gonna return single."

"He's gonna stay the same."

"I don't wanna get married."

He meant it. At least right now. In that moment, he hated himself—and the rest of them—more than ever. Not because they were selling the house and the courtyard, or dividing up their father's inheritance. That house and that courtyard had to be sold, and the inheritance . . .

"I told Baram we should throw a wedding party for you in the house before it's sold," Monira said.

Roonak nodded.

"We're not supposed to talk about these things tonight. Tomorrow night . . ." Baram said. That is when he realized they had already made all the arrangements. Selling the house. The courtyard. Everything.

It was late. Baram and his family left. He got up to go too, but Monira stopped him. "Roonak and I need to talk to you."

What do they want? He thought. Probably part of their agreement.

"We had to agree to sell the house and the courtyard."

What would he do if that is what they said?

He would laugh. A bitter laugh. And he would say, "I didn't come back to guard that broken-down house."

And what if they told him to get married? Why? Because it is their mom and dad's will? Then he'd cry. Not out loud—just in his heart. And he would say, "I didn't come back to carry out the will of the dead."

"We've done nothing for our parents. At least let's not keep them waiting. Let's do what they requested us to do," Monira would say.

Which request? He remembered his mother's death. Right after the revolution's victory. She died on the first day of the civil war. He was not home that day. He was helping carry the wounded—along with some of his comrades—through alleyways, through the streets, behind sandbag trenches, taking them to the hospital. The hospital was overflowing. More packed than ever. Wounded everywhere, and their families . . . That is where he saw Baram. He was shocked. Baram was supposed to be at home. In the basement. Away from the war. Away from stray bullets. But there he was. And not just him—all their relatives were there. His heart dropped. Did someone from the family get hurt? He rushed over. A doctor stepped out of a room. The family crowded around him. "What happened?" they asked.

The doctor dropped his head in grief. "Unfortunately . . ."

Monira and Roonak's screams vanished into the chaos of the hospital. He was frozen. Who? Who's dead? The very first bullet of the civil war stopped his mother's heart. Just like that. She did not say a word. Not even to Roonak, who was sitting right next to her. A sudden death.

"But it took a whole week for my father to die. He kept talking right up to the end. He asked for you more than anyone else," Monira said.

"I'm tired. My head's pounding. I should go," he said.

"I need to tell you something. Just sister to brother."

She led him into a small cozy room, and Roonak came along. He really was tired. And that headache was killing him.

"Can we talk tomorrow? Or maybe tomorrow night?" he asked.

"Impossible. We need to know what you're going to do," the sisters said.

"I wanna finish my story. The story of Farhad and . . ." he did not say it.

"We need to know if you're staying or if you're leaving," they said.

They asked him that before. At the provincial government building. And somewhere else too . . .

He did not know. He said, "I'm gonna extend my visa for another three months."

"Stay here," Jalali replied, "things have changed. It's not like before. You could find work, at a university, or even at our office."

"If you stay, or even if you go back, you should get married," his sisters said. "There's plenty of beautiful, educated girls in this city."

"A girl who understands you, and someone like you . . ." Roonak said.

"I know a girl like that. And she loves you a lot," Monira added.

He sighed, clearly annoyed. "Let's leave that for another night, another time."

He stood up. His sisters did too.

They told him selling the house and the courtyard would take two or three months.

“In those two or three months, you should . . .” They began.

“Two or three months is a small window. I’m afraid it won’t be enough time,” he said again.

Time for what? I had to ask him. “What do you need time for? Marriage?”

He did not respond. Either he did not hear me—or he did and just ignored it. He did not even lift his head. He has been sitting behind his desk ever since he came back from Monira’s house. Hunched over his writing. Over the story of Farhad.

“No worries. You’ll finish it. The story of Farhad is almost done,” I said.

He gave a bitter smile. I did not see it—I could tell from the way his shoulders moved.

“Nobody’s thinking about Farhad,” he said.

SEVENTEEN

All were gathered. In their father's house. In Mirza Sa'id's house. It had been years since this house saw such a crowd. Mirza Sa'id's sons and daughters had arrived in the afternoon. Concordant and congenial. Along with their wives, husbands, and children. The women swept the house. They cleaned the hall and the kitchen. The men had their heads close together, talking. The children, especially Baram's little ones, were playing in the courtyard, among the trees, in the cold air. Their mother called out to them several times from the balcony. She wanted them to come inside. She said they might catch a cold. They would stain their clothes. "Let them be," Baram said, "It'll get dark soon and they'll come in. Let them play in the courtyard for the last time."

For the last time!? Monira and Roonak heard it. Their hearts sank, but they said nothing. He heard it too, but said nothing. What could he say? He knew as well that the children were playing in the courtyard and the house for the last time. He knew that soon, there would be no courtyard and no house left to play in. A while later, the courtyard and the house would collapse. They would tear it down. Surely, they would cut down the trees first, and the sparrows would be homeless. And the neighbors' cats would . . . The two gaunt cats, out of fear of the children's teasing, would take refuge in a corner of the half-ruined, dried-up pool. Their pool would be filled. They would flatten the courtyard. Then they would eat into the house. They would tear down the old doors and windows, the plaster decorations on the walls and niches, and the giant pillars of the balcony. They would tear down the house. Then, a tall building would rise in place of the courtyard and house, growing brick by brick, higher and higher, facing not the sun and the *qebla*, but the street. The building of the city's greatest bank. Mellat Bank. Or was it Melli Bank?

It was dark. The children went inside, and all of them, from the oldest to the youngest ringed around the sifra. Around the old sifra of Mirza Sa'id's house. The takeaway food was served. Then they resumed talking. At first, they spoke of their memories, their old memories of this courtyard, this house, and . . . Then they started talking about selling the courtyard and the house, about dividing the inheritance, and about him getting married.

Baram said, "My wife has a cousin who's a widow. A literate and obedient woman. She's around thirty or so. She's sterile, that's why . . ."

Monira was taken aback. "She's sterile!?"

"Better that she's sterile," Baram said, laughing. "Don't you wanna tell me what kids are good for besides beggin' for money all day?

Monira lost her temper. "Don't ever mention it again."

Baram's wife hit the roof. She bit her lip. "Aunt Monira's right. Don't say that again. Parwana has plenty of suitors. She's not going to marry a man much older than her," she said, addressing Baram.

Baram fell silent. He laughed quietly at himself and at them. "I've found him a girl as fine as a peacock's feather," Monira said. "Young and beautiful. She'll definitely give birth to an army of healthy, kicking sons."

An army!? He looked at the children. At Baram's children and Monira's daughter, Nashmil. He sighed. A cold sigh. The guests fell silent for a moment. In that stillness, he heard the soft munching of a mouse. That small mouse ran along the corners of the walls and disappeared behind his desk. He saw the mouse but could not follow it. Not even after the guests left. His sister, Roonak, did not leave. "I'll stay here tonight in the house of . . ." she said. She did not say, "In the house of our father." She said she would stay with her uncle. Roonak called him "uncle" from the perspective of her own children and her niece, Nashmil.

Likewise, Nashmil wanted to stay the night and so did Baram's older son. "I'd like to stay here tonight, to be with my aunt and my uncle," he told his father. His mother raised an eyebrow, a silent sign of refusal.

"My son, they like to be in pairs. They have a lot to talk about, a sisterly, brotherly conversation."

"No one has the slightest idea what those two are whispering into each other's ears," Baram said years ago. He wanted their father to get tough with them. But Mirza Sa'id said nothing. He knew what Baram was getting at. Lady Ra'na, however, said, "They happen to be brother and sister, why not let them be . . ."

"Aren't Monira and I siblings?"

"They're younger siblings, born one after another. Only two years apart."

The younger brother and sister were always close, friendly and open with each other. They confided in one another and knew all of each other's secrets. It was like that when they were teenagers, and even as they grew older. When he started university, he would come home every weekend and . . . "You and Monira should learn from them and be kind to each other," Lady Ra'na said. Monira was kind to all of them, like her mother. But Baram . . . Baram took after his father more: reticent, often angry, and stubborn.

Roonak tidied up the room. She made the beds. Then she sat down. "Well, talk to me, Uncle. About the years of estrangement and . . ." she said, with sisterly warmth.

Right after his return, he stayed in Tehran for a week. At Roonak's house. He talked with her late into the night. About the years of estrangement and . . . He spoke of the pain he had carried through those years of exile. The pain of distance and separation. The pain of dreams left unrealized. The pain of writing. Writing his own grief and the grief of others. The sorrow of men and women whose dreams never came true. Those whose games . . . the games of life, of love, and . . . Roonak was all ears. She wept with every word. "May your sister die, so you wouldn't live a happy life . . ."

"He who lost something or someone in the past can't live a happy life."

Who said that? Him? Whom or what had he lost? He did not know. He knew. But he was not certain.

"Why didn't you marry? Someone who could fill the emptiness Afsana left behind?" Roonak asked. She was the only one in the family who knew about his love affair with Afsana. She knew Afsana too. First through his poems. He used to write poetry back then. He used to recite his revolutionary poems to his comrades. But his love poems, he shared those with no one but Jalali and sometimes Roonak. "You should introduce this Lady of Rain to me," Roonak once said. The Lady of Rain? That was the name of one of his poems.

"When the revolution wins . . ." he said. But more years passed that day, and Roonak still did not have the chance to see Afsana. She first saw her at their mother's funeral. An unfamiliar girl who came alone and sat quietly in the corner of one of the rooms. She kept staring at his picture. As she prepared to leave, she turned to Roonak at the door and said, "Accept my deepest condolences. I hope this is your last sorrow. I hope your brothers . . ." A while later, Roonak said she was certain that girl was Afsana.

That girl was Afsana. Roonak saw her again. They became friends. So close, like sisters. She even visited her house. A small house at the end of an alley . . .

"Do you still remember that story?" he asked.

Roonak remembered it well. She remembered most of it and especially the ending. The ending? An event that took place years ago, on a cold autumn day. A simple event. A girl whose lover walked away from her and . . . Roonak buried that event deep in her heart for years. She never revealed it to anyone. Not even to him.

A year and a few months after the revolution's victory, the new regime took over the city . . . after a brutal house-to-house war. After the victory of a revolution for which hundreds of thousands of young people had fought and died in the same trenches. The armed warriors in the city ran away, and the state gunners took their place. During those days, the young boys of the city were arrested in groups, and he stayed inside because of Mirza Sa'id, his father, who begged him not to leave the house. But later, he was arrested on the very day he stepped outside to see Afsana. He did not stay in prison long. Just a month and a half. They realized he was not armed, so they set him free. But his own imprisonment, the imprisonment of some of his friends, the secret assassinations, and the execution of many others left him terrified. He was terrified. He was thinking about leaving. Roonak knew it. "What about Afsana, that poor girl . . ." she said.

On the day he was fully prepared to leave, Afsana came to his house. Only Roonak was home that day. She was happy to see Afsana. But Afsana did not go inside. In the courtyard, beside the pool, she took a letter from her purse, and Roonak read it. It was his letter to Afsana. The letter of last goodbye. Afsana burst into tears. Tears poured down her cheeks. Roonak hugged her, as if to console her. He returned soon, carrying a large empty bag. He froze when he saw Afsana. He was embarrassed and lowered his head in shame. Roonak remembered that moment. That bitter moment. She remembered his words too: "I need to leave. There's no other way," he said. Then he walked beneath the trees in the courtyard and sat in his father's chair. Dry leaves fell to the ground and onto his head. Roonak remembered that scene vividly. He wanted to leave them alone. Afsana held his hands. Afsana's trembling, imploring hands did not let him go . . .

maybe hoping for a help or some promising words . . . "If I stay here, I'll be arrested. Every day they take a group. Every night, another comrade of mine . . ."

He could not finish his sentence. "You were arrested too," Roonak interrupted, "but they released you after a while. You weren't armed. You're scared for no reason."

"If I stay here, I'll be hanged. My life, my future . . ."

"And what about my life? My future?" Afsana asked. She said it, sobbing. "If you leave, they'll force me to marry Naseri."

And what did he say? "I wish you happiness."

He said it with a blush. With fear. With a broken heart. Then he stood up, walked around the pool, and climbed the stairs. Afsana was still crying. All her wishes, all her dreams, were draining away. After pacing along the edge of the pool, over the dry fallen leaves, she walked out through the door. Into the alley . . .

Roonak remembered it. Afsana, fading into the alley, farther and farther away. Her shoulders trembling with sobs.

"What do you know about Afsana, Roonak? After I left . . . after she married Naseri . . ." he asked.

"She left here after the wedding," Roonak said. "I asked her friends about her a few times. They said she went to Tehran. They said she was happy."

"Don't you know how and why she died?"

It was the first time he asked. Roonak did not know. Though she went to Tehran after Afsana's marriage, she never saw her. She did not hear anything about her either until the day she read her obituary in the mourning column of a newspaper: WE BELONG TO ALLAH AND TO HIM WE SHALL RETURN.

She called him that same day.

"How many years ago was it?" Roonak asked.

He could not remember. "Afsana died too soon. She died too soon," he said.

I was not with him that morning, when his sister Roonak walked him to the door that opened onto the alley. But upon his return . . . He returned in a hurry. He went into the courtyard, along the edge of the dried, half-ruined pool, and up the stairs swiftly. It seemed he heard the munching sound of the mouse again. He did. And he followed it. He went behind his desk, opened the drawer, and pulled out a stack of papers. Baram's child had already messed up his writings before he could gather and put them away last night. The kid scrambled the pages. He straightened them out, one by one, until he reached the last page. And he read it:

Tired and weary, the blind boys sit shoulder to shoulder in a corner of their small courtyard, holding each other's hands. Each one has a handful of seeds in their fists. Raise their hands, the blind boys. They open their fists and wait. With no eyes, with no sight, they look forward. Hoping that one of the pigeons on the rooftop will choose to nest in their open palms and . . .

"Is that the painting Farhad made of the blind boys?" I asked.

He said nothing. He lifted his head and glanced at the wall of the room. At the painting of the blind boys. Their hands were still raised. He wrote:

A few steps away, Kaleh sits in the doorway or in another corner of the courtyard. She watches her brothers. When will the waiting end? The blind boys' waiting. Kaleh's waiting. Kaleh . . .

Kaleh what? he thought. He lit a cigarette. While thinking, he kept tapping the tip of his pen against the whiteness of the paper, again and again. But the scattered spots sparked nothing in his mind. "I wish Farhad had another painting, too," he said.

"What was Kaleh waiting for?" I asked.

EIGHTEEN

Kaleh wished Farhad would take her for a walk someday. To where? She dreamed they might stroll hand in hand, like engaged couples, through the alleys of the neighborhood and then on to the bazaar. She longed to go to the bazaar with Farhad, even just once, wandering from one shop to the next: perfumeries . . . fabric shops . . . jewelry stores . . . She did not want him to buy her anything. She only hoped that Farhad, like other men, would ask her, "What would you like me to buy for you, baby?"

Kaleh would say, "Nothing."

Then he would insist, "A necklace, a pair of earrings, or at least a ring . . . this necklace is beautiful. You look so elegant with it around your neck." The salesperson would quickly hand it to Farhad, and Farhad would fasten it gently around her neck. The salesperson would hold up a mirror in front of her. The glowing yellow of the necklace against her pale skin, the light in her sparkling eyes, and her gaze shifting from the necklace to Farhad. He would stand behind her. A foot taller. A smile on his lips. He would not take his eyes off Kaleh's neck.

"It really suits you." The sparkle in his eyes would prove it. "Let it stay on your neck," he would say. Then he would turn to the salesman and ask, "How much is it?"

Kaleh would take it off. Not with a crushed heart. "I don't want it," she would say. She wanted nothing but to go out with Farhad. To go to a park, a recreation ground . . . among the trees and through rows of colorful flowers, to walk around the pool and the fountains. Like all lovers who wander hand-in-hand and, when tired, sit beneath the cool shade of a tree or on the soft green meadow, whispering to each other. What are they talking about?

"About themselves, their love, their life and future," Kaleh said.

She was sitting beside Farhad, on the chair in his room. Farhad had his arm curled around her neck. "We need no parks, no recreation grounds, no crowds. This little bit of privacy is enough for us," he said.

She lowered her head into his arms. "This little bit of privacy and . . ." she whispered. "Farhad, tell me the truth. Do you still think the police . . ."

Farhad kissed her on the lips, passionately, and . . . They fell silent.

The old landlady was coughing. She was either in the courtyard or standing by the window of her room, waiting for Farhad and Kaleh to come down the stairs. The old woman knew they were upstairs, in Farhad's room, and that they would come down now or a little later. They would pass through the stairs and into the dark corridor, and then Farhad would open the wooden door. He would glance out quickly to make sure no one was around, and then Kaleh would slip out on the spur of the moment. In that fleeting moment, as Kaleh slipped out under his arm, Farhad would steal a kiss from her cheek and her neck. A smile on Kaleh's face.

The old woman was not aware of that. She only knew that the door would open, Kaleh would slip out, and it would close again. Then Farhad . . . The old woman would wait for him to visit her after saying goodbye to Kaleh, his head lowered like a shameful son, and say, "Kaleh and I have decided to get married. Daya, you should go ask for Kaleh's hand."

The old woman had been waiting for this news for a long time now. Ever since the day Rahim, Kaleh's brother, gave up gambling and found work somewhere. It was Farhad who helped him get the job. A few days after that brawl between Rahim and Kaleh. The one that drew all the neighbors into the . . . After the old woman explained their conflict to Farhad, she said, "Kaleh told me, 'If Rahim doesn't stop gambling and roaming around, if he doesn't find a decent job, I'll hurt myself.'"

"How long can we live like this? How long can I keep hosting his gambling, graceless friends? I was wrong to ever accept this. From now on . . ." Kaleh had said, crying.

Rahim answered, "Where's the job? Go ahead, find me a job . . ."

A week later, Farhad sent word through the old woman that he found Rahim a good job at the shop of one of his comrades. The old woman cheered up. She forgot about the pain in her legs and back. "Wish you all the best, my son. You didn't just settle Rahim's life. You settled Kaleh's too," she said tactfully. Farhad did not understand what she meant. "People never dare to propose to Kaleh because of her hooligan brother. If Rahim's life settles down, I might come to you one day and say, 'My son, Kaleh got married.'"

Did she get married? The old woman said it on purpose. Farhad was startled. His face turned pale.

Yesterday and last night, he sat behind his desk until late, writing nothing. He did not write? He wrote but crossed it out. He wrote, crumpled the page, and threw it away. He wrote and . . .

I said, "It seems . . ."

I knew he did not hear it. I did not say what it seemed like. I did not finish my sentence. I just watched him. He looked like someone being forced into debt slavery. He seemed to be under a lot of pressure. Suddenly, he threw his pencil down in anger. It rolled off the desk. He took a cigarette from the packet and lit it.

"It's useless . . ." he muttered to himself. "I'm never gonna make it." Then he got up from behind his desk. He wandered around the room and stopped near the bookcase. "How are all these books written?" he asked himself. The books were not all stories; he had already read the ones that were. He read them when he could not write. He read dozens of long and short stories—Kurdish, Persian, Iranian, foreign, and . . . It was strange that he classified the stories by language. He might have even sorted the authors according to . . .

"I'm a storywriter from Rojhilat, Eastern Kurdistan," he used to say when he was abroad. "I'm a Kurdish storywriter," he used to say when he was here.

It is strange . . . how writers are categorized by their language and nationality. A storywriter from the East, or from the West . . . a Kurdish or Persian storywriter . . . a writer of a superior language, of a dominant nationality . . . I wish all humans spoke a single, shared language just as they laugh and cry in one language. I wish all storywriters wrote in one language just as they suffer in one language. The pain of writing. The pain of writing and turning pages black. Writing, crumpling, and tossing . . .

He woke at the crack of dawn. He washed his face with a handful of water. Standing in the kitchen, he ate a quick bite, then went back to his room. Back to his desk, where he lit the first cigarette of the day. I said . . . No, I said nothing.

"I should go to Farhad," he said.

I was in Farhad's room, sitting and drinking tea. I poured him a glass and said, "Tea after breakfast." Then I laughed and added, "How come you smoke so much but drink so little tea?" He smiled and said, "Exile has ruined my sense of taste."

I did not say it has also ruined his life. The fire in the brazier has gone out. I emptied the ashes and filled it with fresh charcoal. Then I picked up a glowing ember with the pincers. He looked surprised. "This early in the morning . . . ?" he said. Then he turned his gaze from me to Farhad. Farhad was not awake yet. He was lying near the small window, where the dim morning light was streaming in. "Farhad wakes up late these days," he said.

He was talking to me. I said, "When a man has no choice but to stay at home. When he's unwilling to do anything . . ."

He wrote:

Does not go out. Farhad. He has not left the house since last week. His comrades have said they might be under police surveillance. All of them? They have decided to sever all ties, with each other and with everyone else. For a while. "What shall I do?" Farhad said. He had to leave that house. Or, if leaving was impossible, he needed to burn all the dangerous and incriminating books and papers he kept at home. He must never be seen leaving. He had to do whatever it took to make the people in the alley believe he was not home. Even the owner of the house . . .

Is that even necessary? Deeply trusts the old landlady. Farhad. As deeply as he trusts his own mother's arms. That very night, he gathers all the books and papers and tosses them into the courtyard. The old woman notices. Standing behind the window, something ominous stirs in her heart. An evil tiding. A harbinger of disaster. The old woman steps out of her room. A matchbox in Farhad's hand. The beginning of a burning. It startles her. And so . . . she says nothing. She does not even whisper it to herself. In sorrow, she gazes at the heap of books. "If you need them, I can hide them for you. Or I can take them wherever you want," she says quietly. She speaks softly, afraid of the heart of darkness and the ears of the enemy. Farhad wonders. The old woman knows everything. Since when? He responds to her kindness with kindness.

"No, Daya Gian."

He sets the books on fire. Sets his affections ablaze. The old woman still stands beside him, shivering. She is cold. The fire does not warm her. The flames flicker across the wrinkles on her face, like the grotesque dance of an old woman caught inside the burning and twisting blaze.

"I mustn't leave the house for a few days," says Farhad.

The old woman understands. Just as she senses the fear hidden behind his words. She lifts her gaze from the fire and looks into Farhad's eyes. In his eyes, the flames have dimmed. "Good," she says softly. "May you stay a few days with your old mother . . . ?"

"But no one must know I'm here. And if anyone comes looking for me . . ."

"I must say you're not at home. I must say you've gone to . . . What am I supposed to tell Kaleh?"

What will he say to Kaleh? How can he make her believe that the sweet days of their love might be coming to an end? The question stings. A question that will go unanswered tomorrow, and the day after that.

Sad and silent, Kaleh steps into Farhad's room. She has been crying. Her bright eyes are still wet. "The pomegranate plant has dried, Farhad," she says. Not long ago, she told him the pomegranate had fallen from its delicate branch. She is crying. Kaleh. From now on, how will she let him know that she recognizes his return? "I'm afraid, Farhad. I'm afraid of losing these secrets and symbols."

Looks around Farhad's room. Kaleh. Both his rooms. Since when has he not gone out? She stares at the painting on the easel. Something stirs in her chest. A sense of an impending event. A disaster.

"Farhad, what has happened?"

"I'm tired. I'm sick. I'd rather not go out for a few days."

He is sick. He is tired. But the event, whatever it is, is something else. His truthful eyes reveal it.

"What's wrong?"

He must confess to Kaleh what he has heard from his comrades. Kaleh's tears shift into sorrowful lament. She cannot bear the weight of staying. She leaves the room . . .

Farhad did not know that Kaleh had already spread the news of his departure throughout the neighborhood. But he did know that every day at sunrise, like a waif, Kaleh slipped out through the iron gate of their courtyard and wandered the alleys, street by street, until evening. Now and then, when the right moment found her, she would . . .

Comes to Farhad in doubt and obsession. Feels fidgety. Within and without. Restless is she. Like popcorn on fire. Brings the latest news from the alley. Kaleh. She seals every window seam, pulls the curtains tight. Then . . .

"Don't go, Kaleh. Stay with me a bit."

She does not stay. She cannot resist the pull to leave. Voices rise from the alley. She has to go, lest a dangerous man—a suspect—passes through the alley without her knowing.

"Kaleh, don't go . . ."

"What about the old woman? It's impossible to talk about those days without mentioning his old landlady," I said.

"Oh, the poor old woman!"

The old woman knew her dream of asking for Kaleh's hand in marriage for Farhad would never come true. She rarely left her room, not because of the pain in her back and legs, but because she could not bear to meet Kaleh's eyes. That sorrowful gaze, those frightened, trembling eyes wounded her. So she stayed inside, wrapped in silence, trying either to remember her own forgotten story or not remember at all.

Farhad jolted awake, like someone shaken from sleep by a rending scream. His frightened eyes darted around the room, and his thin, trembling body quivered. I said, "He must have had another nightmare. It's been a while since that rending scream . . ."

He was startled. His gaze shifted from me to Farhad. "A rending scream?!" he said. "So Farhad heard it too."

Farhad stood up. Slowly, with effort. His thin, weakened legs could barely support his withered body. They could not hold him. He tossed away his cigarette and took a step forward, wanting to embrace him. I stopped him.

"Let him be," I said.

Goes to the window. Farhad. Gently draws back the corner of the curtain, peering into the alley. Toward Kaleh's house. Into the small and blue window of Kaleh's house. The trace of the mini pomegranate tree is still there. The curtain is shut. Looks around. Kaleh is not in the courtyard, nor by the iron door. The blind boys are not sitting in the corner. Their hands no longer raised. And the pigeons on the rooftop . . . Rahim has sold most of them. He kept just a pair. A many-hued crowned pair, and . . . He wanted to sell them too, but Kaleh stopped him.

Turns his gaze to the other side of the alley. At the far end of the alley, Kaleh appears. She has worn a veil, a part of it crumpled beneath her armpit. In a hurry is she. Turns her gaze now and then. Sees fear and doubt in her movements. Farhad. And as she nears, in her eyes too. Raises her head. Kaleh. Wind loosens the grip of her hair. Sees her. Farhad. The dance of her disheveled hair he sees. He sees her finger pointing. The folded corner of the curtain slips down. Leaves the window empty. Farhad walks out of the room, too.

"Look how eager he is to welcome her. As if it's the first time he wants to open the door to her," he said.

He said it with a sad smile, joyfully and gloomily.

"It's not the first time, more like the last," I said.

"The last time?" he asked, with sorrow and surprise.

"Kaleh carries bitter news. The news of the arrest of two of Farhad's comrades," I said. "Perhaps the police and SAVAK have discovered Farhad's shelter."

"How long shouldn't you step out of the house?" Kaleh had asked the day before. Farhad laughed. More to ease the sadness in her eyes than out of amusement.

"I'll leave now if you want me to," he said.

That sentence frightened her even more. She lost her calm. "How should we know if there's any so-called threat?" she asked. Then she burst into tears. "Farhad, I'm afraid. Carefree you are, sitting in this room. I fear the cops might rush into the house and . . ."

She could not finish her words. With the help of the old woman, Kaleh prepared whatever was needed for a day and an event like that. Against the wall that connected the courtyard to the rooftop she leaned the ladder. She even marked some paths he could use to escape. Even . . . The old woman dared not tell her it was useless. She did not say that if the police ever wanted to catch him, they would block the rooftop first. The old woman saw it before. Some years ago, the police sealed off the rooftops to catch an escaping man in the same neighborhood.

She repeated her question. "How could we know the danger of arrest is over?"

"One of my comrades will inform me," Farhad said.

"Which one? The one with the glasses?" Kaleh asked. "Give me an address. I'll go get the news myself."

Farhad did not give it to her. "Not needed. I'm sure he'll come. I'm sure one of them will."

When? Farhad had been waiting for a week. Since the Friday before. Yesterday was Friday again. "One of them will appear today. If nothing . . ." he said. He did not say if nothing had happened. But Kaleh understood.

"What if they don't come along?" Kaleh asked. Farhad could not hide his fear.

"They know me. They've seen me a few times in the alley and at the door. I'll go and say."

Farhad did not accept it. "I don't want anyone to burn in my fire. I don't want you to . . ." he said.

Kaleh burst into tears.

"I've been burnt in your fire, Farhad," Kaleh had said the night before, when she called round to his house under the pretext of visiting the old woman.

"They didn't appear today either," she said, warning him. "Give me the address of one of your comrades, or I'll never leave this room."

"Why didn't they come up?" he asked.

Drained and distressed are their steps. The shuffle of their feet can break the silence of the stairs. Cannot awaken the light sleep of the stairs. Sneaks into his room. Farhad.

Disillusioned. Follows him. Kaleh. Like always . . . not like always, she is a shadow growing pale in the last fading rays of sunrise. Bloodless is Kaleh. Her worn-out eyes have shed whatever tears they had in the courtyard. The courtyard of the old woman's house is wet. Wet with Kaleh's tears. The old woman is sheltering the last farewell of the lovers.

"I must go."

Says Farhad. In shame. In shame and tears. No longer confined is he to his manly grandeur.

"You can understand. I have no other way but to leave. Now or a moment later, the police will rush into this house and . . ."

"Take me with you, Farhad. I'll come with you. Take me wherever you go."

Cuddles him. Kaleh. She holds his fearful body tight. His legs. He rushes. She ruins.

He turned his gaze from that view. "I'll go," he said.

He was at Farhad's room. Not his present room. He was at the old woman's house. His eyes were wet, and his gaze was filled with shame.

"But still . . ." I said.

He did not wait for me to continue. He left the room in a hurry and went down the stairs. I followed him too. The old woman was standing at the bottom of the stairs, in the dark corridor. Was she crying? He passed by her. He opened the wooden door and . . .

We were in the alley.

"I wish you didn't leave. Just to listen to her last words," I said.

Kaleh's last words were still, after years, resonating through the emptiness of the alley:

"I can't hold this grief. I can't resist it."

He put his pen down, rested his elbow on the desk, and ran his fingers through his hair. He was reminded of Afsana. Their last farewell.

"Don't you wanna finish this part of the story?" I asked.

"This part will never finish," he said.

NINETEEN

He saw Naseri once again. A cold evening in a crowded teahouse, tucked into the corner of the old city square. For a long while now, he had hardly left the house. Every two or three days, maybe, just to pick up a few essentials. Then, always without warning, he would return. Back home. Back to his writing desk.

"Roonak went back three weeks ago," Monira said, "but you only paid us a fleeting visit . . . You don't come over to my house. You don't pick up your phone. And whenever we try to see you . . ." She broke into tears, and then she went on. "What did you break it off for? If it's because of selling the house and the courtyard, the deal isn't even done yet. The contract hasn't been written. No money's been exchanged. I'm ready to take it all back. If you don't want to sell this house and courtyard, then neither do I. Roonak doesn't either . . ."

"Monira," he said, "it's not about the house or the courtyard. They should be sold someday. And they will be."

"Then what is it?" she asked. "What's eating at you? Who hurt you? Why don't you act like before?"

He sighed, tried to meet her feeling halfway. "Believe me, nobody's hurt me. Nothing's happened. I just haven't been able to come by. I've been wrapped up in something. And now . . ." He paused. "Now I just need to finish what I'm working on before I leave the house."

"I want to wrap it up too," Monira said sharply.

What? He looked at her, puzzled.

"Your marriage."

He laughed.

"Monira, I've told you. I'm not a man of marriage."

Monira lost it. "You're gonna miss your chance. You'll never find anyone better or prettier than Laila. Even Roonak fell for her the moment she saw her. That poor twisted girl, she calls me from Tehran every single day asking about the proposal."

Proposal? "You should come to my house tonight," Monira said. "If you don't . . ."

"But tonight I'm . . ."

She hung up.

I could not help it—I smiled. "Looks like this story's got a happy ending. Proposal, wedding, and all that . . ."

He looked up from behind his desk and stared at me. "I'm afraid this story will never get finished," he muttered. He looked exhausted. For days and nights, he had been writing nonstop. And now, finally, he reached Farhad and Kaleh's last goodbye.

Farhad entrusted the things in his house to the old landlady. Let them be hers. Let her do to them whatever she wished. Also his paintings . . .

The old woman had said she would not touch his paintings. She would leave them untouched inside the rooms and lock the door on them until he came back. The old woman hopefully awaited Farhad's return. She said she would wait for him.

But Kaleh knew there was no return at all. She cried, "I can't hold this grief. I can't resist it." Then disappeared. She got lost for a second time inside the loneliness of those tight, deadlocked alleys. First in the whiteness of Farhad's last canvas and now in his story. The story of Farhad was upon his desk. For some months, every word and sentence had been revised. On page one hundred and something, he slid his eyes from his handwritings to Farhad's last canvas. Farhad's last canvas was still on the wall of his room. He looked at it closely. Drained and frightened were his eyes. Like Farhad's eyes that did not see Kaleh when he wanted to see her in the whiteness of the canvas on the easel. The canvas still had some dark, thin, and twisted lines.

He said, "Like his story . . . with no head or tail . . ."

He said it disappointedly. I got scared. I stood up and approached him. I went to his desk and reached for the papers. The story of Farhad was heavy inside my hand. Heavier than I expected. Then I laughed. A view that would always return.

"This story is over," I said.

My words petrified me.

"It's over?" He looked petrified too. He said that in shock. Then he shook his head in grief.

"After working continuously for some months," he said sadly, "I came back again to the first day and the first sentence I had written."

My hand started trembling under the weight of his writing, and the papers slipped on the desk.

I said, "It had to be like this. You began your story from the last days of Farhad's life. After a revision, you should have . . ."

"Farhad is still inside the loneliness of those deadlocked, tight alleys," he said.

Farhad was under the dim light of the window in his room. His skinny, bony hands ringed around his knees. His head dropped over his shoulder. Like a sitting dead body. A mummified corpse of a man . . . He stood up. He went near the window. The window of his room—or Farhad's? He looked through the glass. It was cold outside. The light flocks of snow from last night still were not melted. They clung to the ground and to the bare branches of the trees in the courtyard beyond the window. Frozen. A big black bird was flying around the courtyard and the house on the other side. He stared at it for a while, hoping it would disappear—fly out of the frame of the window like always.

Then he turned his head, as if being summoned by someone. He put on his coat and wrapped his scarf around his neck.

"Where to?" I asked.

"I'll go out. I wanna know what happened to Kaleh after Farhad left."

Did he say Kaleh? Or Afsana? I said nothing. I was in a dilemma. To sit under the dim light of the window of my room or to wear my coat and wrap my scarf around my neck and leave the room . . . ?

It had been a while since he went outside. Like a man who lost something or somebody and was searching for them in the alleys and on the streets, he was staring at the faces of the people walking. Men and women . . . a throng of ghosts that passed by him quickly, in a hurry. He saw them and he did not. He could see their cold-stricken faces and he could not. Frowned and smiling faces. The quick movements of their hands and legs intermingled. A touching game. The cloud of their breath scattered at the edge of their mouths. He could hear the whispers, the murmurs—and he could not. Sliding words, broken, compound, and complex sentences . . . "Who am I looking for? For Kaleh?" he asked himself many times.

Kaleh was not in these alleys and streets. He knew that. She did not disappear down these alleys and streets. Kaleh disappeared in another place. In a deadlocked and tight alley. In another city—the city of Farhad's story. He had walked away from that city years ago. He had been seeking other people ever since he came back. Seeking those who were from that city. Those who were Kaleh's family. Seeking her brother, Rahim. Seeking the blind boys. The blind boys of the story were two twisted teenagers who would sit beside each other in a corner with their arms stretched out and their fists opened, so that a pigeon could nest on them. Maybe at this very moment, they were sitting beside each other in a corner with their hands open, so that a charitable person passing by in a hurry might drop a coin from the bottom of their pocket into their hands . . . Where?

He saw a man ahead of him, selling lamps out of a basket in his hand. He quickened his steps and approached him. He called him: "*Kaka*, I'm looking for two blind men. Two men of . . ."

The man turned his head. "Am I one of them?" he asked with laughter. He was startled. A man with smallpox, whose empty eye bowls were two terrifying holes.

"No, no, none of them had smallpox. No terrifying hole . . ."

He did not say that. "Where can I find them?" he asked.

"This city is full of blind men and women. In every alley and street, in front of the door of every mosque, around each square . . ." the man said. "Around that square is full of blind men."

He headed toward the square. The square and the pavement around it were crowded as ever. The taxies and the cars were all queued up. In every corner of the square and at the beginning of those streets every one of which led to a part of the city, people were standing in groups waiting for taxies. On the pavement, a lot of people spread different things on the ground for sale and they were advertising by loud cries and chants. And some people . . . He looked at them closely. None of them were blind. Even those beggars sitting by the curbs of the streets were not blind. He approached one of them. He bent down and silently said, "Do you know two blind men stretching their hands and . . ."

The man raised his head. "Two blind men?" he asked, furious. "Why do you think only a blind man needs charity? I need it too. Give me what you want to give them."

Then he showed his amputated leg. Next to him another man raised his fingerless hands. Hopeless, he stood up and passed through the crowd of people. A delicate womanly voice stopped him.

"For the sake of your good looks."

It was the voice of a fat and dark-skinned Romani woman. She did not address him. She stood in the way of a thin, dirty man. The man was struck dumb.

"Oh, my darling . . ."

The Romani woman became rude with him.

"Fifty Tomans," she said boldly.

The man slipped his hand into his empty pocket, then pulled it out.

"I got no money," he said, "but I'm ready to give you a piggyback ride, four times around the square." He laughed. The Romani woman laughed too, her cheeks and thick dark jowls trembling.

"If you've got the guts to ride me just once around without falling," she said. Still laughing, she disappeared into the crowd. The man vanished too.

Three small children surrounded him. "We can polish your shoes," one of them said. Each had a small box hanging from their shoulder. He looked at them but did not say a word. "We'll do a good job. Twenty Tomans . . . Fifteen Tomans."

"Ten Tomans," the smallest one said, almost pleading.

From somewhere nearby—maybe from a music shop—a song played: "Wish Your Eyes Never See Pain" by Abbas Kamandi.

A burst of noise came from the taxi queue. An old woman wearing a *shada* scarf and in a *kolwana* cloak spat a mouthful onto the ground. "It's the end of the world . . . In broad daylight . . ." A young woman stepped out of the line, scared. A boy standing a few steps away shouted after her, "Bravo! New way of marketing, huh? Attracting customers like that."

She vanished.

He picked up his pace again. Faces. People. Movement. Then he saw the statue in the middle of the square. The head of a veiled woman, hands raised. Her index finger pointed toward something. But what? At the base, in bold black letters:

HIJAB IS THE BEAUTY OF WOMEN.

It was not the only writing. Placards hung from the fence circling the square:

THE FIRST WOMEN'S CONGRESS IN A CIVIL SOCIETY

Next to it:

THE NATIONAL KARATE CHAMPION RETURNS TO OUR CITY

And next,

A VOTE FOR [—] IS A VOTE FOR REFORMATION AGAIN AND [—]

He followed the direction of the statue's finger. The song was still playing: "Let My Eyes Carry the Pain . . ."

Then—he heard his name. "Mehraban . . . Mehraban." He stopped. Turned. Two men walked past him, hand in hand. Were they blind? They moved slowly through the crowd, faces down, ashamed.

"Mehraban . . . "

A man standing in the doorway of the teahouse waved at him. His voice was familiar. So was his smile. But he did not recognize him. "You talking to me?"

The man stepped closer, arms slightly open in welcome. "Don't you know me?" He found himself suddenly in the man's embrace inside the crowd. They kissed each other's cheeks. The man's face and lips were cold—but his breath . . . "Why don't you recognize me? Why don't you recognize Comrade Dler?" the man said with a hint of sarcasm.

And then he remembered. A smile settled across his lips. "Kursh, is that you?"

They kissed each other's cheeks again. A porter with a load on his shoulders elbowed past them. Somewhere in the mayhem, a woman screamed. A teenage boy darted away, frightened—yet laughing.

"What are you doing here?" Kursh asked, delighted.

"I'm looking for two blind men."

He was smiling too now. They stepped inside the teahouse. He had been there before. It had not changed. They took a seat in a corner, and Kursh ordered two teas. "So, you were looking for two blind men?" Kursh repeated with amusement. He looked confused. Kursh burst out laughing. "Among all these blind folks . . ."

He did not finish the sentence. Instead, he changed the subject. "I still believe this is the best teahouse in the world. Don't you think so?" His eyes wandered around the room—the ceramic-tiled walls with faded images of old heroes, the rows of wooden chairs and tables, the clinking of cups and saucers, the bubbling of hookahs. It was warm inside. Warm and crowded.

"Nothing has changed in here except for the tea man and the customers," he said.

"Of course, at the moment, two of the customers . . ." Kursh said with a smile.

He chuckled, then gently placed a hand on his shoulder. "Only the people change in here." He kissed him on the cheek again. "Tell me, what are you doing here? Why are you here?"

He turned toward Kursh. His hair was receding, and his mustache and beard had turned gray. He had put on a bit of weight. "But . . . But his look is just the same. The same Comrade Dler," he murmured to himself.

He and Kursh left this place together, years ago. They even spent a few months abroad side by side. Then he went to Turkey and . . .

"I thought you were in Europe. When did you come back?"

"Around five months ago."

"Forever?"

He did not know. He smiled and said nothing. Kursh said, "Even if you came back with that hope, you'll go back after a few months. I don't think your wife and children . . ."

He did not finish. He understood it by his laughter. "So you returned to get married," he said. "People like us, wherever we are, can't get along with women other than the women of our land. Only the women of this land can live with us. Even outside our land. Even in Europe. One or two years ago, Ramazani got married to a woman from here. Mansur Ramazani. Did you know him? He didn't come back. They sent him one of his cousins from here. An eighteen-year-old girl . . ." Kursh burst out laughing. A few customers turned their heads curiously.

"I don't have it in mind to get married."

He had told Monira the same. She just laughed. "You don't need to have that in mind. If I'm your older sister, I know how to get you hitched. And a girl . . ." She did not say anything about an eighteen-year-old girl.

"Laila is a very good girl. And she loves you a lot."

Did Monira, without telling him, already . . . ?

"Well, tell me, how've you been living all these years abroad? What have you done?" Kursh asked.

He did not say he had studied there. He did not say he had lived in a cramped forty-square-meter home. He did not even mention that he had written stories. He said nothing about himself. Or all those years. Instead, he said, "Tell me about you, Kursh."

Kursh had left here for Turkey, but he had returned after some months. He did not stay in Southern Kurdistan long, and he was not armed either. That was why they did not get too tough on him. He was in prison for a few nights, and then he was emancipated. Kursh wanted to return to university and finish his education. He could not. They did not permit him. He stayed at his father's house for a while. A poor house. He had a poor father. His father gave him all his savings so he could settle his life—afraid his son would leave again. He married a girl from the family who only studied the alphabet and nothing more.

"I've lived like a man and now I father six daughters and a son," Kursh said, laughing. He looked at him with veiled grief. "My oldest daughter is fourteen and my son is a toddler." Then he started narrating parts of his life from those years . . . how he got married and ended up buried in misery and problems. His wife and children needed food. They needed clothes. But he was a poor, penniless man, living hand to mouth. He leaned on the comrades for a few years, but gained nothing.

"The same comrades who claimed they wanted to give the poor and working class their rights came to power and divided the land among the farmers," Kursh said. "Some of them became tradesmen, smugglers, and factory owners, and . . ." He shook his head. "They exploited me from morning till evening, worked me like a dog, and didn't pay me enough to fill my stomach or feed my family."

Now, he had enough money to burn. From nights to mornings, he sold cigarettes, warm milk, and cakes. He sold them to the strangers who arrived in the square at midnight, to the drivers of those taxis and cars waiting for nocturnal passengers, to the homeless, and . . .

"So, what do you do during the day?"

"I sleep during the day. Or I come here to the teahouse and . . ."

The teahouse was crowded. The cold outside pushed people in, and they rushed into the teahouse in clusters. He gazed at each and every face—mute, broken, and bony faces eclipsed by the clouds of smoke hanging in the air. His face was bored and tired, just like those years. Just like the ones in Farhad's portraits. He was thinking. Farhad must have come here a lot, painted portraits of these faces. While Kursh was talking, he suddenly noticed someone slipping into the teahouse. A familiar person.

It was Naseri.

Just like the last time: disheveled hair, a thin white beard . . . This time, he was wearing an old coat. Naseri went and sat in a corner on a stool. He was cold. He crouched down, hands in his pockets, a half-burnt cigarette dangling from his lips.

Who gave it to him?

"Kursh, do you know that man?" he asked, surreptitiously pointing to Naseri with his finger. Kursh followed his gesture.

"Don't you know him? Naseri . . . Kawa Naseri . . . The son of . . ." Then he smiled bitterly and shook his head in sadness.

"You have the right not to know him. The game of life made him a stranger even to himself."

"Naseri was a young and well-dressed boy who had a high-end green Peugeot. He sometimes played tembûr." He whispered those words to himself, like the last time he talked to himself and . . .

This time, Kursh heard him.

Kursh said gloomily, "When I see a man like that, I forget my own problems. People like us ended up this way chasing a good, humanistic dream. But a person like Naseri . . ."

He did not finish.

"What happened to Naseri?" he asked.

"He's broken down. He broke down for some years after losing all his father's riches. After his wife passed away . . . he broke down. He was in a sanitarium in Tehran for a long time. He's come back since last year . . . a helpless and harmless man. Doesn't care what people do. He doesn't even talk to no one."

"Well, where does he live? Who does he live with? With his family or relatives?" he asked in surprise.

"He doesn't have much family. His father died a while ago. His uncles aren't around. He seems to be living with his old aunt. The old woman gave him a room and, meal by meal, she . . ."

Someone came and sat beside him. A giant man. He jammed himself into the seat, making him uncomfortable.

"Let's go out," Kursh said.

He still had his eyes on Naseri. The sad and miserable Naseri was smoking. He lit a cigarette too.

"No, please order two more teas, if possible."

Kursh ordered two more teas.

He asked, "Aren't they curious about his present condition?"

Kursh shook his head, pitifully.

"The story of Naseri is a strange one. Everybody only knows shingles and they make up the whole house. Most people say this illness runs in his family. His mother's side. They say his only uncle died in a sanitarium. Before his mother died, she also . . ."

"But in those years, Naseri seemed like a young and reasonable man."

Kursh laughed, as if wanting to ask why he was even asking all these questions—or to say that the distance between reason and unreason is . . . But he did not say that.

Instead, he said, "Money covers the secrets. They say he was incomplete back then, too. He's been incomplete since childhood. A lonely, alienated, and unstable boy who always took refuge at home to play tembûr . . . They say even in those days when everyone in the city, sane and insane, rushed into the streets for demonstrations, he hardly stepped out of his room. And on that day, he finally did—he saw a girl and fell in love. A girl from a poor family. They say that infatuation changed his life. It pulled him out of that loneliness and sadness . . ."

He continued, "That was the time we both saw him. Those days he dressed to the nines and drove that green Peugeot. He played tembûr once or twice at certain ceremonies . . . He was in love back then . . ."

"So to convince the girl . . ."

I said, "Oh, poor Afsana!" When he came back home and quoted Kursh's words, I said, "Poor Afsana . . . So she married a man who was incomplete, who had a screw loose . . ."

He said nothing. He did not yet believe what Kursh had said. He could not trust the evidence or the reasoning. A miserable man like Naseri. A star-crossed man like Naseri—a man who seemed settled, deserving. Someone who says nothing except for asking for cigarettes once in a while becomes a mystery, buried beneath a pile of half-true sayings and stories.

He thought, Jalali surely knows Naseri better than Kursh. Jalali must know the real facts. Why did not he ask Jalali about Naseri before? Why had not Jalali said a single word about Afsana all this time?

"Jalali comes here Friday night, and I'll ask him everything. About Naseri . . . Naseri's breakdown . . . About Afsana . . ." he said, his voice tinged with fear. “I still don’t know why or how Afsana died,” he whispered to himself. “Jalali knows for sure.”

What happened to Afsana after he left?

TWENTY

Was it Sunday or Monday evening when he saw Kursh . . . Comrade Dler? He had told him a story that had set him on pins and needles. Naseri's story. "Everybody narrates his life in some way," he said.

But he did not mention Naseri and Afsana's story. Kursh did not know Afsana, and he was not aware of their love—Afsana and Naseri's. It was only Jalali who knew Afsana, and he certainly would have heard Naseri's story. The story of Afsana and Naseri's marital life. Jalali certainly knew what happened to Afsana after he walked away, after she married Naseri. So why had he not said a word so far? Why had he not mentioned Naseri, or even Afsana? Except for a few references, for narrating some old memories in which Afsana had a part.

Maybe because he never asked.

I'll ask everything about Naseri and Afsana this time he comes along. Will Jalali say the same words Kursh did?

"Naseri was unstable and incomplete since childhood."

Did he surrender Afsana to an unstable and incomplete man?

He would look forward to the answers to those questions until Thursday night, but he could not carry the burden. The first night after he came back home, he wanted to forget all the words Kursh had uttered. Naseri and Afsana and . . . To forget all those who belonged to his past. First, he wanted to think of Laila. Some days ago, Laila had Nashmil hand him the typesetting of her poems. She said, "I'd like him to have a look at them. At the page design and the artistic touch and . . ."

Laila edited some of her poems based on his advice. She changed some words. He had read her poems once more. When they were handwritten, they were more congenial. Also the title of her notebook . . . Eve Does Not Repent Her Sin.

"Which sin?" he asked her. "The sin of cheating Adam?" She shook her head in grief. What did that girl want to say? How did she look at life? He could not fathom it. He could not know her. To the kind heart of . . . Laila dedicated. At first, she dedicated it to the kind heart of her father. Then she dedicated it to his kind heart. In what ways was he generous to her? Her father was not generous to her either. He died before he had the chance. He was killed. "You take after my father so much," she said, with shame. "My dad loved my mum."

When did she say that? Did she say that?

"You can't find a better and prettier girl than Laila. Laila loves you a lot," Monira said.

Why should Laila love him? Afsana had loved him as well. But he walked away from her. Years ago. Like Farhad who walked away from Kaleh. In a deadlock and tight alley . . .

"But Farhad had no other choice but to leave Kaleh," I said. I did not say it that night. I said it the day after—after he called Jalali and said he would like to be with him that night.

"Farhad didn't leave Kaleh of his own will. They arrested Farhad. Arrested him and . . ."

He was on the balcony. He has kept the iron door ajar for a while now, waiting in the cold. Waiting for Jalali's arrival—and at the same time, waiting for the other people of his past. Afsana?

Afsana had gone . . . She walked out of the wooden courtyard door in tears, and he was waiting for his father to come home. To bid him farewell. To kiss his cheeks, to kiss his hands. Since then, he had not told his father about his departure. His father came back. He saw him—and his heart dropped. His father looked older, more exhausted than ever. His eyes could not even roam around the courtyard. He did not perform wudu in the pool water. The pool was cold. It was not clean or see-through anymore. Algae had taken it over. His father climbed the stairs, onto the balcony. He sat in the old chair to rest. He noticed the stork's nest on top of the neighbor's berry tree. The nest was empty. The storks had migrated. He walked up to his father. Greeted him—uncertain, afraid. His father shook his head. "This year, the storks migrated so soon. They left us too soon," he said.

"I'm going to leave you too, Father. I wanna leave."

His father turned to him. Looked him over, head to toe. Two drops welled up in his eyes. The tears started falling, slow and heavy.

"You shouldn't have gone. You shouldn't have left."

Did his father forget he had not left yet? He had left.

Jalali arrived. He brought some food, a little drink, and a few old cassettes—each one capable of reviving a memory from their bygone days.

"When you called and said you wanted us to be together tonight, I freaked out," Jalali said.

He was in the kitchen.

"What did you fear? You think this'd be our last night together?" he said.

Jalali followed him. His fear was more apparent now.

"You want to return?" Jalali asked.

"Return where?" He turned to him, tense. He was scared too—scared of Jalali's look, scared of that question, cold as ice.

"Why do you think I want to return?" he asked.

"I heard you want to sell your house. I heard that after you got your inheritance . . ."

He did not finish. They have not spent a night together in a month. Now he was glad Jalali was there. Glad they were together.

"What else did you hear? Didn't you hear they want me to get married before they sell the house and give me my share?"

Jalali was over the moon. He had heard it.

"Marriage? With who? Laila?"

"Laila? So you heard that too."

He said that with worry in his voice, then stepped out of the kitchen. On the excuse of spreading the sifra, he left. But what he really wanted was the cigarette on the desk in his room. He lit it.

"Monira wants you to get married by hook or by crook," I said.

But he did not hear me. His mind was elsewhere—with Afsana, Naseri, and that story Jalali was about to tell him after a few more sips, once the alcohol loosened his tongue.

Jalali stepped out of the kitchen too. He spread the sifra beside the fireplace—set out a bottle, two glasses, and a little something more. Then he switched on the light bulb. It had gotten dark too fast. He glanced out the window. In that mere darkness, snow was falling fast and heavy.

"I've known Laila Tolu'i for a while," Jalali said with a smile. "Two, maybe three years now. After she finished studying, she was hoping to get hired at our office. Laila's a smart girl. Wise, too. Yeah, she's younger than you, but still . . ."

They sat down at the sifra and took their first shots.

Jalali said, "That day at the museum, when you praised her poems, I thought . . ."

"I want you to talk about someone else."

"Someone else? Who?"

"Afsana."

Jalali was startled—not by the name, but by the look on his face. That serious, agitated look. The way his eyes floated, restless, made Jalali realize just how much he had been hiding. As if for the first time, he saw what was collapsing inside him.

"You still haven't forgotten Afsana?"

"You saw Naseri, didn't you? Did you see what happened to him?"

"I see him every day," Jalali said. "Naseri lives next door. In his aunt's house."

"So you know his story. Everyone knows it by now."

Jalali nodded. It was a bitter story. The kind that could ruin a night.

"Some stories are better left forgotten," Jalali said, still tasting the harshness of the liquor in his throat. "Like Naseri's. What good is there in dragging that story back after all these years?" Then he answered his own question. "Trust me, it ain't good. Not for you, not for . . ."

He did not finish. He did not say "not for Naseri" or "not for Afsana." He let the sentence trail off.

"I came here to help you let the gale carry your grief away. I didn't come to . . ."

"You have to tell me," he said.

So Jalali told him everything.

A month or two after he left, Afsana married Naseri. It was a quiet wedding. Cold, plain. Was it her choice? Or was it just the sad custom of those years? There was no music, no *dahol*, no *zurna*, no dancing, no *chopi-keshan*. Just the groom, holding the bride's hand, taking her to Tehran. To a house, they said, that Naseri's father had bought for him. A beautiful place on the high end of the city. But Jalali did not tell him about the day they came back to visit family. He did not say he had seen them. Did not say he spotted them stepping out of a sleek car near the bazaar. Did not say how shocked he was.

Afsana was more beautiful than ever. Wearing an elegant manteau and matching scarf, an expensive bag slung over her shoulder. Golden-rimmed sunglasses. Her makeup thick, polished. She looked like someone he never met before. Jalali did not even recognize Afsana—only Naseri. Naseri, dressed as always, like someone who belonged to a different world. A lucky man. He startled when he saw Jalali. His face went pale for a moment. Then he looked at Afsana. She did not seem to notice Jalali at all. Naseri grabbed her hand and the two of them disappeared into the bazaar. Jalali did not tell him that seeing them that day reminded him of *him*—his comrade, the one who ran away. Like a scalded cat, Jalali went straight back home and wept for him.

"They stayed in Tehran forever. Even after the death of Naseri's father . . ." Jalali said.

Naseri's father passed away a year after his son's wedding. Here, they held the funeral at the Grand Mosque. Jalali attended as well—maybe just to see Naseri again. To be reminded of him again, and then to go home swiftly . . . This time, Naseri did not resemble a fortunate man. He was mute and unhappy. More unhappy than the only son whose father just died. He sat in a corner of the mosque. Nothing and no one could capture his attention. He did not even see him. His uncles welcomed the people into the mosque. They responded to the expressions of condolence. A few days after the funeral, Naseri returned to Tehran—certainly with Afsana. He seemed to have sold his entire father's inheritance to his uncles. He seemed never to have returned. Or he did, but Jalali did not see him. Did not hear of him.

Until the day he heard the news of Afsana's death.

"How did you hear? How did Afsana die? What did she die of?" he asked.

Jalali did not know. Like Roonak, he also saw the obituary in the newspaper.

At first, he was shocked. Afsana died? Then he cried a bit. Or maybe he did not. He started asking around. He tried to find out where, in which mosque, they had held a funeral for her. They did not hold a funeral in any mosque. He looked for Naseri's uncles—none of them were here anymore. Jalali did not know Naseri's aunt, and he was not her neighbor back then.

"So you don't know the whole story?" he said sadly. He lit a cigarette and took another shot with Jalali.

"Until then, there was no other story that anyone, including me, was aware of," Jalali said. "Until then, it was just a life lost in the chaos of thousands and thousands of other lives. The stories are told or written after the events. The story of Naseri and Afsana only started to heat up after Afsana's death. And also after Naseri came back here."

Naseri returned some years after Afsana died. Jalali first saw him not in the crowd around the square, but in the alley. Jalali had just recently bought that house. One day, when he stepped outside, he saw a miserable, helpless man about to leave a neighbor's house. He did not notice him. But the man stopped him. "Gimme a cigarette."

Jalali recognized him instantly. Naseri?! He did not say it. "I'm not a smoker," he said. Naseri walked past. Jalali stared after him, mouth open. But he did not follow.

"Who's that man? That helpless man?" he asked a shopkeeper in the alley.

The shopkeeper shook his head in grief. "The son of Haji Naseri. He used to be one of the prosperous men in this city," he said.

"So, why's he like this now? What's he doing in this alley?"

"It's a long story. It's been a while since he was pushed out of the sanitarium. Now he lives here with Haji Fatma, his aunt . . ." the shopkeeper said. "They say he's been like this since he was a child. They say the old woman, his aunt, was also incomplete and a maniac."

Kursh said the same thing before. But Jalali said, "Haji Fatma is a reticent, timid old woman. She talks to nobody. She's not even close to the women in the alley. But with my wife . . . sometimes, when I'm not home, she pays my wife a visit and talks about herself and her relatives, about her poor nephew, about Naseri . . . Naseri has always been wretched since childhood, when his mother died and . . . People thought he lacked nothing. But in fact, he had nothing to hold on to. Even during the time he had Afsana, he . . ." Naseri loved Afsana. He would stalk her day and night from the moment he first saw her. When he married her, he fluttered around her like a butterfly.

But Afsana . . .

Afsana must have tried hard to love Naseri. She must have given him a smile. She might have done things he liked. Worn makeup. Made herself look pretty and sat beside him. Listened to him wholeheartedly while he played the tembûr. And with the sound of his music, she must have closed her eyes and tuned her body to it. Sometimes, she must have opened her eyes to give him a languishing look. Given him a loving, soft smile . . . Afsana must have done that. A woman who loves her man would do such things. She would tune her movements, her eyes, and her breath to the music of her man. To the beating of her man's heart. But a man's heart is not just moved by his wife's movements, her smile, and her eyes. A man also hears the beating of his woman's heart. And the beating of Afsana's heart must not have been in tune with Naseri's.

Definitely, Afsana's heart was not with Naseri.

"With whose heart? With that nomad, wanderer?"

"Nomad, wanderer? Who?"

Naseri must have had him in mind. He was abroad at the time. In Turkey.

"What if he called you? What if he's waiting for you to leave me and go to him? What if your marriage with me was all a plan? What if . . ."

Jalali did not say those words aloud. Instead, he said, "Naseri mistrusted Afsana. He may have thought that . . ."

He thought his wife was still in love with her first lover. He thought that nomad wanderer would not leave them be and would return. That is why he left this place—with the excuse of protecting himself and his wife from the tension and struggles here, with the excuse of business and making money, he left.

But Naseri was not a smart or successful businessman. His father used to tell him what to buy and what to sell. As soon as his father died, his uncles . . . his uncles . . .

"A year after his father's death, his uncles turned all their possessions into cash and left," Jalali said. "They went abroad.

It seemed they asked Naseri to come too. It seemed they were supposed to leave together . . . But Naseri . . ."

Naseri did not dare. He was afraid Afsana would . . . in Europe.

Afsana must have talked to him a lot. She must have said that business here was like Satan's game—that he was not fit for it. She must have said that he had no one left here to truly care about him. And she was right. He really did not. And she had no one too. She must have told him to sell what they had and leave. But Naseri would not accept it. He suspected something evil behind what she said.

"You wanna take me to Europe and divorce me there? With that nomad wanderer, you want to . . ." He was in Europe at the time. But how did Naseri know that?

"Put it out of your mind. I'll never leave this land."

Jalali said, "Naseri went broke after the peace between Iran and Iraq. Just like all the other businessmen who lost their fortune . . ."

Jalali was getting drunk. He was drunk. But the bottle was still half full. The sound of the cassette player was faint—a fervent womanly voice that neither of them could hear.

Naseri's mistrust began to grow after his bankruptcy. He doubted not only the one who was abroad, but every other man. All the men in a city of ten to fifteen million. The passersby on the streets. The shopkeepers from whom Afsana bought things. The neighbors.

He moved his house once every two or three months after he was forced to sell it.

And Afsana . . .

Afsana might not have been allowed to step out of the house. She might not have even dared to open the curtains of her room or make a phone call. She must have been under pressure.

A woman is under pressure when the filthy, suspicious gaze of her husband traces her every movement. She must have cried. She must have sworn on everything that she considered no one as a man but Naseri. That she loved him more than anyone else. Even more than her own daughter . . .

"They had a pretty little girl, Awat. They seemed to love her a lot," Jalali said.

Afsana endured that awful burden for the sake of Awat. She was scared. If she divorced . . . if she left her daughter behind . . .

Naseri must have seen that. He must have told Afsana that if she divorced him, he would never let her see Awat again. That if she ever tried to take her daughter, he would do something terrible. Something to himself. Something to the girl. He must have frightened her. A man knows that a woman is a mother, and a mother cannot let go of her child. A man always keeps an ace up his sleeve. That is how he gains power over a woman. That is how he torments her. That is how he puts himself above her. That's how he . . .

He did not ask why Afsana did not complain.

He was scared—scared of what would follow, afraid of the story's ending. How does a story like this end?

In disaster.

He feared disaster.

"Afsana finally had to take him to court. One of those days when Naseri beat her, bruised her face, and terrified their daughter, Afsana took Awat's hand and . . ."

At court, Afsana asked for a divorce. She said she could not go on living with a sick, unstable man. But Naseri refused. He said he loved his wife and daughter, and that everything he did was for their own good. He promised to change. Promised not to bother them anymore. The judge took the papers from her. Told them to reconcile.

But the second time . . .

Jalali was completely drunk. So was he. The bottle was empty, and the long winter night was halfway through. They told the story of Naseri—one of them through what he had heard, and the other through what he imagined. The story of Naseri and Afsana . . .

Jalali said, "But the second time . . ."

Afsana asked for divorce for the second time. In court, she cried. She dropped to her knees and begged. She said she would give up all her rights, all her alimony, as long as she could keep her daughter. She said her husband was a madman, unfit to raise Awat. The judge pitied her. A young woman. A devoted mother, willing to give up everything for her child. He looked at Naseri. Naseri stayed silent the whole time. Head down. Biting his lips. Then he was given the chance to speak. Naseri stood. Looked at the judge. Looked at the people in the room. There was shame in his face. Fear. Doubt. Then he said he was ready to divorce his wife. He said it with tears. Afsana lit up. The judge smiled. Naseri said he was ready to get divorced—to free himself and his daughter from a great danger.

Danger? That startled Afsana.

"What danger? What are you talking about?" the judge asked.

Naseri fell silent for a moment, as if he were preparing himself to unveil a great secret. And then he did. He talked about the time before he married Afsana. About her love for a young man. A rebellious, wild man who ran away because of his crimes. Who escaped Kurdistan and was now in Europe. Naseri spoke of him. Spoke of Mehraban. Said that the dark shadow of that wild man loomed over his life since the very first day of marriage. Said he abandoned his city and left his family out of fear that Mehraban might come back. That he put all of his father's property up for sale and . . .

Afsana was stunned. Her agitated eyes wandered the courtroom, landing on the questioning stares of the audience, then on the judge. The judge's smile vanished. His gaze turned cold—cold as ice.

"It's a lie . . . That man is lying," Afsana said.

Naseri kept speaking. No tears. No shame. Just hatred, bitterness. He claimed that wild man had never stopped haunting them. That he called Afsana from Turkey. Written to her from Europe. Sent people—wild, dangerous people—to follow her. That he wanted Afsana to leave her family and run off with him.

Afsana exploded. Not with rage, but with the panic of an innocent woman falsely accused. She lunged at Naseri like she had lost her mind, tried to silence him, choke his words before they poisoned everything. They stopped her. Court officers. The judge's warning froze her in place. He was angry.

Afsana cried. She screamed, "It's a lie! That man's dishonoring me!"

Naseri kept talking. He reached into his pocket and pulled out three papers. He said he found them among Afsana's personal things. Letters from the wild man. Two old. One recent. He opened the new one. He read it aloud:

"To my darling . . ."

Afsana collapsed. Her body gave way to trembling and broke under it. A woman breaks when she is forced to carry the weight of sins she has never committed. When the cost of defending her innocence crushes her from the inside. Afsana must have loathed her body in that moment. Her heart. Her past. Her present. She might have hated everything about herself.

"Afsana was sacrificed by an illusion," Jalali said. "By the story of a mad lover. Naseri built it all from a single illusion."

He said . . .

He said nothing. Just could not. He could not keep dragging those memories out. That dark day, and all the darker days that came after, were beyond what he could bear to imagine.

Jalali noticed. He stood. He had already stood. He kept pacing the room, heavy with Jalali's painful words and the weight of his own imagination. Naseri's story was not over. Neither was Afsana's. Jalali walked out. He went after him. I stayed behind. Alone. Me—and the bitter fate of writing this story. His story? My story. The story of all those people who were characters in my own story. The story of all those failed loves that were my own lost love. The story of the shattered lives that mirrored my own forgotten life. I was left with the mournful task of writing my story.

And I remembered his question once more: How can this story ever be read?

TWENTY-ONE

He returned home at dawn, when the *baangbejes* were summoning people to prayer. Calling through the loudspeakers mounted atop the mosque towers. *Haya alal salah . . . Haya alal falah . . .* Their voices overlapped, intermingled, echoing through the darkness and loneliness of the city, weaving into the snowflakes that had been falling since nightfall. Falling still, endlessly, as if they would never stop, not now, not ever. He came back home worn and weary. But he could not feel it. He could not feel the cold either. Nothing. He stepped onto the snow in the courtyard and walked toward the stairs. In the hall, he shook the snow from his head and shoulders. Entered. The room was cold. He made the bed and slipped under the blanket. The heater had run out of oil. It was off.

"You'll freeze if you sleep like this," I said.

He could not stand on his feet. He had already contracted a disease.

"You'll get sick," Jalali had said some hours ago, when Jalali stepped out of the room. He put on his coat, wrapped a scarf around his neck, and followed Jalali out of the house. "Where the hell you goin' now?" Jalali asked, drunk, as he shut the courtyard door and walked toward his car. "Why are you out in this cold, in this frigid snow?"

"To have some fresh air. I'm choking."

He was choking. The poison inside Naseri's story . . . The story of Naseri and Afsana . . . has gathered in his lungs. Spread through all his veins. Jalali wiped the snow from the windshield of his car. Then he got in. "Pop in. We'll drive somewhere and . . ."

"I wanna walk a bit. Alone."

Before leaving, Jalali said, "You'll get sick . . ."

Then he drove away.

And into the streets he went. He put his hands in the pockets of his coat and walked down the slope of the small street beneath the falling snow. It was not the first snow of the year, but it was the first heavy one. Snow lay thick on the ground. His feet crunched through the soft, white layer. His footprints along the street were of a calm and conscious man. Light and close were his steps. It was a long line that was crooked in some spots. He slid in somewhere. The trace of his buttocks and elbow were visible on the snow. He kept on walking inattentively. He was walking on the white rug and in the twilight loneliness of the street and among the thin and thick snowflakes. A car passed by the street. The wheels left two tiny streams. They faded quickly. A taxi came close to him. The driver honked at him. He did not turn his head. Did he not hear, or was he reluctant to turn his head? He kept staring straight at the dance of light white snowflakes. The thin and thick snow crystals were falling down the heart of the dark sky. They were falling while dancing in the light of lampposts. They dropped on the shops and houses, on the branches of the street trees, on head and shoulders, and even on his eyebrows and mustache. He moved his legs slowly and softly on the snow that was raised in layers. To where? From that street to another and . . . from that night to another. Other nights of the past years. The nights that he was not here. He was not in this city, not in this land. But his dark shadow upon Afsana's house spoiled her life with Naseri. His black shadow was lying on the white snow. From the tip of his feet to . . .

He was standing with his head raised. The snow on his eyebrows fell. The snow on his eyelashes poured down. He stared at his vicinity. He found himself in a tight alley. A familiar alley. Familiar? The door lamps on his sides illuminated the dancing ceremony of the snowflakes. He was surrounded by the lamps. Surrounded by the dim lights on the closed doors of the houses. He was surrounded by his own shadows. A bunch of dark shadows, getting pale and paler, from the tip of his feet to . . .

He set off. The shadows were turning around him, like the dance of ghosts in the lonely night of an alley. The shadows were moving on the walls of the houses, on the closed doors and the windows. They peeped into the windows. Into the dark rooms. Many people were certainly asleep in those dark rooms. No one was aware of him. No one awaited him. In oblivion, he walked through the alley, softly and slowly. The light of a room at the end of the alley caught his eye. It was glowing behind a bright window, as if it has been lit for years. He wished a shadow, the shadow of a person, would fall across the curtain. Whose shadow? Years ago, it was Afsana's. Afsana in her blue dress, her long hair scattered over her shoulders. He saw her. He saw the shadow. The shadow of Afsana's upper body, large and blurred, shrinking, deepening, until her full image appeared. And then a hand, a white, delicate hand, pulled the curtain aside.

"Hey, you crazy! What are you doing in our alley in that cold snow at midnight?" Afsana had said. Many years ago. It was during those days after the nights when he would pass by her alley several times before dawn. He would linger beneath the balcony of a house across from the window of Afsana's room.

"I missed you," he said. "We haven't seen each other for days."

Afsana gave him a smile. "Are we supposed to see each other every day?" She laughed sweetly. "Well, why don't you move here and be our neighbor? Why don't you rent that old woman's house across from us, the one whose window opens to mine and . . ." She said it as a joke.

"Like Farhad . . ." he said.

She said, ". . ."

He was raving. He had been raving since he returned, since he lay under the blanket. Maybe he was dreaming. Dreaming of Afsana . . . dreaming of Kaleh . . . I was sitting there, looking at him. He was raving as he shivered. He was popping like popcorn on fire. It was getting bright outside.

"It's morning. It's bright," I said.

I woke him up. He moved his head out from under the blanket with struggle. His sluggish eyelids were opening like the black, dirty curtain of a window in a foggy room. He looked at me.

"Can you stand up?" I asked.

He said nothing. He rolled his eyes around the room lethargically. The daylight streamed into the room through the window and the wrinkled curtains. Brightly, it spread across the room. The room was cold. Breath would freeze the moment it was exhaled.

"Stand up if you can. Stand up and . . ." I said.

I did not finish what I wanted to say. He could not. He closed his eyes again. His eyelids were wet. So was his forehead. Frost-like drops of sweat, clear and limpid, settled on his face. He pulled his head back under the blanket again.

"We can see each other every day, even every hour, if you rent the old woman's house. You behind the window of your room, and I behind the window of mine . . ." Afsana had said.

"And when no one's home, you can secretly come to me and . . ." he said.

"Then, together in one room, away from the eyes and ears of people. We can talk 'til we drop and . . ." Afsana said. Many years ago. He had forgotten it. Since the day he had left this place. He did not remember it—not during all the years of distance and exile, not even since the day he returned, not even while he was writing Farhad's story. He did not know . . . That part of Farhad and Kaleh's story was, in fact, a part of his own sweet dream. He did not realize that. The sweet dream of Afsana and himself—one that was forgotten years ago. "Afsana . . . I wish that white and delicate hand . . ."

He was still raving. Like a dying, fevered man, he was calling out to his beloved.

"Kaleh . . ."

I was scared. I was nervous. I did not know what to do. I did not know how to help him. I went toward the window and pulled the curtain slightly aside. It was morning. It was no longer snowing. The sky was clear. The courtyard was crammed with snow, and the tree branches were bent beneath its weight. The world was white. Sunlight was shining on the face of the snow. It stung his eyes. I drew the curtain closed.

"Kaleh gian . . ."

I wished someone could come here. I wished I could bring someone in or call somebody. I wished a storyteller could call one of his characters and ask for something. Can he not?

"Someone will come now, or a moment later," I said. I said it to myself. "There's a voice from outside. It must be Monira."

It was Monira. She opened the courtyard door and came through the snow. On the stairs, in the hall, and behind the door of the room, she stamped her feet on the ground and shook herself off. She opened the door. Her clothes, up to her knees, were wet.

"Good God, what a heavy snow!" she said.

Standing in the doorway, she looked around the room. The sifra was still spread. He was still in his bed. She was surprised. She closed the door behind her. "Look at this room," she murmured to herself. The room was not only untidy and dirty, but also freezing cold. She walked toward the heater. It was off. Clearly it had been off for some time now. She was startled. She panicked. "This heater . . ."

She approached him in fear. He was shivering under the blanket. She pulled the blanket off his face. As if facing a dead body, she went pale in an instant and struck her chest. He woke up. The sound of Monira's footsteps and the cracking of the door had awakened him.

"I'm cold," he said.

It sent shivers down her spine. She hugged his head and touched his face. It was drenched in sweat. His skin burned with fever. "Wish your sister were blind! What happened to you?" Monira cried, tears running down her face.

But he was smiling. A weak, dim smile. A smile meant to calm her down. "It's nothing . . . I'm just sick . . . I'm cold . . ."

His voice could hardly be heard. Monira stood up and restlessly went out of the room. She brought some oil and turned the heater on. She approached him and hugged his head again, moving her hand on his face.

"Wish I was blind not to see you like this! Wish I could die!"

He said nothing. Monira went to the kitchen. There was milk in the fridge. She warmed it and brought it back to him. He slowly lifted himself with effort, with Monira's help. He sipped half a glass of the milk. The warmth of it melted the ice within him. And the warmth of the heater . . . Like a mother tending her sick child, Monira was crying and cursing herself. She gently urged him to drink the rest.

"I knew you were sick. As if someone told me. I just felt it. I've called you a hundred times since early this morning, but you didn't answer." She walked over to the telephone. It was unplugged. She plugged it in and called her husband. Then she called Baram as well. "We need to take you to a doctor. We should . . ."

The heater was burning with a roar. A soothing sound filled the room. The heat reached him. His shivering stopped. Monira wiped her tears and dried her eyes.

"May your sister die! I wish I came here earlier!"

Monira started massaging him. There was a strange stiffness in his back. The veins along his spine stuck out, crawling like snakes beneath her hands. He could not hold himself together. Dizziness . . . The room was spinning around his head. The furniture . . . the walls . . . and Monira . . . He had to recline. Monira moved to spread the blanket over him. He was still in his street clothes. She noticed. The bottom hem of his trousers was still wet. She froze. "I bet you've been outside tonight," she said.

She struck her lap and chest again.

"Out in that cold . . . drunk . . . ?"

He coughed. A dry, relentless cough. Monira stood up and brought him a suit of dry clothes. "How did you survive all those years abroad alone?"

She said it while crying. She changed his clothes. He was like a corpse in her hands. The corpse of a man who . . . Monira spread the blanket over him again. "You haven't changed. You're just the same as when you left," she said. "Reckless and untidy as ever . . . weaker and thinner . . . quieter and more marooned. I thought you changed over these years, that you lived like everybody else. But I was mistaken. Now I'm dead sure I've misunderstood you all these years. You're still young. You haven't grown yet. After all these years of studying and writing . . . after forty or so years of life, you haven't grown. Unlike most people who grow up. Unlike most people who . . ."

Monira thought he could hear, but he could not. Then she heard a knock on the courtyard's iron door. She left the room in a hurry. Her husband brought a doctor, a familiar one.

"What's wrong, man? You came back after all these years just to fall sick?" the doctor said. He said that as a joke. Then he lifted the blanket off his body. He was frailer than ever. His whole body was drenched in sweat. He coughed again. A constant, dry cough.

"His lungs are inflamed," the doctor said.

He injected him. "We have to take him to the hospital. He must . . ." Baram arrived while the doctor was still speaking. Without a word, he lifted him onto his back and rushed out of the room. And out of the courtyard too . . .

TWENTY-TWO

"I'll go back to our house," he said. "I'll go back to my house."

Once again, he forgot that he had walked out of that house and courtyard for the last time. Since the day he was carried out of the house and courtyard, since the day he was taken to the hospital . . . He had been in the hospital for three weeks, and he was to be discharged today. "You can take him home now," the doctor said.

"Take him home?" Baram asked, startled. "But doctor, he's not yet . . ."

Monira blew a fuse. "He isn't yet what?

He still did not feel well. Silent and sorrowful. But he had been treated kindly by the doctors and nurses, unlike the other patients. They had heard he was a writer. A hometown storyteller who had fallen ill after returning home from years of estrangement and exile. He had a fever, along with swelling in his lungs, and was trembling for a week . . . It took two weeks before the doctor was certain that his lungs were clear and the other dangers he has feared was passed. As for the headaches and dizziness . . . "His headaches and dizziness are related to his nerves," the doctor said.

"And what about his silence and sorrow?" Monira asked. "What about how he sometimes forgets things and . . ."

"Wasn't he like this before?"

Was he? Monira did not know. She looked at her husband, then at Baram. Neither of them knew for sure. He had been gone for years, and even when he finally came back, he did not stay with them. "He's weak and anemic. Keep an eye on him. Make sure he eats well. As for the depression, don't leave him alone," the doctor said. "Tell him something funny. Remind him of happy memories . . . There's nothing more we can do here, but at home, you can still . . ."

"I wish you hadn't sold the house. I told you before, selling the house and courtyard . . ." she said.

A week after he fell ill, the paperwork for selling the house was ready. All that remained were the sellers' signatures and the two hundred and forty million Tomans the bank would pay in cash. It was as if a fire had been lit under Baram. He had one foot in the bank, the other in the hospital and at Monira's house . . . Roonak came to visit him too and so did her husband. Baram was no longer alone. Monira's and Roonak's husbands were also . . . One night, they all gathered at Monira's house. All but him. "Now that we're all here, we should finalize the sale," Baram said. "If we don't sign the deed in the next few days, it'll be pushed to next year, and all our efforts will be wasted. God knows, the bank might back out by then, and . . ."

"Our poor brother's lying in a hospital bed, and you're talking about selling the house and courtyard?!" Monira said. "I've said it a hundred times: not until my brother recovers, not until he's released from the hospital, not until he gets married in that house and courtyard, not until we fulfill our parents' will . . ." Monira could not finish. Her voice broke in sobs. Roonak was crying too.

"Thank God our brother is okay. I'll bring him home from the hospital in a week," Baram said. "But once I do, I won't let him stay alone in that ruined, empty house and courtyard . . ."

"We never should've let him stay there by himself," Monira's husband said. "If he was at Baram's place, or even yours, you wouldn't have let him sneak out in the freezing snow like that."

Roonak's husband said, "If you ask me, sell the house while he's still in the hospital. That way, hopefully, when he comes home . . ."

"What about his marriage? What about my parents' will?" Monira said.

The next morning, Baram, Monira, and Roonak signed the contract to sell the house. But not him. A few days later, they brought the contract to the hospital and asked him to sign.

"Is this for the sale of the house?" He did not say he would not sign. He said, "I just have one more day and night of work to do in that house."

Baram laughed. "We'll still have the keys for another month. Once you're better, hopefully . . ."

He signed it.

Again, the dizziness . . . He turned his face away from them and looked outside. Through the hospital window, he stared at the hospital grounds, at the snow that have blanketed the world in white.

"Close your eyes and rest a bit. Don't stare at the snow so much," Monira said.

"What are you looking for in that snow, behind this window?" her husband asked.

And Baram . . . "I'm sorry. I couldn't keep my word. After the payment was made, the bank took all the keys to the doors and rooms," Baram said. "Yesterday, we packed everything up and moved it to Monira's house."

They placed his bed in the guest room at Monira's house. A large room that was sometimes filled with his guests. Aside from his friends and relatives, most of them were writers, poets, and artists. Most were young. Laila visited him too. She would occasionally come to see him at the hospital. And now, at Monira's house . . .

He rarely spoke to the guests. He would murmur a reply to their greetings, then fall silent. After they left and the house grew quiet, he stood up and walked to another room. A small, secluded space with a single window overlooking the courtyard. There too, he sat behind the window, staring out. The snow in the courtyard was melting. Little by little. He watched it disappear. He was thinking. Thinking of Afsana, of the day he walked away from her. Those bitter days. He still did not know how or why Afsana died. He knew nothing about Kaleh after Farhad left . . .

"I need to go. I need to see Farhad," he said.

To see Farhad? Monira looked at him. Fear and surprise in her eyes.

"I have to go and finish my story."

Monira rushed out of the room. She returned with a stack of papers and a pen, placing them gently in front of him. "Here you are. Your pen and papers. Sit down and . . ."

He picked up the pen and let his head fall over the pages. Over the white pages. Every day, he would bend over the blank paper and write nothing. He could not write. Not a single word. "You don't write a single word. So why do you spend so much time in this empty room, just staring at those white pages?" Monira asked. "You're still sick. You need rest. You're depressed. You need to be around people and . . ."

Again, the dizziness . . . He could not bear the crowd. "I like being alone. I'm used to it," he said, his voice heavy with boredom.

"It's a bad habit," she said sadly. "You should break it."

He stared again at the white paper in front of him. His thoughts returned to Afsana. He remembered her. Again. Remembered Kaleh . . .

Monira left the room, her heart heavy. She went to Nashmil and her husband. "If it goes on like this . . ." she said, crying. She did not say what would happen if it went on like this.

"Don't panic. We've never really known him. He's always been like this. Always . . ." her husband said, trying to comfort her. "He needs a change in his life. If he gets married . . ." he said with a smile. "Marriage will help him. A woman is the remedy for all pains: weakness and silence . . . depression . . . amnesia . . ."

Nashmil said, "Miss Laila Tolu'i sends her warmest regards every day, and . . ."

Monira was deep in thought. Laila was a passionate, self-sacrificing girl. She loved him. Only a woman like Laila could bring change to his life. He had to propose. He should have done it long ago.

"I've been wasting time for no reason. I need to do something before it's too late. And . . ." she murmured, smiling. "If Laila comes over this time . . ."

Laila arrived. Monira opened the door and greeted her with warmth, hugging her tightly and kissing her cheeks, just as always. Laila did not seem surprised. She did not ask what happened. "Who else is here?" she asked.

There was no one else. Just Monira—and he was in the small room. "How is he doing now?" Laila asked.

"Thank God, he's better. He's sleeping. He's resting in the small room." Monira placed a hand on Laila's shoulder and gently led her inside.

"I don't want to wake him. I just came to ask how he's doing and . . ."

"We won't wake him," Monira said. "Come on. You and I need to talk."

Laila was surprised. Monira was smiling. Truly smiling. It was a long time since Laila saw that on her face. Not since he fell ill. Maybe he really was better now. That thought made Laila happy too. She wondered why Monira wanted to talk to her. She looked at her. Her gaze and her smile were as kind as ever. As ever? No. It felt like this time, there was something even softer in her. Monira led her into another room. She helped Laila settle in, then stepped out for a moment. One of his photographs hung on the wall. An old picture from his youth. Laila stared at it. He seemed to be looking back at her. A sad gaze . . . Sad? No, a familiar gaze. The same look she had seen for years on the wall of her own room. The same eyes. Her father's eyes.

Monira came back with two cups of tea and a small plate of candy. Every part of her seemed to smile. "I'm sure you're wondering why I wanted to talk to you."

Laila stayed quiet. "I want us to talk about him," Monira added in a low voice. She pointed toward his room. The room where he was supposed to be sleeping. Laila looked surprised. "About him?"

Monira nodded. "Do you know why he became sick . . . ?" She did not let Laila answer. "That freezing, snowy night . . ." Then Monira remembered that Laila already knew what had happened, even though she did not mention it . . . Monira felt rushed. Something was pressing on her mind. Something she needed to say before he woke up. "When a man lives alone . . ."

Monira was not smiling anymore. Just a faint trace of a smile on her lips. Laila sensed it. She understood at once what Monira was about to say. "We've known each other for some time," Monira said. "And I think you know how deeply I care about you, how much I respect you. Not just me. My whole family. My husband, my brother, even Roonak, who's only met you once."

Laila thanked her.

"Believe me, I love you just as I love Nashmil. I care about your life and happiness just as much. You're intelligent, wise, and talented . . . It's a bit awkward to praise someone to their face. But you're wiser than to . . ."

Laila lowered her head. She was sad. The smile has dried on her lips. Monira did not know why. She said . . .

Laila looked up. Her gaze was serious, cold. Monira was taken aback. "Are you proposing to me?" she asked, with a quiet sadness.

It was not the first time Laila would receive a proposal but it was the first time Monira ever made one. "Yes," she said.

She said nothing more. She did not know how to keep the conversation going. Laila asked her question directly, and she answered it. Without the slightest idea of where that question and answer might lead. Laila let out a deep sigh. Her face was full of sorrow. Monira was stunned, but she quickly pulled herself together. "I know he's older than you, but . . ."

Laila gave a bitter smile. So bitter that Monira feared she might burst into tears. "But Mrs. Monira, he's not the kind of man who marries. He didn't come back to get married," Laila said, "and I'm sure he doesn't even know about the proposal."

What was the girl saying? How did she know? Monira did not ask. "You're right," she said, "but he's a shy and decent man. He's always been that way. Maybe he's too shy to talk to you . . . because he's older than you, and he's afraid you'll say no. He's my brother. And even though we were apart for years, I know him well. He loves you. I'm sure of it. Since the first day he met you . . ."

Laila was instantly filled with joy at her words. A sweet, trembling joy moved through her body. Monira felt it too, that sudden spark of happiness. Laila's eyes filled with tears. "I love him too. Since the first day I saw him. Even before that."

It was a difficult but sweet confession. She said it shyly. Color returned to her cheeks. The bitter smile vanished from her lips. Monira lit up. "So you love each other and . . ." she said. "It's not just because he's unwell. He's recovered completely. If he still seems a little sad, silent and sorrowful . . . please . . ."

"Mrs. Monira," Laila said, "he's not the kind of man who marries." Then she turned her face away, wiping her eyes, avoiding Monira's gaze.

"Why do you think that way? . . . I'm sure . . ."

Laila did not mention that, long before Monira proposed to her, she had once proposed to Mehraban. Had she really proposed? When? Where? One day, on a high, quiet hill. She said, "I want to be the character in your new stories." His sad voice still echoed in her ears: "I have no time left to write new stories."

"Let him be, Mrs. Monira. Let him finish his story." She did not say his last story. "He has returned to finish his story."

Laila pointed to something Monira had heard from him a dozen times. Then she stood up, put on her veil, and walked out of the room. Monira followed her. Neither of them spoke. As if there was nothing left to say. Both of them were quiet. As Laila crossed the hall, she heard him just for a moment. He was crying in the small room.

TWENTY-THREE

When I lifted my head from the brazier, I realized he was in the room. My room or Farhad's? A dark, smoke-filled space that smelled of damp and burnt trash. How long has he been there?

"I've been waiting for you. I knew you'd come," I said.

I knew he would come. Since the day he was taken to the hospital. Since the day he was brought to Monira's house. "I need to go see Farhad. I need to finish my story." He used to say that over and over during those days without pause. He had come now. He sat under the dim light of the window. Under the dim light of the window of Farhad's room. In Farhad's place. He rang his thin and bony arms around his knees. His head was dangling over his shoulder. Just like Farhad who used to ring his thin and bony hands around his knees and . . . What a remarkable resemblance he bore to Farhad.

Grey hair and beard. His sunken cheeks and eyes. It was as if he were hiding behind Farhad. Or Farhad, behind him. The story writer and the character of the story were now the same. A person clouded by amnesia for years. Amnesia? A person who had cut himself off from everything—himself, his life, his past. From his parents and . . . from his beloved. From Afsana. Afsana? From Kaleh.

"I don't want to depict Kaleh based on Afsana. I don't want Kaleh to be Afsana, or even to resemble her," he said. He said that at the very beginning of writing his story. "I don't want the story of Farhad and Kaleh to be the story of me and . . ."

He still had not finished his story. The story of Farhad and Kaleh. He tried his best to bring it to an end, especially while staying at Monira's house. In a small, secluded room, he sat staring at the thick whiteness of the pages. Just like Farhad, who used to stare at the whiteness of his canvas. Farhad had not finished his painting either. His last painting.

"But I'll finish my story. The story of Mehraban. The story of a writer who returned after years of distance and exile to write his last story," I said.

His last story? I stood up. I glanced at him as I rose. He was still sitting, arms wrapped around his knees. A cloud of smoke lingered above his head. I walked toward him and stood at the room's window. Like him, who used to stand there and wipe the layer of soot and smoke from one of the small eyes of the window with his palms. I looked out through the glass. At the ruined courtyard. At the trees cut off at the roots. The trees had fallen to the ground with their bare branches. They covered the courtyard. A grand building had collapsed on the other side of the courtyard. Its pillars crumbled. The roof and balcony sunken. A giant black bird sat atop the debris. A frightening sight. Frightening? No. Sad and heartbreaking. I turned my gaze away from the window.

"Stand up. We need to go out," I said.

Where to? He did not ask.

"We need to go to that narrow, dead-end alley where Farhad . . ." I said.

The alley knows, the neighborhood hears—Farhad's leaving is never meant to stay hidden. They ask one another about it. When men meet, whether in teahouses or elsewhere, they ask about him.

"Have you heard Farhad's gone?"

"Don't you know where?"

"Do you think that . . . ?"

They do not go on. Are scared. The men. They fear each other. They fear a spy who might be within one of them. Are not scared. The women. The women of the alley are worried. Their worry deepens when they look into Kaleh's eyes. There's no waiting in Kaleh's tearful eyes.

Questions have left Kaleh's mourning eyes since the day three well-dressed men broke into Farhad's home and searched every corner of his rooms. Her steps no longer carry her forward. Rarely does she leave her house. And hardly ever does she pass through the alley. Goes to no one's house. Kaleh. She does not even respond to the soft tapping of the tawn weavers. Doleful are the women. More doleful than their parents. Than their brothers. They heard the news of Farhad's arrest from their brothers. They wept when they learned he had been taken. They cried for Kaleh. For the death of her dream. Kaleh's sweet dreams were also their own dreams. They are crying for the death of their dreams. They stay in, striking against tawn weaving. Against those red flowers that bloom on the blue background of the rug through the movement of their fingers and the beating of their hearts. Stay-in strike against singing Bartawnana. The tawn weavers. Against their group singing which would resonate inside the alley through the door and the window of their basement. The Bartawnana song of the tawn weavers loosened the feet of each and every passerby. It would steal the passing from their steps. Loosened the feet of the lovers. They stay in strike against their lovers, the lady rug-weavers. They do not sit at the rug loom if not for their brothers' warnings, their fathers' orders, and their mothers' pleas. They do not move a finger without tears. No colors will the rug have this year. The rug trade has grown cold this year. No one will buy a rug woven with yellow-hued flowers . . .

He passed by the gloomy bazaar. By the shops. Carpet shop. Clothes shop. Perfume shop . . . by the jewelry shop. The bazaar was not crowded. It was cold. People were in their homes. I stood at a crossroad. "Which alley should we take?" I asked.

I was in a dilemma. We had Farhad with us before. He would walk ahead. But this time . . . I followed him into a narrow alley. I quickened my steps to catch up. "These narrow alleys are all too similar. Be careful . . ." I said.

He put his hands in the pockets of his coat and walked through the twisting alleys. Just like Farhad. Like that first time, when he seemed rejuvenated. He became younger and . . . The alley was empty.

Vacant is the alley. Vacant and deplorable. As if the graveyard's dust has been sprayed upon it. Upon the roofs and the time-worn edges of the houses. Upon the thatched walls. Upon the windows and . . . they're still blue. The windows. Blue? Grey are they. Tightly shut and latched are the windows. The gaps and the peepholes are covered with paper and glue. No one is there behind the windows. Not even the young, marriageable girls. Curtains are fully drawn. Out of fear of the cold, the wooden and iron doors are locked. Fear of the wind. Only the stubborn and furious wind dares to pass into the alley. From this side of the alley to . . .

The other side of the alley is a dead end. The wooden door of the old woman's house is also locked. The iron door of Kaleh's too. No chance to unleash itself. The wind. Irate and enraged, it clutches the doors and windows of the houses. It tightens its grip on the balconies. It tosses Rahim's pigeons ahead of itself from the rooftop of Kaleh's house. Exhausted and frightened are the pigeons. They scatter across the sky above the alley and the neighborhood. The pigeon pairs are torn apart . . .

"Don't forget that Rahim sold his pigeons after Farhad found him a job . . ." I said.

He stopped. He leaned against the wooden door of the old woman's house, which stood in front of Kaleh's house. He was tired. His fatigue was obvious and if the door was ajar, he would go inside. He would walk through the dark corridor and up the stairs. Into Farhad's room. He did not know what had happened to Farhad's room. That night, when the three officers rushed into the old woman's house in utter silence, they broke down the door to Farhad's room and went inside . . . They must have searched every corner. They must have unpacked everything in the room. What did they take with them?

"I won't let you take anything from this house. These things are in my care. I don't like being indebted to their owner," the old woman said.

"The owner is a criminal," they replied.

Criminal?

"You're the criminals who break into homes by force and . . ." the old woman said.

The men threatened her. One of them pushed her to the ground. The other cursed at her.

"You're a stupid, crippled old woman. You can't understand. The owner of those rooms is a young and foolish student. He ran away from university. He's a spy. He works for outsiders. We've arrested him and we'll kill him. Be sure of this: you'll never see him again, never feel indebted to him. Be sure that . . ." said the third man, who looked older than the others.

The old woman did not hear the rest of his words. She left the room in tears, in grief. She went down the stairs. Kaleh was in the courtyard. The courtyard of the old woman's house. She was shivering like a reed in a gale. She heard the shouting too. When she saw the old woman, she began to cry. Out of fear, the old woman quickly pushed her into a room. Her own room.

"They'll kill him. I know they will," Kaleh said tearfully. The old woman wept too. For Farhad. The dying-young Farhad. For Kaleh. The ill-fated Kaleh . . .

The iron door of Kaleh's house opened. Rahim and three or so others came out. They were his friends. Had they just finished gambling? They did not notice him. He was not meant to be seen. They were chortling. Bursting into laughter. Were they drunk?

"It seems Rahim has quit his job and returned to his old life," I said.

He had quit his job. When he found out Farhad had left. When he learned Farhad had been arrested. He quit it and came home. Did Kaleh not ask why? Did she not scorch him? "Who could've guessed that painter was a criminal," Rahim said with fear. He said it in fear. Kaleh was sitting in a corner. Her head buried in the bowl of her hands, staring off into nowhere. The blind boys sat shoulder to shoulder. "My boss is one of his comrades too. I thought maybe he was a criminal as well. I was scared they'd arrest him too," Rahim said. Kaleh did not lift her head. She said nothing. The blind boys said nothing. Rahim grew agitated.

"You're acting like I was the one arrested. Why do you sink into despair . . . ?" he said. Then he stood up and left. The following morning, he went to see his old friends and . . . Kaleh, sad and silent, was staring at something. At what?

"How long are you gonna mourn? Those guys don't show up to a funeral. Stand up and get ready to welcome them like before," he yelled at her. "What if you've been that fucking painter's accomplice? Have you been a criminal too?"

The iron door was still open. He sneaked into the house like a ghost. Kaleh's house . . .

Kaleh's house is also vacant. Rahim has gone out, and the blind boys are not at home. Alone is Kaleh. Fearful is she. She has been filled with fear since the day Farhad left, since the day she sat in the corner of her small room and buried her head in the bowl of her palms. She does not know what she's afraid of. A mysterious fear has taken root in her heart. She does not know why. She does not know? Kaleh stands up. She clasps the wall and stands up. From that room to the other and . . . She is a stranger to the rooms. A stranger to the things in there too. The picture on the heart of the wall, the forty-piece cloth, the handcrafts in the niches, the flower pot in the window, even the mirrors . . . She remembers. She collects all the mirrors in the house, small and large. Inside her own room, she hangs the mirrors that are to be hung. She leans the mirrors that are to be leaned. She positions four large full-length mirrors in the four corners of the room. Plays a game. Kaleh. She has done it before. A hundred times, since she came to know herself. Came to know herself Kaleh inside the throng of those mirrors. Inside the siege of those reflections, all of which are her. The image of body parts on all four sides. A childish game. She has confessed to it before. A hundred times, each time giving herself a promise to stop. To stop buying mirrors. But could not stop. Kaleh. Not even when she became a grown-up girl. Not even when she came to know Farhad . . .

She was startled the first time she looked for a mirror in Farhad's room and found none.

"How can you live without a mirror?"

"Without a mirror?!"

"How can you ignore yourself and your body parts?"

She stands among them. Inside the mirrors. At the center of the room stands. Kaleh. As she always would. A hundred times, she would pull the curtains. Kaleh would lock the latches on the door. She would turn on the lamp and take off her clothes. Fully nude. She would stand naked before her own eyes. Before the flood of her gazing, frightful eyes. She would strip in each mirror. She would gaze at herself in all of them. She laughs when she tells Farhad for the first time. Farhad was in wonder and awe.

"What are you seeking in those mirrors?"

"Myself. Parts of my body. I fear losing them."

"Losing them?"

Farhad is astonished. Farhad asks no more questions.

Kaleh goes to the window. She pulls the curtain and locks the latch on the door.

"What is that girl going to do?" I asked.

TWENTY-FOUR

A rending scream jolted him awake again this morning. A dry, gut-wrenching scream.

"Afsana . . ." he shouted.

He recoiled in fear. In panic. His eyes darted around the room. Around the murky, smoke-filled room. His wild, panicked gaze could not settle on anything. On the dark walls. On the soot-covered picture frames and broken mirrors tucked into the niches. Blackened and dim. The sleeping clock on the heart of the wall was black and dim too. The window . . . The sun had just risen. A pale, thin light had just slipped through the small eyes of the window. It still carried the rust of the cold and the dark. The cold and darkness of a long night. A long autumn and winter.

"Yeah, that was Afsana . . ." he said. He repeated it like someone unsure of what he had just said. I was sitting a little way off from him. By the brazier, as always. But it gave off no warmth. The burning coals have died, turned to ash.

"It was Afsana's scream. This whole time . . ." he said. His voice trembled. He could barely get the words out. I could not quite catch what he was saying.

I was drained. Did not sleep a wink last night. Since we left Kaleh's house in the evening, since he fell asleep, I had been going over his story. The story of Farhad.

"I've been dreaming of Afsana this whole time," he said.

Farhad dreamt of Kaleh too. In the last part of his story.

When did he write that last part?

Farhad's last dream. The last dream of a painter who . . .

Yet sits the painter, facing the easel and the canvas. He gazes upon the bold, unrelenting whiteness of the cloth—at those tiny, black, contorted lines. Yet he pursues the lines, the painter. At their fraying ends, Farhad seeks Kaleh.

"Kaleh, where are you? I endured. I was shamed. All for this moment, just to find you."

"Why won't you appear? Why do you hide from me?" he calls out, raising his voice.

The whiteness of the canvas stings his eyes. Dizziness and—

A bullet-like pain shoots through his face and neck. "Why won't you appear behind these lines?"

His hand goes numb. Farhad. The brush slips from his fingers, slithers, and falls to the ground. Dizziness and . . . The canvas and easel spin above his head. Collapses flat on his back. Farhad. His eyelashes fall shut.

He loses sight of the painting. Only voices remain. The insidious voices do not leave him be. Even in slumber, even in unconsciousness, they pour down on him. Madness murmurs in his skull, stringing webs everywhere around him. Delusional whispers. They do not let Kaleh's voice reach him.

"Kaleh, raise your voice. Step out of that darkness. I want to see you. Show yourself. I want to know what's happened to you all these years . . . Kaleh, I want to paint you again . . . Paint your delicate, soft face and body . . . Like that time, Kaleh . . . Not like that, in the clear water of the pool . . . This time in . . ."

Farhad cries. He is sleeping, but crying. Kaleh can no longer restrain herself. She appears—not behind the lines of Farhad's final painting, but in his dream. In his last dream.

"Kaleh gian . . . darling . . ."

Kaleh does not hear Farhad. The voice of the man in whose last dream she appears. Not a single word does Kaleh hear. She stands. In a small room, wearing an all-blue dress with tiny red flowers, she lingers among dozens of small and large mirrors. She has been fragmented into countless small and large paintings.

"Kaleh . . . darling?"

Smiles. Farhad. Delighted, he is.

"The bitter days of distance are over. I knew you could endure it."

Does not see him. Kaleh. She does not see the man in whose dream she appeared. She sees no one but herself. But her weary body. She is a stranger to her own body parts. A stranger to her hands, her legs, her belly, her back—even her head and face. They do not obey her. They do not undress. They do not dance. Even her eyes do not see as she wishes. They do not gaze into the mirrors. They do not look at the unknown images. They fixate on the fire in the heater. They watch the dance of its flames.

"The season of coldness is over, Kaleh. We no longer need the fire. Our union warms not just us, but the whole city."

Does not listen to him. Kaleh. She does not listen to the man in whose dream she appears. She listens to no one but the oil-filled gallon of the heater. Her legs lead her toward the heater. Her hands stretch out to grab the oil gallon. Her fingers twist open the lid. A small hole comes into view. Kaleh bends down. She gazes at the oil in the gallon. She sees herself in the oil through the hole. Her own face, reflected in the deathly blackness of the oil. She lifts the gallon.

"What are you doing, Kaleh?!"

The gallon halts above her head. On Kaleh's head. Her left hand loses its strength. The gallon tilts, and the oil spills. It pours over Kaleh's head. Over her soft, disheveled hair. Over her shoulder, chest, and breasts. Over her entire body. The oil is cold. Her skin breaks into goosebumps.

"Kaleh . . ."

Screams Farhad. Kaleh's body is all wet. Her hair clings soddenly to her neck and shoulder. Her blue dress sticks to her skin. She seems naked. Kaleh. Her cold, wet body lies scattered among the mirrors.

Her silent face, her fatigued eyes, her chin, her lips, and . . . All those stranger faces staring at each other, staring at each other's chest, protruding breasts, back and bottom, staring at a blue skin and a garden of small red flowers and . . . They are not scared. They are not petrified. No feelings have they held inside themselves, the fatigued eyes of Kaleh.

"Kaleh . . ."

Hapless is Farhad. He does not know where or how to stop that moment of death, which is to come in mere minutes. In her hand, Kaleh holds a match. She lights it and . . .

"Kaleh, no . . ."

The bottom of her dress catches fire. Flames spiral around her. Her fatigued eyes widen. Her silent face comes to life, like embers. Her hands rise, and Kaleh begins to dance.

"Kaleh . . ."

Kaleh is a yarn of fire, dancing among the dozens of small and large mirrors. The mirrors are a tight, narrow ballroom. The room too. She jumps out of the room. A yarn of fire crashes against the walls of the courtyard, against the iron door and . . . Kaleh is a yarn of fire, surrendering herself to the cold and loneliness of the alley. To the craving arms of the wind. The flames rise with the gale. Fire weaves through the alley, and by Kaleh's scream, her last rending scream, Farhad jolts awake.

He finished his story just as I had predicted. Farhad's story came to an end in the closing days of winter. The closing days of winter in what year?

"I'll finish my story too. The story of Mehraban," I said.

Then I raised my head. He was not in the room. I was alone. I sat beneath the dim light of the window, my thin bony hands wrapped around my knees.

GLOSSARY

Atrchai (Etirçaî) A kind of scented geranium.

Baangbej (Bangbêj) A person who calls Muslims to prayer from a mosque.

Bartawnana (Bertewnane) A traditional form of Kurdish vocal music, usually performed by men and women while weaving Kurdish carpets. It features rhythmic repetition and deep emotional expression. This music serves both as an accompaniment to labor and as a way to preserve and pass down cultural heritage. Though it originated in the weaving tradition, many Kurdish musicians now perform this style beyond its original context.

Bayt (Beyt) A form of Kurdish folklore and oral storytelling intertwined with music. It is typically performed through singing in a fast-paced, emotionally intense vocal style known as Hayran.

Chopi (çopî) A handkerchief in the right hand of the first person in the dance circle, who leads the other dancers. They wave their hand in the wind and spin the chopi as a sign of happiness.

Chopi-keshan (Çopîkêşan) The act of leading a Kurdish dance circle while holding a chopi, guiding the rhythm and movement of the group.

Chirok (Çîrok) A Kurdish word for story. It refers to a narrative form that can be oral or written, often rooted in folklore, collective memory, and cultural identity.

Daf (Def) The daf is a traditional frame drum often used in Kurdish mystical rituals. Its deep, resonant sound carries a supernatural quality that evokes spiritual ecstasy and a sense of divine connection. Today, it has also become part of modern music, with many musicians incorporating the daf into their compositions.

Dahol (Dehol) A traditional percussion instrument, typically used in celebrations, weddings, and folk dances, often played alongside the zurna.

Daya (Daye) A Kurdish word meaning "mother," used both literally and affectionately. Daya can refer to one's biological mother, but it is also lovingly used to address or describe any woman who offers deep care, warmth, and protection, like a mother would.

Gian (Giyan) A Kurdish word meaning "dear."

Jajim (Jajim) A traditional hand-woven Kurdish textile, typically made of wool and characterized by colorful vertical or horizontal stripes. Jajim is often used as a floor covering, blanket, or decorative cloth.

Jamana (Jamane) A traditional Kurdish scarf that is traditionally worn by fighters, and today is often worn by others as a symbol of solidarity with the Kurdish struggle for independence.

Kak (Kak) An honorific Kurdish title meaning "mister" or "older brother," used to respectfully address or refer to a man in formal or polite contexts. The word Kak is typically placed before a person's name and is not used alone.

Kaka (Kake) A casual honorific in Kurdish, meaning "brother" or "buddy," used in informal speech to express friendliness and familiarity. Unlike Kak, the word Kaka is often used on its own to refer to someone affectionately, without needing to be followed by a name.

Kilim (Gilêm) A flat-woven textile traditionally made by Kurdish, Persian, Turkish, and other regional weavers. Kilim rugs are known for their geometric patterns and vibrant colors, and are typically used as carpets, wall hangings, or coverings. Unlike pile rugs, kilims have no knotted surface and are lighter and more flexible.

Kolwana (Kolwane) A flat-woven textile traditionally made by Kurdish, Persian, Turkish, and other regional weavers. Kilim rugs are known for their geometric patterns and vibrant colors, and are typically used as carpets, wall hangings, or coverings. Unlike pile rugs, kilims have no knotted surface and are lighter and more flexible.

Kolwana (Kolwane) A colorful Kurdish garment that covers the back, traditionally worn by women.

Mamosta (Mamosta) An honorific that literally means "teacher," but is commonly used to show respect to people of high social status, such as artists, writers, and generally individuals with knowledge in any field.

Qebla (Qible) God's house. The direction towards which the Muslims do their prayers.

Sarchopi (Serçopî) A Kurdish title for the person who takes the first position in the dance ring, holding a chopi in hand and leading the rhythm and movement of the group during Kurdish dances.

SAVAK (Sawak) The former secret police, intelligence, and security organization of the Pahlavi dynasty in Iran, established in 1957 with the help of the CIA and Mossad.

Sokhma (Soxme) A colorful Kurdish top garment that covers the chest, traditionally worn by women.

Shada (Şede) A traditional Kurdish women's headwrap, similar to a turban or scarf, worn wrapped around the head. Şeda is both a cultural and decorative garment, often used in festive or traditional settings.

Sifra (Sifre) A traditional cloth or spread laid out on the floor or carpet, around which people sit to eat meals. It is commonly used in Kurdish and other Middle Eastern cultures as a communal dining space, often replacing a table during everyday or festive meals.

Tawn (Tewn) A traditional Kurdish weaving device, especially used by women for making hand-woven Kurdish carpets.

Tembûr (Tembûr) The tembûr—also pronounced temura, tanbur, or temira—is a mystical stringed Kurdish instrument played by followers of Yarsan. Yarsan was the primary religion of most Kurdish people before the spread of Islam. Many Yarsanis still live in Kurdistan today, where they play the tembur during gatherings in their assembly houses. The instrument has become an integral part of Kurdish music and defines much of its spiritual character.

Zhala (Jale) A Kurdish name for a kind of Nerium Oleander flower used as an ornament.

Zurna (Zurna) A traditional Kurdish woodwind instrument with a loud, sharp sound, mostly played at weddings, celebrations, and folk dances. It is often accompanied by the dahol (Kurdish drum) and is known for its energetic and festive tone.

ACKNOWLEDGMENTS

We are deeply grateful to Malav Kanuga, Joris Leverink, Sydney Rainer, and the rest of the team at Common Notions Press for stewarding this translation into publicaton with care and deep commitment. We have enormous gratitude also to our dear friend Stephen McKenzie, who enthusiastically reviewed the translation and offered thoughtful and precise word choices. Words cannot fully express our appreciation for his invaluable contributions.

We are sincerely thankful to Aryan Omar Hassan for his thoughtful reading and guidance, which helped shape the natural rhythm and flow of the translation. Without his discerning eye and dedicated efforts, something essential would have been missing.

Our sincere thanks also go to Hanie Moaseqi, who wholeheartedly examined the translation and provided us with insightful feedback.

We warmly thank our cherished friend Saman Zoleikhaei, who lent us a hand in finding fitting English equivalents for some of the more challenging Kurdish words and idioms.

Kawan Mohammadpur wrote a highly informative introduction for this book. A distinguished scholar in the field of Kurdish literature, his words illuminate hidden dimensions of *Birds in a Gale* for English readers. We thank him from the depths of our hearts.

We are truly grateful to everyone who contributed to this project. We owe a special debt to Mr. James Brent Mitchell for his invaluable guidance, unwavering support, and illuminating commentary on the translation.

And finally, to Reşo, Ciwan Haco, Şivan Perver, Nasir Rezazî, and Yedê Şakirî, whose music accompanied every word and breathed life into this translation—our deepest thanks.

ABOUT THE AUTHOR

Ata Nahai is a Kurdish novelist and short story writer who writes in Sorani Kurdish. He is considered one of the foremost novelists in Greater Kurdistan (which includes parts of Iran, Turkey, Iraq, and Syria) and the leading Kurdish novelist in Iran. Born in Baneh in 1960, he graduated from high school in 1978 with a diploma in literature. Due to the revolutionary atmosphere in Iran in 1979 and the subsequent closure of universities for the next four years, he was unable to continue his studies.

Nahai began his literary career by writing short stories and producing essays on the art of fiction. He has published three collections of short stories and three novels in Kurdish and has translated several world short stories and literary essays into Kurdish. In 2002, he won the top vote at the First Conference on Teaching the Kurdish Language in Tehran and became the head of the Kurdish Language Academy in Iran.

Nahai has translated Houshang Golshiri's *Shazde Ehtejab* and Milan Kundera's *The Kafkaesque World* into Kurdish, along with several other short stories by well-known international authors. *Birds in a Gale* was originally written in Sorani Kurdish and co-published by Zhiar Press in Sine and the Kurdish Cultural Institute of Tehran. The second edition was released in Southern Kurdistan (Iraq) by Aras Press. The third and fourth editions were published by Mang Press in Eastern Kurdistan. The novel has been translated into Kurmanji and published by Avesta Press in Istanbul, and the Persian translation was published by Behnegar Press. Nahai was awarded the Aras Prize for Kurdish Literature in 2005 and the Ahmad Hardi Prize for Creativity in Sulaymaniyah in 2008 for *Birds in a Gale*. Additionally, the Persian translation of *Birds in a Gale* and his latest novel, *Dealing Helaleh's Destiny*, won the prestigious Mehregan Prize for Best Novel of the Year in Iran in consecutive years.

ABOUT THE TRANSLATORS

Chiya Parvizpur is a Kurdish author and translator writing in both Kurdish and English. Holding bachelor's and master's degrees in English literature, he uses fiction to preserve and reimagine the folk traditions, myths, and historical memory of his people. By blending the particularities of Kurdish culture with universal literary forms, he seeks to resist cultural erasure and give renewed life to a heritage long under threat.

For Parvizpur, translating into English is just as vital as creating in Kurdish. He has brought major Kurdish novels—often shaped by the collective suffering of the Kurdish people—into English. Through both endeavors, he works to ensure that the Kurdish voice, suppressed for over a century by the nation-states of the region, can be heard worldwide. He believes that although the Kurds have no country, their literature stands alongside that of any nation.

His debut novel, *The Smell of Wet Bricks*, published in English by TP London and in Kurdish in Kurdistan, launched a planned trilogy. The second volume, *Twenty-Four Seconds of Shehin's Life*, written in Kurdish and weaving multiple Kurdish languages, was banned in Kurdistan by Iran's Ministry of Culture and Islamic Guidance. He published it abroad to reach the Kurdish diaspora, and it went on to win the 2024 KAL Literary Prize.

Parvizpur's translation work includes the novels *Birds in a Gale* and *Dealing Helaleh's Destiny* by Ata Nahai, *Gabor* by Seyyed Qader Hedayati, and *The Shadeless Border* by Jiyar Jahanfard, and he plans to translate other powerful novels.

When he's not writing, Parvizpur plays the tembûr, an ancient Kurdish instrument whose sound is threaded into his work. His work explores fading identity, music, mythology, and the blend of tradition and modernity, all grounded in anti-colonial resistance. Through his creative writing and translations, he fights for the survival and renewal of Kurdish culture.

Hourieh Maleki Qouzloo (Huri) is a Kurdish writer and translator with a deep love for language and storytelling. For more than twenty years, she has shared that love in the classroom, teaching language and literature, and now teaches at international schools in Stavanger, Norway. Her curiosity about people and cultures has led her to explore the theme of identity in her academic work, resulting in several published articles, and she is currently pursuing her second master's degree in English and Literacy Studies at the University of Stavanger.

Huri has brought contemporary Kurdish literature to new audiences through her English translations of *Birds in a Gale* by Ata Nahai and *Gabor* by Seyed Qader Hedayati. Her love for Kurdish literature began in the earliest days of her childhood, when the poems and stories her parents read to her settled in her heart like a lullaby. That early connection to literature has stayed with her, growing stronger over the years and finding its voice in her novel, short stories, and translations. She is currently working on her Kurdish-language novel *Prishkei Henar* and is preparing a collection of short stories, hoping to see both in print soon.

Her mother tongue is Kurdish, and she is fluent in English, Persian, and Turkish, with a working knowledge of Arabic, French, and Norwegian. To her, language is an inseparable part of identity, with each new language opening a door to another world and offering fresh ways to understand people and their stories.

TRANSLATORS' NOTE

All aspects of the work on this translation were done equally by the two of us and the order of our names is purely alphabetical.

ABOUT COMMON NOTIONS

Common Notions is a publishing house and programming platform that fosters new formulations of living autonomy. We aim to circulate timely reflections, clear critiques, and inspiring strategies that amplify movements for social justice.

Our publications trace a constellation of critical and visionary meditations on the organization of freedom. By any media necessary, we seek to nourish the imagination and generalize common notions about the creation of other worlds beyond state and capital. Inspired by various traditions of autonomism and liberation—in the US and internationally, historical and emerging from contemporary movements—our publications provide resources for a collective reading of struggles past, present, and to come.

Common Notions regularly collaborates with political collectives, militant authors, radical presses, and maverick designers around the world. Our political and aesthetic pursuits are dreamed and realized with Antumbra Designs.

www.commonnotions.org
info@commonnotions.org